EYES OF TERROR

Eyes of Terror
and Other
Dark Adventures

by

L. T. Meade

Swan River Press
Dublin, Ireland
MMXXI

Eyes of Terror
by L. T. Meade

Published by
Swan River Press
Dublin, Ireland
September MMXXI

www.swanriverpress.ie
brian@swanriverpress.ie

Dust jacket design by Meggan Kehrli
from artwork © Brian Coldrick

Typeset in Garamond by Steve J. Shaw

With thanks to John Connolly
for his continued support

Published with assistance from Dublin UNESCO
City of Literature and Dublin City Libraries

ISBN 978-1-78380-750-5

Swan River Press published
a hardback edition of
Eyes of Terror in September 2021.

Contents

Introduction

In December 1898, the influential *Strand Magazine* (1891-1950), famous for its fictions of crime, detection, and the uncanny, proclaimed Irish-born author L. T. Meade (1844-1914) one of its "most popular contributors". Featured alongside H. G. Wells in the *Strand* series "Portraits of Celebrities at Different Times of Their Lives" (1898), Meade was declared not only a "literary celebrity", but also "one of the most industrious modern writers of fiction". The praise was well-deserved; over the course of a professional career that spanned four decades, Meade edited a high-quality girls' literary magazine and authored close to three hundred novels as well as countless short stories and articles on a wide variety of subjects for readers of all ages. Though she was considered one of Arthur Conan Doyle's most able competitors in the *Strand*, her fame did not long survive her, and she is generally best remembered for her formulaic girls' fiction. However, recognition of Meade's significance as a *fin-de-siècle* professional woman writer is now increasing. More recently, Meade has been credited with popularising—if not inventing—the medical or scientific mystery, a subgenre of crime fiction that blended modern science and medicine with the uncanny and the occult. Even so, Meade's interest in the uncanny remains largely unexamined. *Eyes of Terror and Other Dark Adventures* is the first modern collection to showcase Meade's uncanny fiction by bringing together an array of sensational tales published at the height of her professional career.

Born on 5 June 1844 at Bandon, Co. Cork, Elizabeth ("Lillie") Thomasina Meade was the eldest daughter of Church of Ireland minister Richard Thomas Meade, Rector of Killowen and subsequently of Nohoval. Like most girls of her class at that time, she was educated at home by a governess. By her own account, Meade decided to become a writer at an early age ("How I Began", *Girl's Realm*, Nov. 1900). Despite her parents' initial disapproval, she published her first novel *Ashton-Morton* in 1866. Following her mother's death in 1874 and her father's remarriage soon after, Meade moved to London to establish herself as a professional writer.

Meade launched her career with a series of successful novels about the lives of London's poor. Inspired by the bestselling waif stories of evangelical author Hesba Stretton (1832-1911), and informed by sensational slum narratives circulated in the press, Meade published *Lettie's Last Home* (1875), a pathetic tale of a child who is beaten to death by her mother, an alcoholic baby-farmer. An early example of Meade's awareness of current issues and marketable trends, *Lettie* exploited public outrage over the shocking details of baby-farming lately exposed by journalists and reformers. *Scamp and I* (1877), the story of a faithful dog and an endearing orphan who refurbishes old shoes in a dank slum cellar, proved to be Meade's most popular waif story. It was also one of her most successful novels, with multiple editions and translations published over the next sixty years. According to Meade in "How I Began", *Scamp* was the novel that made her name and secured her career. Though she moved to other genres in the following decades, Meade continued to write about urban poverty, child welfare, and related social issues in works such as *A Princess of the Gutter* (1895) and *Mary Gifford, M. B.* (1898).

With her career established, Meade married London solicitor Alfred Toulmin Smith in 1879 at a ceremony performed by her brother Gerald, then Rector of Killarney, at Christ Church, Cork. She returned to London where she continued to write as L. T. Meade. Marriage and the birth of four children in the 1880s (one died in infancy) did not alter her dedication to the professional life or significantly alter her rate of production. By the middle of the decade, prompted by recent critical developments in girls' education, Meade turned her interests to the girls' school story, the subgenre she brought into fashion with her bestselling first school novel, *A World of Girls* (1886). Some of her most memorable schoolgirl stories featured rebellious but good-hearted Irish girls "exiled" to English schools for "taming". Meade's colourful characters were patterned after Princess Glorvina of Inismore in Sydney Owenson's fiercely nationalistic novel, *A Wild Irish Girl* (1806). In the 1890s, Meade expanded her range to exploit public debates surrounding women's higher education with her first college-girl novel, *A Sweet Girl Graduate* (1891).

Meade's status as a leading author of girls' fiction was recognised in 1887 when she became the editor of a new upscale girls' literary magazine *Atalanta* (1887-1898), a position she held for the next six years. The editorship brought her considerable prestige and opportunities to take leadership roles in feminist-oriented literary and professional associations. *Atalanta* under Meade's editorship was known for its emphasis on women's culture and its progressive articles on women's education, employment, the arts, and literature. Meade used her position to attract contributions from prominent authors such as Christina Rossetti, Frances Hodgson Burnett, Robert Louis Stevenson, and H. Rider Haggard. She also published Irish writers including poet and novelist Katharine Tynan, who considered Meade a friend and mentor.

Meade entered an important new period in her career after resigning her editorship of *Atalanta* in 1893. Though she remained a dedicated girls' writer, her publishing interests expanded to include the emerging genre of mystery and crime fiction. Inspired by the phenomenal success of Arthur Conan Doyle's Sherlock Holmes series launched in the *Strand* in 1891, Meade formed a critical relationship with the magazine. At the same time, she formed highly productive collaborative associations with two medical doctors: Metropolitan Police surgeon Edgar Beaumont (1860-1921), writing as "Clifford Halifax, M. D."; and Eustace Robert Barton (1868-1943), writing as "Robert Eustace". Meade's collaborators supplied her with medical and scientific information while she did the actual writing. Generally narrated by a medical doctor or an amateur scientist who often functions as the protagonist, plots typically turn on manifestations of insanity, addiction, mesmerism, and new scientific discoveries. Meade-Barton narratives are particularly inclined toward unusual scientific devices, rare or "impossible" (not yet realised) medical information, and generous infusions of the uncanny and the occult. Storylines frequently focus on family secrets, disputed legacies, larceny, fraud, bigamy, abduction, and murder, while gothic settings include ancient ruins, remote country houses, asylums, and dilapidated castles. As in all her popular fiction, regardless of genre and audience, Meade did not hesitate to exploit the success of others. She deliberately referenced literature her readers knew, in this case, gothic and uncanny fiction by authors such as Edgar Allan Poe, Charles Dickens, Wilkie Collins, Joseph Sheridan Le Fanu, Mary Elizabeth Braddon, Rider Haggard, and Conan Doyle.

Stories from the Diary of a Doctor, Meade's first *Strand* series, was launched in July 1893. The twelve part Meade-Beaumont series narrated by "Clifford Halifax" attracted considerable interest prompting a second twelve-part *Strand* series in 1895.

Many of the stories are a blend of several sensational narrative forms. Uncanny, unaccountable, or extraordinary incidents occur in stories such as "The Heir of Chartelpool" (1893) in which Halifax performs successful brain surgery in his sleep while guided by an impelling "Power" or "Presence". Others involve miracle cures by means yet unknown to science but, according to the authors, "within the region of practical medical science" as in "Creating a Mind" (1895) in which Halifax performs a life-threatening operation to expand a child's skull. Gothic, horror, or occult incidents occur in "A Death Certificate" (1893) and "To Every One His Own Fear" (1895) where Halifax saves cataleptic patients from live entombment, and in "The Horror of Studley Grange" (1893) in which Halifax investigates the appearance of an "appalling apparition" at the home of one of his patients. Incidents involving insanity, drug use, and exotic poisons occur in a number of stories including "The Hooded Death" (1895) where Halifax intervenes to prevent an addict "with the cunning and cleverness of the Evil One" from destroying his wife. Mesmeric influence is the focus of Halifax's attention in "My Hypnotic Patient" (1893), "The Red Bracelet" (1895), and "With the Eternal Fires" (1895), a particularly surreal tale involving an English schoolboy kidnapped and imprisoned in a derelict temple of Hindu fire worshippers by a vengeful mesmerist.

"Very Far West" (1893), reprinted in the present collection, is arguably the most unsettling story in the series. It is a strange, dreamlike tale, redolent with the menace and eroticism characteristic of some of Poe's best works. Here Halifax is lured to a dark house in a solitary square by a beautiful woman seeking medical assistance for her father. Though Halifax narrowly escapes from what is essentially a house of terror, the experience leaves him haunted and suffering "strange thrills of horror" that render him unable to perform many of his medical operations for some time. The story concludes on an uneasy note intensified by the fact that the house, its location, and its occupants remain a mystery; in his traumatised state, Halifax is unable to identify the deadly house when questioned by the police, thereby drawing into question its very existence and raising doubts about the adventure itself.

Within months of the conclusion of the second series of *Stories from the Diary of a Doctor*, Meade and Beaumont introduced *The Adventures of a Man of Science* (1896), an eight-part *Strand* series, collected as *A Race with the Sun* (1901). Though the narrator-protagonist Paul Gilchrist is a "scientific man of leisure" rather than a medical doctor, he is frequently called upon to treat a variety of medical conditions including brain disease and insanity. Described as "a keen observer of human nature and a noted traveller", Gilchrist maintains a private laboratory in London where he conducts experiments leading to new treatments for disease. Two stories in the series, "The Sleeping Sickness" and "The Panelled Bedroom", stand out as examples of occult fiction. The first concerns an instance of chiromancy where Gilchrist investigates the case of a widow murdered after her death is foretold by a celebrated palmist. Using modern scientific methods, Gilchrist solves the crime through the analysis of a blood smear taken from the crime scene. In "The Panelled Bedroom", selected for this collection, Gilchrist is represented as a clairvoyant and a hypnotist of a "higher order". On this occasion, he encounters a dangerous female mesmerist while on a holiday visit to the country mansion of an old friend. When Gilchrist disrupts the woman's plot to gain control of her cousin's fortune using mesmeric techniques, he is threatened with demonstrations of her power. Gilchrist describes his sense of unease and "very real horror" when she appears spectre-like in his bedroom—a "ghastly", "grotesque" chamber with a strange arrangement of panels and hidden doors that remind him of a certain deadly hotel room in Collins's "A Terribly Strange Bed" (1852).

The Meade-Beaumont partnership lasted through the 1890s. In addition to their *Strand* series, the authors published a number of successful novel-length medical mysteries. Notable examples include *The Medicine Lady* (1892), a story of gender transgression and medical intrigue; *This Troublesome World* (1893), featuring seduction, addiction, insanity, blackmail, secret identities, revenge, and murder; and *Dr. Rumsey's Patient* (1896), involving drug abuse, brain disease, and a family curse. By 1897, however, the partnership was on the wane, and Meade began to collaborate with Eustace Robert Barton ("Robert Eustace").

The six-part Meade-Barton series, *A Master of Mysteries: The Adventures of John Bell—Ghost-Exposer*, was launched in *Cassell's Magazine* in 1897. The introduction of occult detective John Bell as the narrator-protagonist marks a significant development in Meade's contribution to the genre. Bell is a professional exposer of ghosts whose business is to "clear away the mysteries of most haunted houses" and other haunted spaces, and to "explain by the application of science, phenomena attributed to spiritual agencies". Although Bell is not the first occult detective in fiction, he is uncommon among his fictional contemporaries in that he accepts no other cases; exposing supernatural phenomena constitutes his entire occupation. Despite the relative uniqueness of Bell's character, the series itself is not particularly original; "The Mystery of the Circular Chamber" and "To Prove an Alibi" invoke Collins's "A Terribly Strange Bed", while "The Warder at the Door" and "How Siva Spoke" concern family curses and disputed legacies. More interesting are "The Eight-Mile Lock", in which Bell attributes supernatural phenomena on a canal to the activities of a jewel thief with a cleverly designed submarine; and "The Mystery of the Felwyn Tunnel", which appears in this volume.

"The Mystery of Felwyn Tunnel" is an eerie tale reminiscent of Dickens's nightmarish story "No. 1 Branch Line: The Signal-Man" (1866), drawn from Dickens's experience of a horrifying train accident at Staplehurst in Kent the previous year. In "The Mystery of the Felwyn Tunnel", Bell investigates two unexplained deaths near a lonely railway tunnel reputed to be haunted. As in Dickens's text, the site is represented as "weird" and "uncanny". According to Bell, "a more dreary place it would have been difficult to imagine"; the tunnel is described as "damp and chill"; its walls oozing and "covered with green, evil-smelling fungi". However, unlike "The Signal-Man" where a sense of the uncanny lingers beyond the story's conclusion, Meade's tale ends on a reassuring tone as Bell discovers a scientific reason for the mysterious deaths.

Meade and Barton introduced another occult detective some years later in the character of narrator-protagonist Diana Marburg, a professional palmist and thought reader in *The Experiences of the Oracle of Maddox Street* published in *Pearson's Magazine* (1902). Despite the promise of occult or supernatural events, the stories offer minimal evidence of "strange mysteries of the unseen world". Though Marburg gives séances and identifies criminals using palmistry, she solves crimes using more conventional methods of detection. Her "marvellous detective abilities" are attributable to quick thinking, close observation, and expert deduction using science and the latest forensic methods including fingerprint identification as in "Finger Tips".

In "The Dead Hand", reprinted here, Marburg uses her occult skills to confirm an act of murder and identify a suspect, but she discovers the murderer's *modus operandi* and proves her case only after a meticulous investigation of the crime scene. In spite of its interesting premise, *The Oracle of Maddox Street* was less successful than the John Bell series—only three "experiences" were published; the stories were reprinted in

The Oracle of Maddox Street (1904), a collection of Meade-Barton stories drawn from several popular magazines.

Of the many Meade-Barton collaborations, *The Brotherhood of the Seven Kings* (1898) and *The Sorceress of the Strand* (1902/3) stand as the authors' most successful. Both series are narrated by English gentlemen with scientific interests and connections with Britain's foremost law enforcement agencies, but the focus is on the fascinating recurring female criminals. *The Brotherhood* guaranteed Meade's recognition as a *Strand* celebrity author, but the series is also significant for the introduction of one of the first female gang leaders in English literature: the deadly Madame Koluchy, "chief and queen" of the sinister "Brotherhood of the Seven Kings", a secret society with Italian associations akin to Count Fosco's "Brotherhood" in Collins's *The Woman in White* (1860). Koluchy and her equally dangerous successor, Madame Sara in *The Sorceress of the Strand*, establish the character of the beautiful female criminal who is skilled in witchcraft and the occult, proficient in the administration of mysterious drugs and lethal poisons, experienced in the use of explosives, and expert in the modern sciences to which few women of the period had access. Both women are exotic foreigners who present themselves as medical professionals able to perform wonderful cures. The characters are modelled after Lady Audley and Lydia Gwilt, celebrated female villains in Braddon's *Lady Audley's Secret* (1862) and Collins's *Armadale* (1866), respectively. But Sara also draws on the notorious "Madam Rachel" (Sarah Rachel Russell [c.1814-1880]), a notorious mid-century criminal who began her very successful career as a "beautifier" in upscale Bond Street by telling fortunes in a London slum market. Koluchy and Sara are unsettling because they traverse gender boundaries, foil patriarchal networks of power and influence, and repeatedly vanish before they can be brought to justice. The crimes Koluchy and Sara commit include fraud, blackmail, robbery, kidnapping, torture, murder, and acts too "ghastly", "grotesque", and "horrible" to describe. Seductive, scheming, and treacherous, they possess "snakelike" abilities to hypnotise their victims and a determination to stop at nothing to achieve their respective ends. Both women are said to haunt the dreams of the men who repeatedly fail to apprehend them.

In "The Doom", the final story in *The Brotherhood*, reprinted here, narrator Norman Head, Koluchy's former lover, states that his apprehensions "never slumbered": "I began to see that cruel face in my dreams, and whether I went abroad or whether I stayed at home, it equally haunted me". Additionally, as beautiful, ageless women with foreign associations and occult powers of fascination, they draw on the character of the female vampire and the social and cultural anxieties she represents in popular gothic fictions such as Le Fanu's "Carmilla" (1871/2), Florence Marryat's *The Blood of the Vampire* (1897), and Bram Stoker's *Dracula* (1897). The latter is specifically referenced in "The Star-Shaped Marks", one of the later stories in the series. In "The Doom", set in a picturesque town near Lake Windermere, what begins as a pleasant holiday for the narrator, a Christmas respite from the business of London and the ongoing search for Koluchy, turns into a deadly affair when Head's best friend and confidante falls victim to the woman's machinations. In the series' sensational conclusion, Head tracks Koluchy to her London laboratory where she stages a dramatic exit that evokes the final moments of Ayesha, the ageless African sorceress queen in Rider Haggard's *She* (1886/7).

In addition to her serialised stories, Meade also published stand-alone uncanny stories that were later reprinted in miscellaneous collections, often with the addition of a narrative frame. One such example, included in this volume, is "The Woman with the Hood", a little-known ghost story that originally appeared in the Christmas number of the *Weekly Scotsman* (1897). Narrated by a doctor, the story is a classic account of a restless spirit, the victim of a long-ago crime, seeking acknowledgement. Called to a country house to attend an heiress tormented to the point of insanity by a spectral figure, the narrator is charged with finding a solution. Though the spirit is ultimately put to rest, the story concludes uneasily with the crime unsolved and questions remaining.

"Followed", a Meade-Barton story, appeared in the *Strand* in 1900 and later in *Silenced* (1904), a collection of medical-scientific mysteries published in the *Strand, Cassell's*, and *Woman at Home* between 1897 and 1902. Set in a "queer" house on Salisbury Plain near Stonehenge, "Followed", reprinted here, is an eerie tale of a young woman's terrifying visit to the home of her future mother-in-law, a woman with a "wild and uncanny" foreign appearance, a jealous attachment to her son, and a passion for venomous snakes. The woman is attended by a devoted black servant who possesses a strange ability to manage his mistress's fits of madness as well as her dangerous creatures. Left alone with the woman while her fiancé attends to business in the City, the young protagonist has reason to fear for her life. She manages to escape the dreadful house and take refuge at Stonehenge only to discover that danger has followed her to the mystical site.

"The Man Who Disappeared", another story from *Silenced*, reprinted here, is a Meade-Barton collaboration first published in the *Strand* in 1901. The story begins when the narrator, a London lawyer, receives a request from a Spanish woman seeking a house to rent near London. Her conditions are specific: the house must be surrounded by a park, situated in the vicinity of a large moor or common, and have extensive cellars or basements suitable for a laboratory. Such a place is soon found—a "gruesome mansion, situated on a lonely part of Hampstead Heath"—and the lease is arranged. Shortly after, the secluded house becomes the scene of a ghastly murder.

"Eyes of Terror", the final story in this volume, was published by Meade in the *Strand* in 1904 and collected in *The Oracle of Maddox Street*. In this tale involving a disputed legacy and the supernatural, a young woman grieving the recent death of her father is troubled by strange encounters with a terrifying apparition that takes the form of two gleaming eyes. Fearing that she is the victim of a family curse or a malevolent spirit, she enlists the aid of a physician whose work "lies altogether in the regions of original research". Once engaged, the physician has little difficulty determining the true cause of the hauntings.

Meade's commercial success can be attributed to her dedication to the professional life and her capacity to "write to order" across genres. In "How I Write My Books", published in *The Young Woman* (January 1893), reprinted here as an appendix, Meade writes that she maintained a strict writing schedule—over two thousand words every day with the assistance of shorthand writers—and never waited for inspiration. One of her greatest strengths was her ability to create memorable female characters in a wide range of contexts, from bold tomboys and wild Irish schoolgirls to women doctors, philanthropists, criminals, detectives, terrorists, and spies. In addition to her fascinating criminals Madame Koluchy and Madame Sara, some of Meade's most notable creations include Anna Beringer, "the clever[est] lady detective in the whole of London" and the "bloodhound" chosen to track Koluchy to her lair; deadly Olga Krestofski, a committed Nihilist in *Stories from the Diary of a Doctor* (1895); and treacherous Mademoiselle Francesca Delacourt, a double agent and "head of a most dreadful gang of spies" in *The Heart of a Mystery* (1901).

Notwithstanding her recognition as a literary celebrity by the *Strand*, Meade's fame was short-lived. Despite her remarkable industriousness and versatility, in the decades following her death on 26 October 1914, she was remembered as the author of schoolgirl fiction judged to have little merit. More recently, however, critics have come to recognise a wider range of Meade's literary and professional activity and to regard her as a significant *fin-de-siècle* New Woman writer. In Ireland, where Meade's reception has been mixed largely due to her orientation toward the English literary market, interest in Meade is also increasing and her contributions to Irish literature are the focus of a growing number of literary and critical studies.

Despite decades of neglect, there is still much for modern readers to discover in the work of L. T. Meade. *Eyes of Terror and Other Dark Adventures* represents not only a valuable contribution to the work of expanding Meade's literary profile but also an important addition to the collection of uncanny and occult fiction by Irish women writers published by Swan River Press.

Janis Dawson
Victoria, British Columbia
March 2021

Eyes of Terror

Very Far West

L. T. Meade with Clifford Halifax, M. D.

I was a rather young-looking man until the incident which I am about to relate took place. I will frankly confess that it aged me, telling for a time on my nerves, and rendering my right hand so shaky that I was unfit to perform operations of a critical and delicate character. I had just got back to town after my summer holiday when the circumstance occurred which sends strange thrills of horror through me even now.

It was a fine night towards the end of September. I had not many patients at this time, and felt a sudden desire to go to the theatre. Hailing a hansom, I ordered the man to drive me to the Criterion. I was in evening dress, and wore a diamond ring of remarkable value on my finger. This ring had been the present of a rich nabob, one of my patients, who had taken a fancy to me, and had shown his preference in this manner. I dislike jewellery as a rule, and never wear it; but to-night I slipped the ring on my finger, more from a sudden whim than for any other reason. I secured a good seat in the front row of the dress circle, and prepared for an evening's amusement.

The play was nothing in particular, and the time of year was a slack one with regard to the audience. Soon the curtain was raised, and the players began their performance. They acted without much spirit, the regular company being away on tour.

I was beginning to regret I had come, when my attention was arrested by the late arrival of a couple, who seated themselves in the chairs next to my own. One of them was a man of striking appearance, the other a very young and lovely girl. The man was old. He had silvery white hair, which was cut rather close to his head—dark eyes, a dark complexion, and a clean-shaven face. His lips were firm, and when shut looked like a straight line—his eyes were somewhat close to his very handsome, aquiline nose. He was a tall man, with broad shoulders, and held himself erect as if only twenty-five instead of sixty years had gone over his head.

His companion was also tall—very slender and willowy in appearance, with a quantity of soft blonde hair, a fair face, and eyes which I afterwards discovered were something the colour of violets. I am not a judge of dress, and cannot exactly describe what the girl wore—I think she was in black lace, but am not certain. I remember, however, quite distinctly that her opera-cloak was lined with soft white fur; I also know that she held in her hand a very large white feather fan, which she used assiduously during the performance.

The girl sat next to me. She had an opera-glass, and immediately on her arrival began to use it for purposes of criticism. I guessed, by her manner and by her gently-uttered remarks to her companion, that she was an habitual playgoer, and I surmised, perhaps correctly—I cannot say—that she knew something by actual experience of amateur acting.

Bad as the play undoubtedly was, it seemed to interest this beautiful girl. Between the intervals, which she occupied examining the actors, she made eager remarks to the gentleman by her side. I noticed that he replied to her shortly. I further noticed that not the slightest movement on his part was unperceived by her. I felt sure that they were father and daughter, and was further convinced that they were intensely attached to each other.

I have never considered myself an impressionable character, but there is not the least doubt that this girl—I think I may say this couple—interested me far more than the play I had come to see. The girl was beautiful enough to rouse a man's admiration, but I am certain that the feeling in my breast was not wholly that. I believe now that from the first moment I saw her she threw a sort of spell over me, and that my better judgment, my cool reason, and natural powers of observation were brought into abeyance by a certain power which she must have possessed.

She dropped her fan with some awkwardness. As a matter of course, I stooped to pick it up. In doing so my hand inadvertently touched hers, and I encountered the full gaze of her dark blue eyes.

When the first act came to an end, the invariable attendant with ices put in an appearance.

"You will have an ice?" said the girl, turning eagerly to the gentleman by her side. He shook his head, but motioning to the woman to approach, bought one and gave it to his young companion.

"This will refresh you, Leonora," he said. "My dear, I wish you to eat it."

She smiled at him, and, leaning back comfortably in her chair, partook with evident gratification of the slight refreshment.

I was careful not to appear to watch her, but as I turned for the apparent purpose of looking at a distant part of the audience, I was startled by the fixed gaze of the man who sat by her side. His closely-set dark eyes were fixed on me. He seemed to look me all over. There was a sinister expression in the thin lines of his closely-shut lips. The moment I glanced at him he turned away. I felt a sudden sense of repulsion. I have had something of the same feeling when I looked full into the eyes of a snake.

The curtain rose, and the play went on. The girl once more had recourse to her opera-glasses, and once more her full attention was arrested by the commonplace performance. About the middle of the act, her elderly companion bent over and whispered something to her. Her hand trembled, the opera-glass slid down unnoticed on her lap. She looked at him anxiously, and said something which I could not hear.

"I shall be better outside," I heard him whisper in response. "Don't be anxious; I'll come back as soon as ever I am better."

He rose and made his way towards the nearest entrance.

As he did so, I turned and looked after him.

"Is he ill?" I whispered to myself. "He does not look it. How anxious that poor girl is. Her hand is trembling even now."

When the man got as far as the entrance door he turned and looked at the girl, and for an instant his cat-like eyes gave me a second swift glance. Again I felt a sensation of dislike, but again the feeling quickly passed.

I wish to repeat here, that I think my judgment was a little in abeyance that evening. I felt more attracted than ever by my next-door neighbour, and yet I am certain, positively certain, that the feeling which actuated me was not wholly admiration.

The play went on, but the girl no longer looked through her opera-glasses. She sat listlessly back in her chair. Now and then she turned impatiently towards the door, and then, with a quick sigh, glanced at her programme, or used her large feather fan with unnecessary force.

The minutes went on, but the old gentleman did not return. Once the girl half rose from her seat, pulling her opera-cloak about her as she did so; but then again she sat quietly back, with a sort of enforced calm.

I was careful not to appear to watch her, but once her eyes met mine, and the unspeakable anxiety in them forced me, involuntarily, to bend forward and make my first remark to her.

"Can I do anything for you?" I whispered. "Are you anxious about your companion?"

"Oh, thank you," she replied, with a long-drawn sigh. "The gentleman is my father. I am very anxious about him. I fear he is ill."

"Would you like me to go and see why he has not returned?" I asked.

"If you would be so kind," she answered, eagerly.

I rose, and went out into the lobbies. I went quickly to the gentlemen's cloak-room, and put some questions to the attendant.

"Is there an elderly gentleman here?" I asked—"tall, with white hair and a somewhat dark complexion. He left the theatre half an hour ago, and his daughter is afraid that he has been taken ill."

The man who had charge of the room knew nothing about him, but another attendant who was standing near suddenly remarked:—

"I think I know the gentleman you mean. He is not ill."

"How can you tell?" I replied.

"Well, about half an hour ago a man answering exactly to your description came out of the theatre. He came from the dress circle. He asked for a cigar, and lighted it. I lost sight of him immediately afterwards, but I think he went out."

I returned to give this information to the anxious girl. To my surprise it did not at all comfort her.

"He must be ill," she replied. "He would not leave me alone if he were not ill. I noticed that an attack was coming on. He is subject to attacks of a serious character. They are of the nature of fits, and they are dangerous, very dangerous."

"If he were ill," I replied, "he would have sent you word in here, and have got you to go to him. He may merely have gone out to get a little air, which relieves him."

"I do not know. Perhaps," she replied.

"And when he is at home," I continued, "if he really has gone home without you, he will naturally send at once for a doctor."

She shook her head when I made this last remark.

"My father will never see a doctor," she said; "he hates the medical profession. He does not believe in doctors. He has such a prejudice against them, that he would rather die than consult one."

"That is a pity," I answered, "for in cases like his, I have no doubt that there is much alleviation to be obtained from men who really understand the science of medicine."

She looked fixedly at me when I said this. Her face was quite piteous in its anxiety. I could see that she was very young, but her features looked small and drawn now, and her eyes almost too large for her little face.

"I am very anxious," she said, with a sigh. "My father is the only relation I possess; I am his only child. He is ill—I know he is very ill. I am most anxious."

She pulled her opera-cloak once more tightly about her, and looked with lack-lustre eyes on the stage. Our conversation had been so low that no one had been disturbed by it; we were obliged to keep our heads close together as we conversed, and once, I am sure, her golden hair must have touched my cheek.

"I cannot stand this any longer," she exclaimed, suddenly. "I must go out—I won't wait for the end of the play."

She rose as she spoke, and I followed her, as a matter of course. We found the lobbies almost deserted, and here I suddenly faced her and tried to use argument.

"You are unnecessarily sensitive and alarmed," I said. "I assure you that I speak with knowledge, as I am a member of the medical profession, against which your father has such a prejudice. A man as ill as you describe your father to be would not stop to light a cigar. I took the liberty of having a good look at your father when he was leaving the theatre, and he did not appear ill. A medical man sees tokens of illness before anyone else. Please rest assured that there is nothing much the matter."

"Do you think," she answered, flashing an angry glance at me, "that if there is nothing the matter, my father would leave me here alone? Do you think he cares so little about me that he would not return to take me home?"

I had no reply to make to this. Of course, it was scarcely likely that any father would leave so beautiful a young girl unprotected in a theatre at night.

"And," she continued, "how do you know that the gentleman who asked for a cigar was my father? There may have been somebody else here with white hair."

I felt convinced that the man who lit a cigar and the father of this young girl were identical, but again I had no answer to make.

"I must go home," she said. "I am terribly anxious—my father may be dead when I get home—he may not have gone home at all. Oh, what shall I do? He is all the world to me; if he dies, I shall die or go mad."

"I am sure your fears are exaggerated," I began, "but perhaps the best thing you can do is to go home. Have you a carriage—shall I see if it has arrived?"

"My father and I have a private hansom," she answered. "It may not have come yet, but perhaps it has. I will go with you, if you will allow me. You wouldn't recognise the hansom."

"Then take my arm," I said.

I led her downstairs. I am not impressionable, but the feel of her little fingers on my coat-sleeve was, to say the least of it, sympathetic. I earnestly wished to help her, and her exaggerated fears did not seem unnatural to me.

The private hansom was waiting just round the corner. It had arrived on the scene in good time, for the play would not be over for nearly another hour. I helped the young lady in. She was trembling very much, and her face, lit up by the gaslight, looked pale.

"Would you like me to see you home?" I asked. "I will, with pleasure."

"Oh, if you would be so kind!" she answered. "And did not you say that you are a medical man? If my father is ill, it might be possible for you to prescribe for him."

"He will not allow it, I fear," I answered. "You say he has no faith in doctors."

"No more he has, but when he gets these strange, these terrible seizures, he is often unconscious for a long, long time. Oh, do please see me home, Dr. ——"

"Halifax," I answered.

"Thank you, so much. My name is Whitby—Leonora Whitby. Please, Dr. Halifax, come home with me, and prescribe for my father if you possibly can."

"I will come with you with pleasure," I answered. I stepped into the hansom as I spoke.

She made way for me to seat myself by her side. The sweep of her long black lace dress fell partly over my legs. The hansom driver opened the little window in the roof for directions.

"What address am I to give?" I said to Leonora Whitby.

"Tell him to go back," she answered, quickly.

"Go back," I shouted to the man.

He slapped down the little window and we started forward at a brisk pace. It was not until long afterwards that I remembered that I was going away with a strange girl, to a place I knew nothing about, the address even of which was unknown to me.

It was a splendid starlight night; the air was very balmy. It blew into our faces as we travelled westward. First of all we dashed down Piccadilly. We passed Hyde Park Corner, and turned in the direction of those innumerable squares and fashionable houses which lie west of St. George's Hospital. Leonora talked as we drove together. She seemed to be almost in good spirits. Once she said to me very earnestly:—

"I do not know how to thank you. It is impossible for me to tell you how deeply indebted I am to you."

"Don't mention it," I answered.

"But I must," she replied. "I cannot be merely conventional, when I am treated so unconventionally. Another man would not have noticed a girl's anxiety, nor a girl's distress. Another man would not have lost half the play to help an anxious girl. Another man would not have put complete faith in a stranger as you have done, Dr. Halifax."

"I do not know that I have done anything more than a man in my profession ought to be ready to do at all times," I answered. "You know, or perhaps you do not know, that a doctor who really loves his profession puts it before everything else. Wherever it calls him, he is bound to go. You have asked me to visit a sick man with you—how is it possible for me to refuse?"

"You are the first doctor who has ever come to our house," she answered.

A great blaze of gaslight from a large central lamp fell on her face as she spoke. I could not help remarking its pallor. Her eyes were full of trouble. Her lips were tremulous.

"You are the first doctor who has ever come to our house," she repeated. "I almost wish I had not asked you to come."

"Why so? Do you think your father will resent my visit—that he will regard it as an intrusion?"

"Oh, it isn't that," she answered. Then she seemed to pull herself together as with a great effort.

"You are coming, and there's an end of it," she said; "well, I shall always be grateful to you for your kindness."

"I hope I may be able to assist your father."

When I said this her face grew brighter.

"I am sure you will," she said, eagerly. "You look clever. The moment I saw your face, I knew you were clever. The moment I looked at your hands, I saw capabilities in them. You have got the hands of a good surgeon."

"What can you know about it?" I answered, with a laugh.

"Oh," she said, with an answering laugh, "there are few things I do not know something about. You would be an encyclopaedia of all kinds of strange knowledge if you led my life."

"Well," I said, "I, of course, know nothing about you, but will you answer one pardonable question? Where are we going? I do not quite recognise this part of town, and yet I have lived in London the greater part of my days. Are we going east, west, north, or south? I have lost my bearings. What is your address?"

"We are going west," she replied, in a perfectly cold, calm voice. Then, before I could interrupt her, she pushed her long feather fan through the window.

"Take the short cut, Andrews," she called to the driver. "Don't go the round. We are in a great hurry; take the short cut."

"Yes, miss," he shouted back to her.

We were driving down a fairly broad thoroughfare at the time, but now we turned abruptly and entered the veriest slums I had ever seen. Shouting children, drunken men and women filled the streets. A bad smell rose on the night air.

Was it possible that this beautiful, refined-looking girl lived in so repulsive a neighbourhood? But no, it was only as she expressed it, a short cut. The horse was a fleet one, and we soon found ourselves in a lonely and deserted square. We pulled up at a house which had not a light showing anywhere. I got out first and helped Miss Whitby to descend from the hansom.

"Will you kindly inquire if your father has returned?" I asked her; "for if not, there does not seem much use in my coming in."

"Oh! come in, in any case for a moment," she answered, in a cheerful tone. "I can see that the servants have all gone to bed, so I must let myself in with this latch-key, but I shall find out in a moment if father has returned. Just come in and wait in the hall until I find out."

She raised her beautiful face to mine as she spoke. Her opera-cloak fell away from her slim shoulders. One white slender hand was raised to push back a refractory lock of golden hair. There was a solitary gas lamp at the corner, and it lit up her willowy figure. I looked at her with a sense of admiration which I could scarcely disguise. We entered the house.

"By the way, can you tell me if there is a cab-stand anywhere near?" I asked, suddenly, "as when I have done with your father, I should like to hasten home, and I have not the least idea what part of the world I am in."

"West," she answered, "very much west. When you leave this house, all you have to do is to take the first turning on your right, and you will find a cab-stand. There are night cabs always on the stand, so it will be perfectly easy for you to get home whenever your duties here are ended."

We were now standing inside the house. The heavy hall door suddenly slammed behind us. We were in pitch darkness.

"What a worry the servants are," exclaimed Miss Whitby's voice. "I always desire them to leave matches and a candle on the hall table. They have neglected my orders. Do you mind staying for a moment in the dark, Dr. Halifax?"

"Not at all," I replied.

She rushed away. I heard her footsteps getting fainter and fainter as she ascended the stairs. She was evidently going to seek matches up several stories. I was alone in the strange house. Silent as the grave was the dark hall. I turned my head to see if any stray beams of gaslight were coming through the fan-light. I found that there was no fan-light. In short, the darkness was of the Egyptian order—it might be felt.

The moments passed. Miss Whitby was a long time coming back. As I stood and waited for her, the darkness seemed to me to become more than ever Egyptian.

I heard a faint sound beneath me. Where did it come from? Did the servants, who kept such early hours, sleep in the cellars? I sprang in the direction of the hall door. Could I have found the lock I would certainly have opened it, if for no other reason, than to let in a little light.

Fumble as I would, however, I could not discover any hasp, handle, or bolt. The next instant a glimmer of light from above streamed gratefully down, and I heard the swish of Leonora's evening dress.

"I beg a thousand pardons," she exclaimed, as she joined me. "What must you think of my leaving you so long in that dark, dismal hall? But the fact is, I could not resist the temptation of finding out whether my father had returned. He has: he is still in his bedroom. Now, will you come upstairs with me?"

She ran on in front, and I obediently followed. On the first landing we entered a sitting-room, which was gaily lighted with a couple of lamps covered with soft gold shades, and on the centre table of which a meal was spread.

"Sit down for a moment," said Miss Whitby; "you must have some refreshment. What can I give you? I am always stupid about opening champagne bottles; but perhaps you can do it for yourself. This is *Jules Mumm*. If my father were here I am sure he would recommend it."

"I don't care for anything," I replied. "If your father is ill, I should like to see him. Have you told him that I am here?"

"No. Do you think I would dare? Did not I tell you how he hated doctors?"

"Then perhaps he is not ill enough to need one," I said, rising to my feet. "In that case I will wish you good evening."

"Now you are angry with me," said Miss Whitby; "I am sure I am not surprised, for I *have* taken a most unwarrantable liberty with you. But if you only would have patience! I want you to see him, of course, but we must manage it."

She sank down on a sofa, and pressed her hand to her brow. She was wonderfully beautiful. I can frankly state that I had never seen anyone so lovely before. A strange sensation of admiration mixed with repulsion came over me, as I stood by the hearth and watched her.

"Look here," I said, suddenly, "I have come to this house for the express purpose of seeing your father, who is supposed to be ill. If you do not take me to him immediately, I must say good-night."

She laughed when I said this.

"It's so easy to *say* good-night," she replied. Then, of a sudden, her manner changed. "Why do I tease you," she said, "when you have been more than kind to me? In truth, there never was a girl in all London who had less cause for laughter than I have now. There is one being in the world whom I love. My fears about my father have been verified, Dr. Halifax. He has just gone through one of those strange and terrible seizures. When he left the theatre I knew he would have it, for I am so well acquainted with the signs. I hoped we should have returned in time to see him in the unconscious stage. He has recovered consciousness, and I am a little anxious about the effect on him of your presence in the room. Of course, beyond anything, I want you to see him. But what do you advise me to do?"

Her manner was so impressive, and the sorrow on her young face so genuine, that once more I was the doctor, with all my professional instincts alive and strong.

"The best thing to do is this," I said. "You will take me to your father's room, and introduce me quite quietly as Dr.

Halifax. The chances are a hundred to one that when he sees a real doctor, his prejudices against the imaginary ones will melt into air. One thing at least I can promise—he shall not blame you."

Miss Whitby appeared to ponder over my advice for a moment.

"All right," she said, suddenly. "What you suggest is a risk, but it is perhaps the best thing to do. We will go upstairs at once. Will you follow me?"

The house was well furnished, but very dark. There was a strange and unusual absence of gas. Miss Whitby held a lighted candle in her hand as she flitted upstairs.

We paused on the next landing. She turned abruptly to her right, and we entered a room which must have been over the sitting-room where the supper was laid. This room was large and lofty. It was furnished in the old-fashioned style. The four-post bedstead was made of dark mahogany. The wardrobe and chairs were of the same. When we entered the room was in darkness, and the little flicker of the candle did not do much to light it up.

Leonora laid it down on a table, and walked directly up to the bed. A man was lying there stretched out flat with his arms to his sides. He was in evening dress, and it did not take me an instant to recognise him as the old man who had accompanied the girl to the theatre. His eyes were shut now, and he looked strikingly handsome. His whole face was so pale, that it might have been cut in marble. He did not move an eyelid nor stir a finger when I approached and bent over him.

"Father," said Miss Whitby.

He made her no answer.

"He is unconscious again—he is worse," she exclaimed, clasping her hands, and looking at me with terror.

"No, no," I answered. "There is nothing to be alarmed about."

I said this in confidence, for I had taken hold of my patient's wrist, and found that the pulse was full and steady. I bent a little closer over the man, and it instantly flashed through my mind with a sensation of amazement that his unconscious condition was only feigned.

I remembered again the sinister expression of his eyes as he left the theatre, and the thought which flashed then through my brain returned to me.

"He does not look ill."

I put his hand back on the bed, but not too quietly, and asking Miss Whitby to bring the candle near, deliberately lifted first one eye-lid and then the other. If the man were feigning unconsciousness he did it well. The eyes had a glassy, fixed appearance, but when I passed the candle backwards and forwards across the pupils, they acted naturally. Raising an eye-lid I pressed the tip of one finger on the eye-ball. He flinched then—it was enough.

"There is no immediate cause for anxiety," I said, aloud. "I will prepare a medicine for your father. When he has had a good sleep he will be much as usual. Have you anyone who will go to the nearest chemist's?"

"I will go, if necessary," she replied. "The servants have gone to bed."

"Surely one of them could be awakened," I answered. "In a case of this kind, you must not be too regardful of their comforts. I will sit with Mr. Whitby, while you run and rouse one of your servants."

"Very well," she said, after a pause; "I will do so."

"Won't you take the candle?" I asked.

"No," she replied, "I can find my way in the dark."

She left the room, closing the door behind her.

The moment she had done so, the patient on the bed moved, opened his eyes, and sat up. He looked full at me.

"May I ask your name?" he inquired.

"Dr. Halifax—I have been asked to prescribe for you by your daughter."

"You sat near us at the Criterion?"

"I did."

"Did my daughter ask you to come home with her?"

"Not exactly—I offered to do so—she seemed in distress about you."

"Poor Leonora," he said—and then he glanced towards the door.

"Did she tell you that I place no faith in your profession?" he asked again, after a pause.

"She did, and that being the case, now that you are really better, I will leave you."

"No, don't do so. As you have come in one sense uninvited, I will put you to the test—you shall prescribe for me."

"Willingly," I replied; "and now, as it is necessary for a doctor and his patient to clearly understand each other, I may as well tell you at once that, the moment I saw you, I knew that you were not unconscious."

"You are right, I was perfectly conscious."

"Why did you feign to be otherwise?" I asked.

"For Leonora's sake, and—my God, I cannot stand this any longer!" He started upright, then fell back with a groan.

"Lock the door," he said; "don't let her in. I am in agony, in frightful agony. I suffer from *angina pectoris*."

"Leonora knows nothing of this," he gasped. "I conceal it from her. I let her imagine that I suffer from a sort of epileptic fit. Nothing of the kind. This hell fire visits me, and I keep it from Leonora. Now that you have come, give me something, quick, quick!"

"I would, if I had the necessary remedy by me," I replied. "If you will allow me, I will write a prescription for your servant. I can get what is necessary at the nearest chemist's. If you prefer it, I will go myself to fetch what is required."

"No, no—stay—not in this room, but downstairs. Leonora will take your message. I hear her now at the door. Let her in—keep your own counsel. Do not betray me."

"I can let her in, in a moment," I answered; "but first let me say that I think you are doing very wrong. Miss Whitby has, I am convinced, presence of mind and strength of character. She would bear to know the true state of things. Sooner or later she must find out. If you give me permission, I will tell her. It is best for me to tell her."

"What I suffer from will kill me in the end, will it not?" inquired Whitby.

"What you suffer from, I need not tell you, is a serious malady. I have not, of course, gone carefully into your case, and it is impossible to do so until the paroxysm of pain is over. In the meantime, trinitrin will give you immediate relief."

"Let me in, please," called Leonora's voice through the keyhole.

"In one moment," I answered. Then I turned to the sick man.

"Shall I tell your daughter, Mr. Whitby? She must have heard us talking. She will know that you have at least returned to consciousness."

"You can tell her that I am in some pain," he replied, "that I have recovered consciousness, and that you are going to administer trinitrin; now go. Promise me that you will reveal nothing further to-night."

He groaned as he spoke, clutched the bed-clothes, and writhed in agony.

"I will promise to do as you wish," I said, pity in my tone.

I unlocked the door, and stood before Miss Whitby.

"My father is better; he has recovered consciousness," she exclaimed at once.

"He wishes to be alone and quiet," I replied. "Darkness will be good for him. We will take the candle and go downstairs."

I lifted it from the table as I spoke, and we descended together to the sitting-room.

"Is your servant coming for the message?" I inquired.

"Yes," she answered. "He will be dressed in a moment."

"Then, if you will give me a sheet of paper and a pen and ink, I will write my prescription," I said.

She fetched me some paper at once; a pen and ink, and a blotting-pad.

"Write," she said. "After you have written your prescription, and the servant has gone to fetch the medicine, you must tell me the truth."

I made no reply at all to this. I wrote for a certain preparation (trinitrin) and a hypodermic syringe. I handed the paper to Miss Whitby. She stood for a moment with it in her hand, then she left the room.

"The servant is a long time coming down," she said when she returned. "How slow, how unsympathetic servants are, and yet we are good to ours. We treat them with vast and exceptional consideration."

"You certainly do," I replied. "There are few houses of this kind where all the servants go to bed when their master and mistress happen to be out. There are few-houses where the servants retire to rest when the master happens to be dangerously ill."

"Oh, not dangerously, don't say that," she answered.

"I may be wrong to apply the word 'danger' just now," I replied; "but in any case, it is important that your father should get relief as soon as possible. I wish you would let me go to the chemist myself."

"No, the servant is coming," she answered.

Heavy footsteps were heard descending the stairs, and I saw through the partly open door the outline of a man's figure. Leonora gave him the paper, with directions to hurry, and he went downstairs.

"Now, that is better," she said, returning to the room. "While we wait you will eat something, will you not?"

"No, thank you," I replied.

The food on the table was appetizing. There were piles of fresh sandwiches, a lobster salad, and other dainties; but something in the air of the place, something in the desolation of the dark house, for this was the only well-lighted room, something in the forlorn attitude of the young girl who stood before me, suspense in her eyes, anxiety round her lips, took away the faintest desire to eat.

If what the man upstairs said was true, his tortures must be fiendish. Leonora asked me again to eat—again I refused.

"Will you open one of those bottles of champagne?" she said, suddenly. "I am faint, I must have a glass."

I did her bidding, of course. She drank off about half a glass of the sparkling wine, and then turned to me with a little additional colour.

"You are a good man," she said, suddenly. "I am sorry that we have so troubled you."

"That is nothing," I replied, "if I can be of benefit to your father. I should like to come here to-morrow and go carefully into his case."

"And then you will tell me the truth, which you are concealing now?" she answered.

"If he gives me permission," I replied.

"Oh, I knew there was something which he would not tell," she retorted; "he tries to deceive me. Won't you sit down? You must be tired standing."

I seated myself on the first chair, and looked round the room.

"This is a queer, old-fashioned sort of place," I said. "Have you lived here long?"

"Since my birth," she answered. "I am seventeen. I have lived here for seventeen years. Dr. Halifax?"

"Yes, what is it?"

"Do you mind my leaving you alone? I feel so restless, impatient, and nervous; I will go to my father until the messenger returns."

"Certainly," I replied; "and if he gets worse call to me, and I will come to you immediately; he ought not to be left long alone. I am anxious to give him relief as speedily as possible. This injection of trinitrin will immediately do so. I hope your messenger will soon return from the chemist's."

"He will be back presently. The chemist we employ happens to live at a little distance. I will go upstairs now."

"Very well," I replied, "make use of me when you want me."

She smiled, gave me a long glance with an expression on her face which I could not fathom, and softly closed the door behind her. It was a padded door, and made no sound as it closed.

I sat down in an easy chair; a very comfortable one, with a deep seat. I shut my eyes, for I was really beginning to feel tired, and the hour was now past midnight. I sincerely hoped the servant would soon return with the medicine. I was interested in my strange patient, and anxious to put him out of his worst tortures as soon as possible. I saw, as in a picture, the relief which would sweep over Leonora Whitby's face when she saw her father sink into a natural slumber.

She was evidently much attached to him, and yet he had treated her badly. His conduct in leaving her alone at the theatre, whatever his sufferings might have been, was scarcely what one would expect from a father to so young and lovely a girl. He had deliberately exposed his own child to the chances of insult. Why had he done this? Why, also, had he only feigned unconsciousness? How very unconventional, to say the least, was his mode of treating his child. He gave her to understand that he suffered from epileptic fits, whereas in reality his malady was *angina pectoris*.

Here I started and uttered a sudden loud exclamation.

"My God!" I said to myself. "The man cannot suffer from *angina pectoris*, his symptoms do not point to it. What is the matter with him? Did he feign the agony as well as the unconsciousness? He must have a monomania."

I could scarcely believe that this was possible. I felt almost certain that his tortures were not assumed. That writhing at least was natural, and that death-like pallor could scarcely be put on at will. The case began to interest me in the strangest way. I heartily wished the servant to return in order to see some more of my most peculiar patient.

After a time in my restlessness I began to pace up and down the room. It was large, lofty, and covered from ceiling to floor with book-cases, which were all filled with bright, neat-looking volumes. Books generally give a cheerful aspect, but, for some reason which I could not account for at the time, these did not.

I might look at one, however, to pass away the time, and I went up to a goodly edition of Dickens's works, intending to take down a volume of *Martin Chuzzlewit* to read. I put my hand on the book, and tried to draw it out of the case. To my amazement, I found that this book and all its companions were merely dummies. In short, the room which looked so full of the best literature, was empty of even one line of respectable print.

I sat down again in my chair. The supper on the table did not in the least tempt my appetite—the champagne could not allure me. There was a box of cigars lying temptingly near on the mantelpiece, but I was not disposed to smoke.

I made up my mind that, if the servant delayed his return much longer, I would open the door, call to Miss Whitby, tell her that I would go myself to the chemist's, and bring the medicine which was necessary for my patient's relief. I felt that movement was becoming indispensable to me, for the gloom of the house, the queerness of the whole of this adventure, were beginning at last to tell on my nerves.

Suddenly, as I sat back in the depths of the easy chair, I became conscious of a very queer and peculiar smell. I started to my feet in alarm, and rushing to the nearest window, tried to open it. I discovered that it was a solid frame from bottom to top, and was not meant to move. In short, it was a window which could not open. I tried the other with similar results. Meanwhile, the smell got worse—it rose to my head, and rendered me giddy.

What was the matter? Had I been entrapped into this place? Was my life in danger? Was there a fire in one of the rooms underneath? Yes, this was probably the solution of the enigma—a room had caught fire in the old house, and Leonora Whitby and her father knew nothing of it. I felt a passing sense of relief as this idea occurred to me, and staggered rather than walked to the door. The smell which affected me resembled the smell of fire, and yet there was a subtle difference. It was not caused by ordinary fire.

I reached the door and turned the handle. I was gasping for breath now, and felt that I had not a moment to lose in getting into purer air. I turned the ivory handle of the door frantically. It moved in my grasp—moved round and round, but did not open. In short, I was locked in—I was becoming asphyxiated. I felt my heart throbbing and my chest bound as by iron.

At this desperate instant I saw, to my relief, an unexpected sight. There was another door to the room. This door was evidently not meant to be noticed, for it was completely made up of the false books, and when shut could not be detected. I noticed it now, for it was slightly, very slightly, ajar. I rushed to it, flung it open, and entered another room. Then, indeed, my agony reached its climax. A man in evening dress was lying full length on the floor, absolutely unconscious, and probably dead. I staggered towards him, and remembered nothing more.

I came to myself, I do not know when—I do not know how. I was in a hansom. I was being driven rapidly through streets which were now almost deserted, in some direction, I knew not where. I could not recall at first what had occurred, but memory quickly returned to me. I saw the face of the dead man as he lay stretched on the floor. I saw once again that dreadful room, with its false books, its mockery of supper, its mockery of comfort. Above all things, I smelt once again that most horrible, suffocating odour.

"Charcoal," I muttered to myself. "There must have been a charcoal furnace under the room. I was duped into that den. Leonora Whitby, beautiful as she appeared, was in league with her father to rob me and take my life; but how have I escaped? Where am I now—where am I going? How, in the name of all that is wonderful, have I got into this hansom?"

There was a brisk breeze blowing, and each moment my brain was becoming clearer. The fumes of the charcoal were leaving me. I was vigorous and well—quite well, and with a keen memory of the past once again. I pushed my hand through the little window, and shouted to the driver to stop.

"Where are you taking me?" I asked. "How is it that I am here?"

He pulled up immediately, and drew his horse towards the pavement. The street was very quiet—it was a large thoroughfare—but the hour must have been nearly two in the morning.

"Where are you taking me?" I repeated.

"Home, sir, of course," replied the man. "I have your address, and it's all right. You sit quiet, sir."

"No, I won't, until you tell me where you are taking me," I answered. "How did I get into this hansom? You cannot drive me home, for you do not know my address."

"Ain't it St. John's Wood Avenue?" replied the man. "The gent, he said so. He gave me your card—Mr. George Cobb, 19, St. John's Wood Avenue."

"Nothing of the kind," I called back, in indignation. "My name is not Mr. George Cobb. Show me the card."

The man fumbled in his breast-pocket, and presently pushed a dirty piece of paste-board through the window. I thrust it into my pocket.

"And now tell me," I said, "how I got into this cab."

"Well, sir," he replied, after a brief moment of hesitation, "I am glad you're better—lor', it isn't anything to fret about—it happens to many and many a gent. You was dead drunk, and stretched on the pavement, sir, and an old gentleman with white 'air he come up and he looks at yer, and he shouts to me:—

" 'Cabby,' says he, 'are you good for a job?'

" 'Yes, sir,' I answers.

" 'Well, then,' says he, 'you take this young gentleman 'ome. He's drunk, and ef the police see him, they'll lock him up—but ef you get down and give me a 'and, we'll get 'im into your 'ansom—and this is where he lives—at least, I suppose so, for this card was found on 'im.'

" 'Right you air,' I says to the old gent, and between us we got you into the cab, and 'ere we are now a-driving back to St. John's Wood Avenue."

"Cabby, I have been the victim of the most awful plot, and—and," I continued, feeling in my pockets excitedly, "I have been robbed—I only wonder I have not been murdered."

As I spoke I felt for my watch and chain—they had vanished. My valuable diamond ring, the motive, probably, of the whole horrible conspiracy, had been removed from my finger. My studs were gone, and what money I possessed—amounting, I am glad to say, to not more than £2 or £3—was no longer in my possession. The only wonder was why my life had been spared.

"Drive to the nearest police-station. I must give information without a moment's delay," I said to the cabman.

But that is the end of the adventure. Strange, incomprehensible as it may seem, from that day to this I have never solved the enigma of that dark house in that solitary square.

West, very far west, it lies, truly; so far that the police, whom I instantly put on the alert, could never from that day to now obtain the slightest clue to its whereabouts.

For aught that I can tell, Leonora Whitby and her father may be still pursuing their deadly work.

When I read in the papers of sudden and mysterious disappearances I invariably think of them, and wonder if the experiences of the victim who has vanished from all his familiar haunts have been anything like mine—if he has waited, as I waited, in that terrible lethal chamber, with its false books and its padded doors—if he has tasted the tortures of asphyxia and stared death in the face, but unlike me has never returned from the Vale of the Shadow.

The Panelled Bedroom

L. T. Meade with Clifford Halifax, M. D.

[We have taken down these stories from time to time as our friend, Paul Gilchrist, has related them to us. He is a man whose life study has been science in its most interesting forms—he is also a keen observer of human nature and a noted traveller. He has an unbounded sympathy for his kind, and it has been his lot to be consulted on many occasions by all sorts and conditions of men.]

The Perownes of Queen's Marvel belonged to one of the oldest families in Staffordshire. Their country seat was remarkable for all that renders family mansions attractive. Some parts of the house were centuries old. There was the tapestry-room, the picture-gallery, the hall with its splendid suits of mail-armour; the wide, white marble stairs; then, again, there was the old painted glass in the Gothic windows; the Henry IV chapel, where prayers were still read morning after morning; and in addition, the many modern rooms with every available comfort. The house stood on a slight eminence, and commanded an extensive view of the neighbouring country. Acres and acres of broad lands surrounded the ancient mansion—there was the Queen Anne garden, with its trees cut in many grotesque shapes—there was the old paddock and the bowling alley, and in addition, of course, the modern gardens, with their smooth, rolling lawns, and their tennis courts.

At the time of my visit to Queen's Marvel, King Winter was in the height of his reign. I made one of a large Christmas party, and I found myself on my arrival surrounded by many old friends and acquaintances.

Edward Perowne, the present owner, was an imposing looking man of about sixty years of age. He had a fine face with aquiline features, a very upright carriage, and the courteous manner which belongs more or less to a bygone school. He came into the hall to greet his guests, accompanied by his pretty daughter-in-law, and a blooming girl whom he introduced to the assembled company as his grandchild.

The weather, for the time of year, happened to be perfect—there was frost in the air and sunshine overhead. Tea was served in the hall, and afterwards we strolled about the grounds. It was somewhat late when I sought the apartment allotted to me, and I had only time to dress for dinner. My servant, Silva, had laid out my evening dress, and was waiting to help me to get into it. I told him that I should not require his services further, and he left the room.

As I dressed I noticed for the first time the great beauty of the room which had been allotted to my use. It boasted of three doors, which at this moment stood slightly ajar—one opened on to the landing, one into a dressing-room and bath-room combined, and one into a small and beautifully furnished sitting-room. This room contained writing-table, easy lounge, many comfortable chairs, also cabinets full of curios, and a large bookcase filled from ceiling to floor with some of the best modern books. I entered the room, but finding I had no time to examine the books more particularly just now, returned to my bedroom, closing as I did so all three doors. When I did that, I gazed around me with momentary perplexity. I found myself in a very spacious bedroom, being nearly thirty feet in length; but what principally arrested my attention was a certain air of emptiness which struck me as strange. On examining the room more closely, I perceived that there was scarcely any furniture—the bed occupied an alcove in a distant corner; a large fire blazed cheerily in the opposite corner; there were a few chairs and one or two tables scattered about, nothing else—no wardrobe, no chest of drawers.

For a moment I felt even annoyed; then I began to examine the walls carefully—they were all made up of panels decorated in white and pale blue. Going near them I discovered in each what looked like a spring. I touched it: immediately the panel revolved on a pivot, and revealed furniture of different kinds within. Behind one was a very deep wardrobe, capable of holding a lady's voluminous dresses. I went to the next panel and touched the spring, and immediately a complete set of drawers of every size and description were revealed to me. Another, when pressed, showed a little table; another, a wardrobe of different construction. In fact, each panel all round the room was really hollow and held furniture of every sort and description, all by this strange means pushed out of sight except when required for use.

But the most remarkable fact about the room was that the three doors which I have already mentioned were also in panels, and when shut absolutely disappeared. The effect was strange, grotesque, and I felt that under certain conditions it might even be ghastly. Standing now in the middle of the room, I was, to all appearance, in a room without any door. I smiled to myself at the pleasant deception, and, as the gong sounded at that moment, prepared to make my exit. To do this I had to overcome a certain difficulty. Familiar as I seemed with the room, I could not for a moment find the right door. I went to one panel after another, each exactly alike, looking in vain for any handle. No handle was to be seen, but I presently saw a button in a certain panel at one end of the room. I pressed it, and a door immediately opened. I found myself then in my prettily furnished sitting-room, which, like the bedroom, was brilliantly lighted from above with electricity. I went through it, and, going downstairs, joined the rest of the guests.

We sat down, between thirty-five and forty, to dinner, and I found myself near the pretty girl who was my host's grand-daughter. Her name was Constance Perowne, she was nearly seventeen years of age, and was as gay and bright and happy looking as the heart of man could desire. She chatted volubly to me, and immediately volunteered to tell me who the different guests were.

"I always spend my holidays at Queen's Marvel," she began; "there is no place in all the world like it. You know," she added, dropping her voice to a low tone, "my father is dead, so mother lives altogether here with grandfather. That is mother sitting opposite: is she not pretty?"

I looked across the table, and encountered the gentle gaze of a lady of about five-and-thirty, who bore but a slight resemblance to the brisk, handsome girl by my side.

"Now I will tell you who the other people are," she continued. "Please listen very attentively, for I am going to begin right away. And first of all I will commence with those in whom I am myself most interested. Do you see that lady at the further end of the table? —she is nearly as old as mother—she is in black velvet, with a diamond star in her hair. Her name is Louisa Enderby. She is my cousin, her mother is grandfather's only daughter. Grandfather married twice, and Louisa Enderby's mother is his daughter by his first wife. My father was dear grannie's only child. Louisa has spent the greater part of her life abroad. She knows Italy, and Spain, and Corsica, and India—she has also been in Ceylon and Japan, and I believe even China. She is quite a wonderful woman, and, first and greatest of all, the most amazing mesmerist you ever came across."

I glanced in the direction of the lady, and saw a heavily built woman with thick, dark eyebrows, eyes somewhat closely set, with an unpleasant habit of looking up from under the heavy brows; a swarthy complexion, and full, red lips—her chin was cleft in the middle, and there was a good deal of obstinacy about the lower part of her face. Miss Enderby was undoubtedly a plain woman, and yet when her eyes met mine I felt a curious thrill, not exactly of sympathy, certainly not of admiration, but of a sensation which might have been a mixture of both. I could not account for it. I only knew that I was intensely interested in the lady, and would like to hear more about her.

When I entered the drawing-room after dinner, a young girl was seated in an easy chair, and Miss Enderby was standing close to her. To my surprise, and even annoyance, I saw that the victim was no other than the happy, bright girl, Constance Perowne. Obeying the orders of the mesmerist, she was now gazing fixedly at her. Miss Enderby looked quiet and very resolved—her eyes were dark with excitement, and two burning spots glowed on her cheeks.

"Remember, I have no wish to make this experiment," she said, turning and speaking to the rest of us with a curious light coming into her deep, queer eyes; "but I have yielded to the persuasions of my many young friends. While I make the necessary passes I must ask everyone to remain as quiet as possible; the slightest noise will distract the attention of the subject of my experiments. Now, then, Constance, you must endeavour to fix your thoughts fully upon me; do not allow them to dwell on outside objects; look me full in the eyes—I will make the passes, and you will doubtless soon fall asleep."

"Oh, dear, it does seem horrible. How can you submit, Connie?" cried a merry girl who stood a few paces away.

Constance laughed.

"I long for the experience," she cried; "it promises to be quite delightful. Now, please, Louisa, begin—I am to fix my eyes on your face—well, I am doing so."

Miss Enderby bent towards her and took hold of both of her hands; she then commenced the usual passes which are supposed after a time to produce hypnotic sleep. I soon perceived that Miss Perowne was not going to be an easy subject—she fidgeted in her chair, her bright eyes glanced away from those of the mesmerist—the passes were made gently and without intermission, and gradually they began to take effect. The young girl's eyes were now steadily fixed on the hypnotist, who gazed back with intensity and firmness. After a time Constance began to complain of a tingling and pricking sensation in her skin—soon afterwards I noticed that her eyelids began to twitch, then to droop, then they slowly closed—she uttered a deep sigh, and Miss Enderby, removing her gaze, announced to us all that Constance was in a mesmeric sleep. The rest of the visitors now crowded round her and began to ask questions through the mesmerizer. What followed was really too absurd to be quoted. Constance answered each remark, however silly.

In some surprise Perowne came up and gazed at her—he shook his white head, and turned to me.

"This is humbug," he said. "Connie is pretending—I shall give her a fine talking to to-morrow. Come into my study, won't you, Gilchrist? I really cannot stand this sort of child's play any longer." He nodded to one or two of his guests, and abruptly left the room.

He and I were looking over some valuable photographs in his study when, half an hour later, one of the younger girls rushed in, with a very pale face.

"Is Mr. Gilchrist here?" she cried.

"Yes," I answered; "what is the matter?"

"Please come into the drawing-room—someone says you know about mesmerism. We cannot wake Connie, we have all tried; but she is in such a queer state, crying and moaning. I think Miss Enderby is really frightened."

"This comes of outsiders meddling with what they know nothing about," I said, rising and speaking with some annoyance.

"Why, what can be the matter?" said Mr. Perowne. "You surely do not take this seriously?"

"Yes, I do," I answered. "Mesmerism is a real power. Miss Enderby has doubtless got the gift to a certain extent. She put your grand-daughter into a real mesmeric sleep, but now, finding she cannot immediately rouse the sleeper, she has in all probability become agitated and nervous. Her state of mind is communicated by sympathy to the patient. If you will allow me, Mr. Perowne, I will go immediately to the drawing-room."

"But do you understand this thing yourself?"

"Yes; I have studied mesmerism with some care."

"You believe in it?"

"Fully—but pray do not keep me now."

I hurried back to the drawing-room, followed by Mr. Perowne and the girl who had brought us the message. We found Constance still lying back in the chair in which she had been mesmerized. Her face, which had been serene and even beatific when I last saw it, was now full of suffering, and I thought it highly probable that if any more attempts were made to rouse her by Miss Enderby, she might be seized with spasms or even convulsions. The mesmerist, with a scarlet face and agitated and highly nervous manner, was grasping the poor girl's hands, speaking in her ear, and trying to drag her from her chair.

"Let her alone," I said, "do not touch her, please. When you become calm again you must reverse the passes, but this can only be done when you are quiet and cool."

Miss Enderby started back and stared at me attentively—her face went white to her lips. I noticed that she began to tremble. I had no time then to attend to her, however; all my sympathies were centred round Miss Perowne.

"Mischief will ensue if this young lady is agitated or worried any more," I said; "counter-influences can only do her serious harm. Let her have her sleep out, even if it lasts for a couple of hours; it cannot do her the slightest injury."

I spoke with a voice of authority, and after a time saw that I was making an impression on the agitated company. I lifted Miss Perowne very gently to a neighbouring sofa, and then sitting down near her motioned to everyone else to leave that part of the drawing-room.

They did so—the expression of suffering left the young girl's pretty face, and she slept on calmly. Miss Enderby stood near, watching her victim for a time, then she turned abruptly on her heel. A moment later I saw that she had left the room, but as she was in no condition to make the reverse passes, and as I thought it extremely unlikely that Miss Perowne would sleep for more than two hours, I did not interfere with her departure.

My prognostications turned out to be correct: between eleven and twelve Miss Perowne awoke quite naturally, looked around her, smiled, and asked where she was.

I took her hand and spoke to her gently.

"You are in the drawing-room," I said; "you need not be frightened—you have been subjected to an experiment. Miss Enderby put you to sleep."

"Then I have been mesmerized at last?" said Constance, springing to her feet.

"Yes, but think no more about it. Go to bed and dream of your Christmas pleasures."

"Is Louisa in the room?" she asked, a deep flush coming into each of her cheeks.

"No, you will see her in the morning."

"Go to bed at once, Constance," said her mother, now coming forward and taking both the girl's hands in one of hers. "Go, darling; you look quite excited."

"But, mother, there is nothing the matter with me. I have just had a lovely sleep, and am not in the least tired."

"Very well, but all the same, go to bed now. Good-night, my dear girl."

The pretty girl kissed her mother affectionately, held out one of her hands to me, and presently left the room. I took the opportunity to express my opinion to Mrs. Perowne that her daughter was a very unfit subject for such dangerous experiments.

I went upstairs and once more glanced round my apartment. As far as appearances went, I was in a room without any means of exit—each panel looked exactly like its fellow. There was no outward evidence of the big, hanging wardrobe, the capacious chest of drawers, the ordinary furniture of a bedroom. All the tables, with the exception of a small one near the bed, had disappeared—several of the chairs had also been put out of sight—the three modes of entrance were as if they did not exist. I could not but be conscious of a certain sense of puzzledom, which might, in a nervous person, even arise to a feeling of discomfort. I sat for a little longer by the fire thinking of Miss Perowne, and of Miss Enderby's remarkable face—then, feeling tired, I undressed and got into bed.

I must have awakened suddenly some hours later, for the fire was out and the chamber was in complete darkness. I found myself broad awake and listening intently. There was not a stir, not a sound in the silent room, but a sense of intense discomfort pervaded every atom of my frame. I could not account for my feelings, for I am by no means given to nerves in the ordinary sense of the word. I do not even know that I was nervous at that moment—I only felt intensely restless. Presently an irresistible impulse to rise came over me. I must yield to it—I stretched out my hand, felt along the wall, and turned on the electric light. In the brightness which immediately ensued the peculiar emptiness of the room once again struck me with a sense of oppression. I lay still for a moment longer, struggling with the inclination to rise—at last it became irresistible; I got up and put on my dressing-gown. When I had done so I felt inclined to laugh at myself—my real wish was to return to bed, but a counter-wish which I had never experienced before impelled me to walk to the opposite end of the room. The three modes of exit so artfully concealed in panels were all, I knew, situated in that direction. In the bright light I could distinctly see the small buttons which when pressed silently opened the panel doors. I approached the centre one, pressed the button, the door revolved noiselessly back, and I perceived that I was on the threshold of the little sitting-room which I have before mentioned. To my astonishment it was bright with electric light, and standing by the mantelpiece I encountered the figure and somewhat arrogant gaze of Miss Enderby.

What did she want with me? How had she got into my private sitting-room in the dead of night? My momentary surprise gave place to indignation.

"What are you doing here?" I asked.

"I have come to speak to you, Mr. Gilchrist," she replied; "I have something to say to you. It will not occupy much of your time."

"Pray be seated," I said; "but permit me to observe that this visit is most extraordinary."

"Not more so than my motive," was the calm reply. "A glance revealed to me this evening that you and I are *en rapport*, as we say in our phraseology. You can influence me, and I can influence you. We are both hypnotists, although you at the present moment are not fully aware of the magnitude of your own gift. I am anxious to pursue a certain course of action which you can, if you will, baulk me in. I wish you to understand that you do so at your peril."

"What do you mean?" I asked.

"To-night, after I left the room, you used your counter-influence with Mrs. Perowne to withdraw Constance from my society. Now, my intention is to see much of Constance—I wish to get her into my power—I mesmerized her to-night for the first time; I intend to mesmerize her again. But for the sudden and complete failure of nerve, which, alas! I am subject to at the most crucial moment of my life, you would not have appeared again on the scene. As it is, I am forced to betray to you what I would far rather conceal. I am a hypnotist up to a certain point—beyond that point I find my powers desert me. Now, you are a hypnotist of a much higher order—in fact, without knowing it yourself, you are a 'clairvoyant'. You can help me if you will—you can oppose me if you choose. I want you to promise not to oppose me—it is for that reason I have visited you to-night."

Having spoken in this strange way, she drew herself up, and gazed fixedly at me. I was also standing, and I looked fully back at her. Her face was full of light, her eyes were extraordinary—she was a very plain woman, but she had undoubtedly the queer gift of an almost unfathomable fascination.

"You promise?" she said, when I was silent.

"I do not know what you mean," I said; "but I may as well say at once that I distinctly disapprove of your influencing Miss Perowne. I do not think it right that young and healthy girls should be subjected to the hypnotic trance. I shall use what counter-influence I possess against you, if that is your intention—it is only fair that you should know that."

"You do it at your peril," she answered; "but you will doubtless think better of this presently. I will visit you again to-morrow night; expect me."

She glided towards the door, opened it, and went out. I returned to my bed.

At breakfast, on the following morning, I observed that all the other guests were present with the exception of Miss

Enderby. It occurred to me to wonder if she had become ashamed of her nightly visit, and did not wish to meet me at breakfast. I was seated near the elder Mrs. Perowne, and I turned to her with a question.

"I notice that Miss Enderby is absent," I said; "I hope there is nothing the matter with her?"

"Miss Enderby?" answered the old lady. "Oh, she never sleeps here. She and her mother occupy a house on the south side of the Park. Louisa went away almost immediately after Constance became better last night—she was out of the house long before eleven o'clock."

"Then how did she get back again?" was my mental comment. "How had she managed to visit me in my sitting-room?"

Absorbed in these thoughts, I scarcely replied to Mrs. Perowne, who must have wondered at my abstracted manner. Soon after breakfast we made up a riding party and went out for a long excursion. I found myself riding near Miss Perowne, who was mounted on a spirited horse and looked lovely in her habit. Her eyes were bright, her complexion clear; all evidence of the emotion which had been aroused last night had now completely left her blooming face. She expressed pleasure at finding herself in my company, and amused and entertained me with her girlish conversation.

"Do you know," she said, "that mother made me give her quite a solemn promise this morning?"

"What about?" I asked.

"That I would not allow Louisa to mesmerize me again."

"I am glad you have made Mrs. Perowne that promise; and now, shall we talk of something else?"

"Willingly," replied Constance. "How lovely the day is! Let us gallop across that stretch of turf."

I assented—she whipped up her horse, and we very soon distanced the other riders to a considerable extent. We halted presently for breath by the roadside, and Constance pushed the tumbled hair out of her eyes.

"I cannot help feeling sorry I made that promise to mother," she began, slightly panting as she spoke. "It has been quite an old wish of mine that Louisa should mesmerize or hypnotize me. Mother says that Louisa was always a very queer child, not a bit like any of us, and when she was quite young she was sent abroad to be educated. She came home when she was nearly grown up, just before the—the dreadful tragedy of grandfather's life occurred."

"What was that?" I asked, looking at the lovely face of the young girl.

"It was about my father, Mr. Gilchrist. He was my grandfather's only son. He married when he was very young, only twenty-one, and he died before"—here her voice slightly faltered—"months before I was born. Mother sometimes speaks of him, but not very often. I will show you his photograph if you will come to my private sitting-room some day. I love his photograph—and sometimes I feel that he is near me. Dear father, everyone loved him so much, and he met his death in such a dreadfully tragic manner. He was drowned while fishing about two miles away from Queen's Marvel. He fell into Lock-Overpool. Mother nearly lost her reason at the time; and as to grandfather, he shut himself up and would not see anyone for years and years—it is only lately that he has at all got over it. You see, he had no other child except Aunt Kate, and for some reason she was never a special favourite of his."

"Then who inherits Queen's Marvel?" I asked.

Constance turned her gentle eyes full upon my face.

"At some very far distant date I do," she answered. "It is a great inheritance for such a little person as I am, and I would much, much rather have nothing to do with it, but grandfather says I must take my responsibilities; and he is going to have me carefully trained—he wants me to be a good business woman and to understand all about the estate; but, Mr. Gilchrist, we are spending too much time chatting; we ought to turn our horses' heads homeward now."

Some fresh guests had arrived during our absence, and the evening which followed was all that was gay and entertaining. Miss Enderby, dressed again in her black velvet, with the one diamond star in her dark hair, was, notwithstanding her plainness and peculiar physiognomy, the life and soul of the party. She had a somewhat deep voice, with penetrating notes in it—whenever she spoke people turned to look at her or to listen to her sentence. She seemed scarcely to trouble herself to entertain, and yet she entertained without effort—her stories were gay, forcible, and to the point—she led the conversation when it languished, and when it grew bright and witty, sustained it at that level.

In the drawing-room she gave us some music—I asked her if she could sing, but she said she had not a note in her voice. Her music, however, like herself, was arresting and convincing—it seemed immediately to penetrate beneath the surface, to stay the thoughts, to quicken the brain, to rouse the intelligence; she improvised a good deal, and presently a number of the guests clustered round the grand piano to listen to her. From grave to gay she wandered—from the solemn to the trivial, from the deep and the passionate to the light and airy. I found myself involuntarily approaching nearer and nearer to her side. Suddenly she stopped in the middle of a sonata, raised her full greenish eyes to my face, smiled somewhat vaguely, and rose from her seat.

"Go on, go on," said several of the guests.

"No, enough; I am not in the humour," she answered. She glided away, and I presently saw her leaving the room.

By-and-by it was time for us all to retire to our respective rooms. I went to mine, poked up the fire, flung myself into an easy chair, and gave myself up to thinking of Louisa Enderby. She was a very plain woman—she was not even specially young, and yet no attractive girl had ever a stronger power of arresting the imagination, of touching—was it the heart, or some other more bewildering, more intangible force? Once again I recalled her visit of the previous night—it was strange, incomprehensible. Her manner of to-day, too, was absolutely baffling—during the whole evening she had never favoured me with special attention, but neither had she made the slightest attempt to avoid me.

As she rose suddenly from that music which was haunting my ears even now, she had, it is true, given me one glance, a glance which set my pulses beating, but which in itself only puzzled and disturbed. I sprang suddenly from my chair; I resolved to think of Miss Enderby no more. I was tired; I would go straight to bed, and to sleep. I had scarcely laid my head on my pillow before slumber visited me—slumber healthy and dreamless; but once again, as twenty-four hours before, I awoke in solitude and darkness to find myself listening intently. In the first moment of waking, I forgot where I was; Miss Enderby's very existence was blotted from my brain; then memory rushed over me. I recalled what had happened the night before; a sensation, not of nervousness, but a sort of peculiar and very real horror, visited me. I remembered Miss Enderby's promise to come to see me again on this night. Would she keep it? No; ridiculous, impossible! She did not sleep in the house. If she had managed by some underhand means to creep back to Queen's Marvel on the previous night, she surely could not perform this feat twice undiscovered.

I resolved once again to banish her from my mind, and turning on my pillow tried to resume my interrupted nap. This I found impossible. The same queer sense of restlessness which had overpowered me on the previous evening occurred again. I had almost a sensation as if I were struggling with someone who wanted to pull me from my pillow. Unable to resist the queer and overpowering desire to rise, I sat up in bed, felt along the wall until my hand came in contact with the electrical communication, and turning the handle I once more filled the room with brightness. The chamber looked queer and empty as it had done on the previous night. Its emptiness now began to impress me disagreeably. I almost wished that it had been my fate to be put into an ordinary bedroom. I began to recollect old stories which had troubled me in my long-ago boyhood—stories of rooms with collapsing walls, of rooms with traps of different kinds, all set for the destruction of unwary travellers.

I remembered one tale in particular of a certain hotel in France, where the top of the bed came down upon the visitor and crushed him to atoms. With an effort I shook myself out of this unpleasant memory. I was not staying at an hotel. On the contrary, I was in the modern wing of a happy English home. No more luxurious chamber could be found in the length and breadth of the land. It was queer that I should be the victim of, not nerves, but a state of horror which I could not in the least account for or understand. I looked again in the direction of the three doors: they were invisible. It occurred to me as quite possible that these doors, which could only be opened by touching a spring, might be easily locked in the same way, and that the miserable inmate of this room might find no door out of which to make his exit. I should, of course, laugh at these forebodings when daylight arrived, but they now impressed me disagreeably, and I sat up in bed with my heart beating hard.

"Ridiculous," I said to myself. "I will not be forced out of my bed to-night."

I was about to turn off the electric light, when once again, and more powerfully than before, the desire to rise overwhelmed me. I could not resist it. It was as impossible for me now to lie in bed as if I had been a child trying to resist the mandates of a stern parent. I rose as I had done on the previous night, and put on a warm dressing-gown which stood near. When I had done so I laughed aloud in a hollow manner.

"This is too absurd," I murmured. "I shall just get straight back to bed, and take a good dose of quinine in the morning—the fact is, I cannot be well." I approached the bed, but a power which I could not withstand kept me from getting into it, and now a queer sensation visited me. I no longer felt the least desire to oppose the influence which was undoubtedly exercising its sway over all my actions. I walked hurriedly across the room, pressed the button of the centre door, opened it as I had done on the previous night, stood again on the threshold of the little sitting-room, and once more encountered the fixed and intent gaze of Louisa Enderby. She was standing then, as she had done the night before, on the hearth—she wore her black velvet dress and the diamond star glittered in her hair. When she saw me a ghost of a smile flitted across her face, then it vanished. I noticed that her features were drawn, as if in mental agony—her queer, greenish eyes burned with a curious light.

"Well," I cried, "this is most extraordinary. Will you please explain how you have got into the house?"

"That does not concern you, Mr. Gilchrist," she replied. "I said I should visit you again—I have kept my word. We hypnotists never break our engagements. Will you please sit down?—I have something to say to you."

I found myself impelled to sit.

"You perceive," she said, with a playful and yet intensely disagreeable smile, "that against your will you are more or less under my power. I have come here, no matter how. Suffice it to you that I am in this house. You were in a calm and peaceful slumber when the near vicinity of my presence made itself felt to you. You awoke; you felt restless and uncomfortable. I willed you to come to me in this room. You struggled against my will. In the end I conquered, as I knew I should. You are here—I will you now to listen to me quietly."

"Say what you have to say, and be quick about it," I answered.

"I warned you last night that you would do no good to yourself by interfering with me. Against my will you used your influence to-day to put Constance against me. Why did you do so?"

"Because I consider the hypnotic influence bad for any healthy young girl," I answered.

"Indeed. Then, notwithstanding your undoubted power as a mesmerist, you do not thoroughly understand the curative influence of the gift which you possess."

"That is neither here nor there," I answered, impatiently. "Miss Perowne is quite well. My motto always is to let well alone."

Miss Enderby continued to gaze at me fixedly. The haggard look deepened on her face.

"You are doubtless aware of the value of the young life which you seek to protect."

"I fail to understand you," I answered.

"Folly!" she interrupted; "you must know what I mean. Constance as the only child of her father inherits Queen's Marvel."

I nodded to this self-evident fact, but did not speak.

"And I," she continued, "as the only child of my mother, inherit nothing beyond a miserable pittance, and even that is not mine while my mother lives."

I did not reply—she continued to fix me with her eyes.

"In order to influence you," she said, "I see I must tell you my story. I will do so as briefly as possible. My father died when I was four years old—he died in a lunatic asylum, where I shall doubtless follow him some day, but not yet, if I can help it. After his death I lived for a time in this house with my mother, but at seven years old I was sent to France to be educated. I was never like other children—I was always moody and peculiar—from my earliest days I was filled with a strange bitterness of spirit—I rebelled against the fate which had given me existence. I received an extraordinary education—just the worst sort for a nature like mine. The lady who had charge of me had dipped from her earliest years into the strange science which we call mesmerism. She quickly discovered that I was a medium, that I had extraordinary occult powers—she encouraged them, she trained me—I became, after a year or two of her manipulations, a very valuable clairvoyant. When still quite young, she took me with her to India, and we both studied mesmerism amongst the Hindus. Shortly after completing my eighteenth year, I came back again to England; my friend had died—my mother was anxious that I should live with her, and I came to her to the house which she now inhabits. My uncle, my mother's step-brother, the heir to this vast property, had just been married. I hated him for living at all; but for him I should have been the heiress of Queen's Marvel. I longed for the place with an avarice, with a passion, which you who are born to wealth can scarcely comprehend. I smothered my sensations, however, and tried to make myself agreeable to the family. I was never beautiful, but I had the power of fascination. In particular, I fascinated my uncle; he was young, only a few years my senior; he was handsome, fully endowed with all that can render life delightful. He had exactly what I had not—a perfect temper, a sweet and generous spirit. I hated him for those gifts as much as I hated him for his wealth.

"Perhaps you have already heard that my Uncle Gerald died when out fishing—he was found drowned in Lock-Overpool, which is part of our river about two miles from here. His fishing-rod was floating on the water, he had a blow on his head, and it was supposed that he had fallen from the rock into the deep part of the pool; and as he had his waders on, he, of course, sank immediately. That was the story credited by the country, and a verdict of 'Found drowned' was returned by the coroner. Now, I will tell you how he really came by his death."

I had been sitting, as she had desired me, up to that moment. Now I rose. The light in her eyes, the queer sort of terror on her face, absolutely startled me. She suddenly crouched slightly downwards, became rigid for a moment, as if she were going to have a cataleptic fit—but then, making a great effort, straightened herself once more.

"Why do you drag my soul from me?" she said.

"I ask for no confidences," I replied, but as I said the words I found myself looking firmly into her eyes. "All the same," I continued, "I know you will give them to me."

"Yes," she panted, "I cannot help myself. The truth for the first time passes my lips."

She now stood stock-still, her eyes were fixed on me as firmly as if she were in a trance, her words came out rapidly.

"The uncle whom I hated, who stood between me and this great property, *did not meet his death by accident!* I was fond of accompanying him on his fishing expeditions. Although no one knew it, I went with him on that special day. He waded into deep water, and I sat on the bank and watched him. He was not far from the pool. I had always had a horror of Lock-Overpool; its depths, its blackness—for it lay partly under a deep, overhanging cave—had always fascinated me. I found myself now gazing into its gloomy depths—as I did so, that demon which seemed to have got into me at my birth suddenly rose and took mastery of me.

" 'Uncle Gerald,' I cried, 'will you do me a favour?'

" 'What is that?' he asked.

" 'I have a fancy for that green fern which grows right in the depths of the rock above Lock-Overpool: will you get it for me?'

" 'With pleasure,' he replied—he admired me, he generally had the power to draw out what little good I possessed. He returned to the shore, and without removing his waders went carefully along the ledge of rock which jutted considerably out over the pool—his gaff lay on the bank—his back was to me—I followed him cautiously—madness was doubtless in my soul—I struck him a heavy blow with the iron instrument on the back of his head—he fell as if he were shot, bounded against a rock, and sank like a stone to the bottom of the pool. With his waders on I knew he had no chance of rising. The moment I had done the deed I repented; I threw his fishing-rod on the water, and rushed home, mad with fright and terror. No one had seen me leave the house, and no one had seen me return; not the faintest ghost of suspicion was ever attached to my name; but from that moment my life has been a torment. Now you know all. I did the evil deed for the sake of the property, but in the end Fate has conquered, for my uncle's widow, unknown to me, was about to give birth to a child. Three months after my uncle's death Constance was born; she is in the direct succession, and inherits the bulk of the property. By-and-by she will marry and her husband will take her name. Now, Mr. Gilchrist, I mean to get Constance under my influence; I do not wish to commit murder a second time, but I must have Constance Perowne as my tool. If you dare to defy me you will suffer."

She stopped speaking suddenly, flung her arms down to her side, and stared straight past me towards the other side of the room.

"I want you to go away," she said, after a long pause. Her voice had altered, it had become feeble and faint. "You trouble me; I am *en rapport* with you, you are in close sympathy with me; you can even read my thoughts. I came here to-night because I could not help it; I have told you this because I could not help it. Now, will you go—will you leave me alone?"

She suddenly fell on her knees; she approached nearer and crouched at my feet.

"Get up," I said; "you do not know what you are saying—there is the door; you must leave me now."

"Not until you have promised," she said.

"I will not promise."

"Then you are in peril. At least let me advise you to sleep in another room. Farewell." She walked slowly through the open doorway, closed the door after her, and vanished.

I did not go to bed again that night. Overpowered by the emotions which Miss Enderby's terrible tale had aroused, I paced up and down my chamber. When the first dawn began to break I dressed myself and went out. The day just beginning was Christmas Eve.

Against my will my steps wandered in the direction of Miss Enderby's house. I did not want to go to her, and yet I was impelled to do so. Suddenly I saw her turning a corner and coming to meet me—she was dressed in a neat costume, and looked both fresh and calm. She came up and wished me "Good-morning" in a pleasant, everyday voice.

I stared hard at her; she met my gaze without flinching; her face was as indifferent as it had been on the previous night.

"You are out early," she remarked. "At this time of year there is nothing to tempt one abroad before breakfast."

"I came to meet you," I answered.

"Indeed!" she replied, raising her brows in well-acted astonishment; "then perhaps you will turn, for I am coming to breakfast at Queen's Marvel."

Her coolness half maddened me. As we slowly returned to the house I resolved to put her to the test.

"You wonder why I am out so early," I said. "I will tell you. I have had a restless night; after such a night as I have just gone through one often feels the better for a walk."

"I am sorry you slept badly," she replied, and now I noticed, or thought I noticed, a light awakening in her eyes; "but I forgot," she added; "your restlessness can doubtless be accounted for—you sleep in the panelled room."

"Yes—it is a luxurious apartment."

"Very," she replied, and the ghost of a smile played round her lips.

"The panelled room is provided with every comfort," I continued, "and not the least of its charms is the sitting-room, with the cabinets and curios which belong to it. The sitting-room is a good place for a rendezvous."

"An excellent place," she replied. "Mr. Gilchrist, we must hurry unless we wish to be late for breakfast."

"There is plenty of time," I answered, and now I stood perfectly still and compelled her to face me.

"I want to ask you a question, Miss Enderby," I said. "Why did you twice visit me in the dead of the night in the sitting-room which is connected with the panelled bedroom?"

"I never visited you," she cried. "What in the world do you mean?"

"You must be mad, or you are acting a part," I replied. "You know you came to see me last night, and the night before, in the sitting-room adjoining the panelled bedroom."

"No," she answered; "it is you who are mad. I do not even sleep in the house," but now her face turned ghastly, she panted, and, suddenly losing her self-control, grasped both my hands. "Tell me what you mean," she cried.

"I will," I answered. "On the first night of my arrival you compelled me to get up; you compelled me to go to my sitting-room; you were there waiting for me; again last night you visited me, and on that occasion you told me—"

"My God! what?" she asked, in a low voice, which was almost like a hiss, "what did I say?"

"You told me the secret of Lock-Overpool."

When I said these words, she gave a cry like that of a hunted animal—she turned away from me and covered her face with both her hands.

"I feared this," she gasped, after a moment. "Something told me that you were exercising an awful power over me. Mr. Gilchrist, why do you mesmerize me? Why do you force me to come to you? Why do you drag that, that—oh, I must say no more; you have frightened me. I wish you would leave Queen's Marvel. What can I do to make you go?"

"Nothing at present," I answered, with coolness. "You have imparted to me a very ghastly secret. I am not prepared to say yet what I shall do about it."

With a mighty effort she recovered herself, the fear left her eyes—she stood up once more quite cool and composed, and faced me.

"You had a bad dream," she said. "You had a bad dream, nothing more."

We were interrupted at that moment by the hearty voice of Mr. Perowne himself.

"Halloa! there you are," he cried.

Miss Enderby ran forward to meet him. She looked quite composed—there was a smile round her lips, and pleasant words came from her mouth.

"I am coming to breakfast with you this morning, grandfather," she said.

He gave her a friendly nod, then turned to me, and we three returned to the house.

From that moment Miss Enderby avoided me. As far as I could tell, her eyes never once encountered mine. That night, too, I had no mysterious and restless desires as I slept in the panelled room. I was not compelled to leave my bed. Miss Enderby did not again intrude upon the hours devoted to slumber. The story she had told me, however, did not lessen its influence on my mind.

I felt puzzled how to act with regard to it—it was either true, and Miss Enderby was a murderer, a most dangerous person to have abroad; or she was mad. I resolved as soon as possible to get some particulars with regard to the death of Constance Perowne's father. Whether Miss Enderby's tale told to me in so strange a manner was true or false, however, it had lain in oblivion for eighteen years, and I determined not to cast a shadow upon the Christmas festivities by taking any steps in the matter just then. The further mystery of her visits I was unable to fathom—she had either come to me in a state of clairvoyance, or I had dreamt the whole thing—the latter supposition I did not believe for a moment; the former seemed to be the most likely solution. The little-understood science of mesmerism accounts for even more mysterious events than the strange visitations I had undergone. Miss Enderby, who knew the ways of the house well, might easily have secreted the key of a side door, and so found her way to my sitting-room without difficulty.

During the week which supervened between Christmas Day and New Year's Day, Miss Enderby was in and out of the house continually. As usual she was the life of the place—counselling Constance, helping her grandfather, entertaining the guests as no one else could entertain them. As the days went by, however, I began to notice in Constance herself a subtle change—she did not look well—the bright, laughing light in her eyes was subdued—once or twice when in my neighbourhood I thought I heard her sigh.

On New Year's Night there was to be a grand ball, to which the county was invited. The evening before Constance was standing near me—I touched her on her arm.

"You are sad about something," I said. We happened to be alone. She turned her sweet young face, looked at me fully, and then burst into tears.

"Don't, don't," she sobbed. "*Don't* drag my secret from me."

"I do not want to," I answered, gently; "but you look in trouble. Can I help you in any way?"

"I do not think so; I am only unhappy because I am disobeying mother."

"In what way?"

"Louisa has mesmerized me again. She asks me about you, and—but there she is coming—please do not tell her I have said anything."

She flitted away, and I turned in another direction.

Next day we dined early, and I went up to my room after dinner to rest for a short time before the festivities of the evening began. I was seated by my fire, reading the current number of the *Nineteenth Century*, when a very light tap came on one of the doors of my room.

Before I had even time to say "Come in," the door opened and the lovely, ethereal young form of Constance Perowne stood on the threshold. She was in her ball-dress, which she had not put on at dinner; a circlet of pearls formed a coronet round her head; she carried a large white feather fan in one hand, and her gloves in the other. I noticed as she stood on the threshold that she slowly unfurled the fan.

She looked at me vaguely—there was a peculiar expression in her eyes. It needed but a glance to show me what had occurred—the girl was in a state of trance or mesmeric sleep. I went up and spoke to her.

"What is the matter?" I asked. "What do you want?"

"There is a box of old silver in a safe at the back of one of the panels," she replied. "I have come to fetch it." She looked past me, answering my questions but not apparently seeing me. I glanced at her eyes; they were dull, and totally unconscious of vision—nevertheless, I knew that she was seeing acutely with the inner sense of the clairvoyant. I did not reply to her, and she walked across the room.

Now, in my peregrinations round this curious chamber I had carefully investigated the contents of every panel except one—that one had, to all appearance, no spring, and although I had felt carefully along the wall, I was never able to open it. It was to this special panel now that Constance Perowne directed her steps. Without the slightest hesitation she pressed her finger against an ornamental trail of ivy, which had been painted on the woodwork—when she did so the panel revolved back as the others had done, and revealed inside a long and narrow safe, made of solid iron. The safe was about three feet to four feet deep. The moment it opened Constance went in, threw her fan and gloves on the floor, and raising her arms began with all her might and main to pull forward a heavy iron box which stood on a shelf.

"It is so heavy," she panted; "I cannot lift it."

"Let me help you," I replied.

Just as if she were in an ordinary state, she stepped out of the safe, and I went in. She stood on the threshold—I stretched up my arms to take down the box, and as I was in the act of doing so, suddenly found myself in complete darkness. The spring door of the panel had come to; I was shut up in a living tomb. I called loudly, but the mesmerist was quite incapable of hearing me. The place in which I found myself was not only dark and narrow, but also, I was quite certain, almost sound-proof. It was a safe built of solid iron, and, doubtless, hermetically sealed. I stood still for a moment to take in the awful position. All too quickly I guessed what had occurred. Miss Enderby had planned this terrible catastrophe; she had made Constance her tool, and had sent her into my room to entrap me into the iron chest. The perspiration stood out on my forehead. I knew that unless I could find a quick mode of exit my hours were numbered; nay, more, that I had but a few minutes to live. I should all too quickly absorb the air in this narrow chamber, and in a very short time should die of asphyxia. For a moment despair seized me—then I resolved to have a fight for my life. Making a rapid calculation, I thought it probable that there was enough air in the safe to last me from ten minutes to a quarter of an hour. I felt in my pocket, took out a silver case which contained matches, and struck one—already the confined space of my living tomb was taking effect upon me—there was a loud buzzing in my ears—my heart throbbed with difficulty—I panted as one does who is suffering death from suffocation. I did not dare to strike another match, for the light would further exhaust my limited supply of air; but in a brief glance round my tomb, I saw just over my head and behind the iron box what looked like a bolt. I tapped the wall at this place—it sounded hollow. Dizzy and reeling, but putting forth herculean strength, I endeavoured to pull the heavy iron box from its position, and then flung myself madly against the wall where it sounded hollow. Already I was almost unconscious, but with the strength of a madman I flung myself against the solid iron. Miracle of miracles, it gave way!—I felt a cold breath of air, and in less than a minute was myself again. Lighting another match, I found myself on the edge of some steep steps which went down into apparently bottomless depths. I descended them carefully, striking a match from time to time to guide my steps. Very charily I got to the bottom of the steps, and then pursued my way along a very narrow and winding passage, which presently brought me to an old door thick with cobwebs, in which was a rusty lock. This door had evidently not been opened for many years. Seizing a bar of iron which happened to be on the floor, I pushed back the hasp of the lock—a breath of cooler, fresher air immediately greeted me, and I found myself out of doors and in the direction of the servants' part of the house. As quickly as possible I once more entered the house and regained my chamber by means of the servants' staircase. I went in, shut the door, flung myself into a chair, and sat for some time thinking over the position of affairs. Whether Miss Enderby was mad or sane, my plain duty now was to acquaint her relations with the awful occurrence which had just taken place—it was not safe to have such a woman at large. Doubtless even now she thought that I was dead, as I assuredly should have been but for the discovery of the secret door at the back of the safe.

After resting for about an hour I carefully changed my dress, and went down to the ball-room. I heard the merry strains of music going on below, and entered the ball-room by one of the side doors. The first person I saw was Constance Perowne—her cheeks were blooming—she looked radiant in her white dress—the light of youth and happiness shone in her hazel eyes. When she saw me she smiled; she was, as I knew afterwards, perfectly unconscious of the terrible deed she had just committed. I did not trouble her with any remark, but went further into the room. I stepped up to an open window and, partly concealing myself behind a curtain, began to look around. I was now able to watch Miss Enderby without being seen myself. She was dressed, as usual, in black velvet, which on this occasion was cut low, and exhibited a lovely white throat and well-shaped arms. The diamond star glittered in her dusky locks; her queer, green eyes were full of light; I fancied I saw a malignant smile round her lips. Doubtless she supposed herself now quite safe—her secret being, as she imagined, in the keeping of the dead. She was dancing with a handsome man, who evidently was succumbing to her fascinations. She was talking to him, showing the gleam of her white teeth, and the queer, mesmeric light in her eyes. He laughed and seemed amused as he listened. Gradually they approached my side—I stepped back a little. They both paused close to me, and I heard her at that moment utter a sigh. I then observed that, notwithstanding her apparent mirth, she was the victim of an uneasy terror. Seen close, her face looked haggard.

I could not resist the temptation to stretch out one of my hands and lay it on her shoulder. She was talking to her partner at the moment, and they were in the act of resuming the waltz. When she felt my hand she turned slowly and looked back at me. As her eyes met mine terror blanched her face, an expression of horror altered each feature—she sank away from the firm touch of my hand nearer and nearer to the ground, looking back at me as she did so all the time with an indescribable and most terrible expression. I have not the least doubt that she thought I was a ghost—it was impossible for her to believe that I could have found any way out of my living tomb. With a loud cry she sank the next moment in a sort of fit at my feet. Some people rushed forward and bore the fainting woman out of the ball-room. When she recovered partial consciousness she was insane. A doctor was summoned, who ordered the utmost quiet, and no one could understand the queer seizure.

Within a week from that date, Miss Enderby died, without ever having one gleam of returning sanity. Doubtless the shock of seeing me when she thought I had quitted the world had completely overbalanced her already too excitable brain. With her death, the necessity for disclosing her terrible secret no longer existed.

As to Constance, she is my special friend, and always will be, and I hope to her dying day she may never know what a near escape she had of taking my life.

The Mystery of the Felwyn Tunnel

L. T. Meade with Robert Eustace

I was making experiments of some interest at South Kensington, and hoped that I had perfected a small but not unimportant discovery, when, on returning home one evening in late October in the year 1893, I found a visiting card on my table. On it were inscribed the words, "Mr. Geoffrey Bainbridge". This name was quite unknown to me, so I rang the bell and inquired of my servant who the visitor had been. He described him as a gentleman who wished to see me on most urgent business, and said further that Mr. Bainbridge intended to call again later in the evening. It was with both curiosity and vexation that I awaited the return of the stranger. Urgent business with me generally meant a hurried rush to one part of the country or the other. I did not want to leave London just then; and when at half-past nine Mr. Geoffrey Bainbridge was ushered into my room, I received him with a certain coldness which he could not fail to perceive. He was a tall, well-dressed, elderly man. He immediately plunged into the object of his visit.

"I hope you do not consider my unexpected presence an intrusion, Mr. Bell," he said. "But I have heard of you from our mutual friends the Greys of Uplands. You may remember once doing that family a great service."

"I remember perfectly well," I answered more cordially. "Pray tell me what you want; I shall listen with attention."

"I believe you are the one man in London who can help me," he continued. "I refer to a matter especially relating to your own particular study. I need hardly say that whatever you do will not be unrewarded."

"That is neither here nor there," I said; "but before you go any further, allow me to ask one question? Do you want me to leave London at present?"

He raised his eyebrows in dismay.

"I certainly do," he answered.

"Very well; pray proceed with your story."

He looked at me with anxiety.

"In the first place," he began, "I must tell you that I am chairman of the Lytton Vale Railway Company in Wales, and that it is on an important matter connected with our line that I have come to consult you. When I explain to you the nature of the mystery, you will not wonder, I think, at my soliciting your aid."

"I will give you my closest attention," I answered; and then I added, impelled to say the latter words by a certain expression on his face, "if I can see my way to assisting you I shall be ready to do so."

"Pray accept my cordial thanks," he replied. "I have come up from my place at Felwyn to-day on purpose to consult you. It is in that neighbourhood that the affair has occurred. As it is essential that you should be in possession of the facts of the whole matter, I will go over things just as they happened."

I bent forward and listened attentively.

"This day fortnight," continued Mr. Bainbridge, "our quiet little village was horrified by the news that the signalman on duty at the mouth of the Felwyn Tunnel had been found dead under the most mysterious circumstances. The tunnel is at the end of a long cutting between Llanlys and Felwyn stations. It is about a mile long, and the signal-box is on the Felwyn side. The place is extremely lonely, being six miles from the village across the mountains. The name of the poor fellow who met his death in this mysterious fashion was David Pritchard. I have known him from a boy, and he was quite one of the steadiest and most trustworthy men on the line. On Tuesday evening he went on duty at six o'clock; on Wednesday morning the day-man who had come to relieve him was surprised not to find him in the box. It was just getting daylight, and the 6.30 local was coming down, so he pulled the signals and let her through. Then he went out, and, looking up the line towards the tunnel, saw Pritchard lying beside the line close to the mouth of the tunnel. Roberts, the day-man, ran up to him and found, to his horror, that he was quite dead. At first Roberts naturally supposed that he had been cut down by a train, as there was a wound at the back of the head; but he was not lying on the metals. Roberts ran back to the box and telegraphed through to Felwyn Station. The message was sent on to the village, and at half-past seven o'clock the police inspector came up to my house with the news. He and I, with the local doctor, went off at once to the tunnel. We found the dead man lying beside the metals a few yards away from the mouth of the tunnel, and the doctor immediately gave him a careful examination. There was a depressed fracture at the back of the skull, which must have caused his death, but how he came by it was not so clear. On examining the whole place most carefully, we saw, further, that there were marks on the rocks at the steep side of the embankment as if someone had tried to scramble up them. Why the poor fellow had attempted such a climb, God only knows. In doing so he must have slipped and fallen back on to the line, thus causing the fracture of the skull. In no case could he have gone up more than eight or ten feet, as the banks of the cutting run sheer up, almost perpendicularly, beyond that point for more than a hundred and fifty feet. There are some sharp boulders beside the line, and it was possible that he might have fallen on one of these and so sustained the injury. The affair must have occurred some time between 11.45 PM and 6 AM, as the engine-driver of the express at 11.45 PM states that the line was signalled clear, and he also caught sight of Pritchard in his box as he passed."

"This is deeply interesting," I said; "pray proceed."

Bainbridge looked at me earnestly; he then continued:

"The whole thing is shrouded in mystery. Why should Pritchard have left his box and gone down to the tunnel? Why, having done so, should he have made a wild attempt to scale the side of the cutting, an impossible feat at any time? Had danger threatened, the ordinary course of things would have been to run up the line towards the signal-box. These points are quite unexplained. Another curious fact is that death appears to have taken place just before the day-man came on duty, as the light at the mouth of the tunnel had been put out, and it was one of the night signalman's duties to do this as soon as daylight appeared—it is possible, therefore, that Pritchard went down to the tunnel for that purpose. Against this theory, however, and an objection that seems to nullify it, is the evidence of Dr. Williams, who states that when he examined the body his opinion was that death had taken place some hours before. An inquest was held on the following day, but before it took place there was a new and most important development. I now come to what I consider the crucial point in the whole story.

"For a long time there had been a feud between Pritchard and another man of the name of Wynne, a platelayer on the line. The object of their quarrel was the blacksmith's daughter in the neighbouring village—a remarkably pretty girl and an arrant flirt. Both men were madly in love with her, and she played them off one against the other. The night but one before his death Pritchard and Wynne had met at the village inn, had quarrelled in the bar—Lucy, of course, being the subject of their difference. Wynne was heard to say (he was a man of powerful build and subject to fits of ungovernable rage) that he would have Pritchard's life. Pritchard swore a great oath that he would get Lucy on the following day to promise to marry him. This oath, it appears, he kept, and on his way to the signal-box on Tuesday evening met Wynne, and triumphantly told him that Lucy had promised to be his wife. The men had a hand-to-hand fight on the spot, several people from the village being witnesses of it. They were separated with difficulty, each vowing vengeance on the other. Pritchard went off to his duty at the signal-box and Wynne returned to the village to drown his sorrows at the public-house.

"Very late that same night Wynne was seen by a villager going in the direction of the tunnel. The man stopped him and questioned him. He explained that he had left some of his tools on the line, and was on his way to fetch them. The villager noticed that he looked queer and excited, but not wishing to pick a quarrel thought it best not to question him further. It has been proved that Wynne never returned home that night, but came back at an early hour on the following morning, looking dazed and stupid. He was arrested on suspicion, and at the inquest the verdict was against him."

"Has he given any explanation of his own movements?" I asked.

"Yes; but nothing that can clear him. As a matter of fact, his tools were nowhere to be seen on the line, nor did he bring them home with him. His own story is that being considerably the worse for drink, he had fallen down in one of the fields and slept there till morning."

"Things look black against him," I said.

"They do; but listen, I have something more to add. Here comes a very queer feature in the affair. Lucy Ray, the girl who had caused the feud between Pritchard and Wynne, after hearing the news of Pritchard's death, completely lost her head, and ran frantically about the village declaring that Wynne was the man she really loved, and that she had only accepted Pritchard in a fit of rage with Wynne for not himself bringing matters to the point. The case looks very bad against Wynne, and yesterday the magistrate committed him for trial at the coming assizes. The unhappy Lucy Ray and the young man's parents are in a state bordering on distraction."

"What is your own opinion with regard to Wynne's guilt?" I asked.

"Before God, Mr. Bell, I believe the poor fellow is innocent, but the evidence against him is very strong. One of the favourite theories is that he went down to the tunnel and extinguished the light, knowing that this would bring Pritchard out of his box to see what was the matter, and that he then attacked him, striking the blow which fractured the skull."

"Has any weapon been found about, with which he could have given such a blow?"

"No; nor has anything of the kind been discovered on Wynne's person; that fact is decidedly in his favour."

"But what about the marks on the rocks?" I asked.

"It is possible that Wynne may have made them in order to divert suspicion by making people think that Pritchard must have fallen, and so killed himself. The holders of this theory base their belief on the absolute want of cause for Pritchard's trying to scale the rock. The whole thing is the most absolute enigma. Some of the country folk have declared that the tunnel is haunted (and there certainly has been such a rumour current among them for years). That Pritchard saw some apparition, and in wild terror sought to escape from it by climbing the rocks, is another theory, but only the most imaginative hold it."

"Well, it is a most extraordinary case," I replied.

"Yes, Mr. Bell, and I should like to get your opinion of it. Do you see your way to elucidate the mystery?"

"Not at present; but I shall be happy to investigate the matter to my utmost ability."

"But you do not wish to leave London at present?"

"That is so, but a matter of such importance cannot be set aside. It appears, from what you say, that Wynne's life hangs more or less on my being able to clear away the mystery."

"That is indeed the case. There ought not to be a single stone left unturned to get at the truth, for the sake of Wynne. Well, Mr. Bell, what do you propose to do?"

"To see the place without delay," I answered.

"That is right; when can you come?"

"Whenever you please."

"Will you come down to Felwyn with me to-morrow? I shall leave Paddington by the 7.10, and if you will be my guest I shall be only too pleased to put you up."

"That arrangement will suit me admirably," I replied. "I will meet you by the train you mention, and the affair shall have my best attention."

"Thank you," he said, rising. He shook hands with me and took his leave.

The next day I met Bainbridge at Paddington Station, and we were soon flying westward in the luxurious private compartment that had been reserved for him. I could see by his abstracted manner and his long lapses of silence that the mysterious affair at Felwyn Tunnel was occupying all his thoughts.

It was two o'clock in the afternoon when the train slowed down at the little station of Felwyn. The station-master was at the door in an instant to receive us.

"I have some terribly bad news for you, sir," he said, turning to Bainbridge as we alighted; "and yet in one sense it is a relief, for it seems to clear Wynne."

"What do you mean?" cried Bainbridge. "Bad news? Speak out at once!"

"Well, sir, it is this: there has been another death at Felwyn signal-box. John Davidson, who was on duty last night was found dead at an early hour this morning in the very place where we found poor Pritchard."

"Good God!" cried Bainbridge, starting back, "what an awful thing! What, in the name of Heaven, does it mean, Mr. Bell? This is too fearful. Thank goodness you have come down with us."

"It is as black a business as I ever heard of sir," echoed the station-master; "and what we are to do I don't know. Poor Davidson was found dead this morning, and there was neither mark nor sign of what killed him—that is the extraordinary part of it. There's a perfect panic abroad, and not a signalman on the line will take duty to-night. I was quite in despair, and was afraid at one time that the line would have to be closed, but at last it occurred to me to wire to Lytton Vale, and they are sending down an inspector. I expect him by a special every moment. I believe this is he coming now," added the station-master, looking up the line.

There was the sound of a whistle down the valley, and in a few moments a single engine shot into the station, and an official in uniform stepped on to the platform.

"Good-evening, sir," he said, touching his cap to Bainbridge; "I have just been sent down to inquire into this affair at the Felwyn Tunnel, and though it seems more of a matter for a Scotland Yard detective than one of ourselves, there was nothing for it but to come. All the same, Mr. Bainbridge, I cannot say that I look forward to spending to-night alone at the place."

"You wish for the services of a detective, but you shall have someone better," said Bainbridge, turning towards me. "This gentleman, Mr. John Bell, is the man of all others for our business. I have just brought him down from London for the purpose."

An expression of relief flitted across the inspector's face.

"I am very glad to see you, sir," he said to me, "and I hope you will be able to spend the night with me in the signal-box. I must say I don't much relish the idea of tackling the thing single-handed, but with your help, sir, I think we ought to get to the bottom of it somehow. I am afraid there is not a man on the line who will take duty until we do. So it is most important that the thing should be cleared, and without delay."

I readily assented to the inspector's proposition, and Bainbridge and I arranged that we should call for him at four o'clock at the village inn and drive him to the tunnel.

We then stepped into the waggonette which was waiting for us, and drove to Bainbridge's house.

Mrs. Bainbridge came out to meet us, and was full of the tragedy. Two pretty girls also ran to greet their father, and to glance inquisitively at me. I could see that the entire family was in a state of much excitement.

"Lucy Ray has just left, father," said the elder of the girls. "We had much trouble to soothe her, she is in a frantic state."

"You have heard, Mr. Bell, all about this dreadful mystery?" said Mrs. Bainbridge as she led me towards the dining-room.

"Yes," I answered, "your husband has been good enough to give me every particular."

"And you have really come here to help us?"

"I hope I may be able to discover the cause," I answered.

"It certainly seems most extraordinary," continued Mrs. Bainbridge. "My dear," she continued, turning to her husband, "you can easily imagine the state we were all in this morning when the news of the second death was brought to us."

"For my part," said Ella Bainbridge, "I am sure that Felwyn Tunnel is haunted. The villagers have thought so for a long time, and this second death seems to prove it, does it not?" Here she looked anxiously at me.

"I can offer no opinion," I replied, "until I have sifted the matter thoroughly."

"Come, Ella, don't worry Mr. Bell," said her father, "if he is as hungry as I am he must want his lunch."

We then seated ourselves at the table and commenced the meal. Bainbridge, although he professed to be hungry, was in such a state of excitement that he could scarcely eat. Immediately after lunch he left me to the care of his family and went into the village.

"It is just like him," said Mrs. Bainbridge, "he takes these sort of things to heart dreadfully. He is terribly upset about Lucy Ray, and also about that poor fellow Wynne. It is certainly a fearful tragedy from first to last."

"Well, at any rate," I said, "this fresh death will upset the evidence against Wynne."

"I hope so, and there is some satisfaction in the fact. Well, Mr. Bell, I see you have finished lunch, will you come into the drawing-room?"

I followed her into a pleasant room overlooking the valley of the Lytton.

By-and-by Bainbridge returned, and soon afterwards the dog-cart came to the door. My host and I mounted, Bainbridge took the reins and we started off at a brisk pace.

"Matters get worse and worse," he said the moment we were alone. "If you don't clear things up to-night, Bell, I say frankly that I cannot imagine what will happen."

We entered the village, and as we rattled down the ill-paved streets I was greeted with curious glances on all sides. The people were standing about in groups, evidently talking about the tragedy and nothing else. Suddenly as our trap bumped noisily over the paving-stones, a girl darted out of one of the houses, and, made frantic motions to Bainbridge, to stop the horse. He pulled the mare nearly up on her haunches, and the girl came up to the side of the dog-cart.

"You have heard it?" she said, speaking eagerly and in a gasping voice. "The death which occurred this morning will clear Stephen Wynne won't it, Mr. Bainbridge?—it will, you are sure, are you not?"

"It looks like it, Lucy, my poor girl," he answered. "But there, the whole thing is so terrible that I scarcely know what to think."

She was a pretty girl with dark eyes, and under ordinary circumstances must have had the vivacious expression of face and the brilliant complexion which so many of her countrywomen possess. But now her eyes were swollen with weeping and her complexion more or less disfigured by the agony she had gone through. She looked piteously at Bainbridge, her lips trembling. The next moment she burst into tears.

"Come away, Lucy," said a woman who had followed her out of the cottage; "Fie—for shame! don't trouble the gentlemen; come back and stay quiet."

"I can't, mother, I can't," said the unfortunate girl. "If they hang him, I'll go clean off my head. Oh, Mr. Bainbridge, do say that the second death has cleared him?"

"I have every hope that it will do so, Lucy," said Bainbridge, "but now don't keep us, there's a good girl; go back into the house. This gentleman has come down from London on purpose to look into the whole matter. I may have good news for you in the morning."

The girl raised her eyes to my face with a look of intense pleading. "Oh, I have been cruel and a fool, and I deserve everything," she gasped, "but, sir, for the love of Heaven try to clear him."

I promised to do my best.

Bainbridge touched up the mare, she bounded forward, and Lucy disappeared into the cottage with her mother.

The next moment we drew up at the inn where the inspector was waiting, and soon afterwards were bowling along between the high banks of the country lanes to the tunnel. It was a cold, still afternoon; the air was wonderfully keen, for a sharp frost had held the countryside in its grip for the last two days. The sun was just tipping the hills to westward when the trap pulled up at the top of the cutting. We hastily alighted, and the inspector and I bade Bainbridge good-bye. He said that he only wished that he could stay with us for the night, assured us that little sleep would visit him, and that he would be back at the cutting at an early hour on the following morning; then the noise of his horse's feet was heard fainter and fainter as he drove back over the frost-bound roads. The inspector and I ran along the little path to the wicket gate in the fence, stamping our feet on the hard ground to restore circulation after our cold drive. The next moment we were looking down upon the scene of the mysterious deaths, and a weird and lonely place it looked. The tunnel was at one end of the rock cutting, the sides of which ran sheer down to the line for over a hundred and fifty feet. Above the tunnel's mouth the hills rose one upon the other. A more dreary place it would have been difficult to imagine. From a little clump of pines a delicate film of blue smoke rose straight up on the still air. This came from the chimney of the signal-box.

As we started to descend the precipitous path the inspector sang out a cheery "Hullo!" The man on duty in the box immediately answered. His voice echoed and reverberated down the cutting, and the next moment he appeared at the door of the box. He told us that he would be with us immediately, but we called back to him to stay where he was, and the next instant the inspector and I entered the box.

"The first thing to do," said Henderson, the inspector, "is to send a message down the line to announce our arrival."

This he did, and in a few moments a crawling goods train came panting up the cutting. After signalling her through we descended the wooden flight of steps which led from the box down to the line and walked along the metals towards the tunnel till we stood on the spot where poor Davidson had been found dead that morning. I examined the ground and all around it most carefully. Everything tallied exactly with the description I had received. There could be no possible way of approaching the spot except by going along the line, as the rocky sides of the cutting were inaccessible.

"It is a most extraordinary thing, sir," said the signalman whom we had come to relieve. "Davidson had neither mark nor sign on him—there he lay stone dead and cold, and not a bruise nowhere—but Pritchard had an awful wound at the back of the head. They said he got it by climbing the rocks—here, you can see the marks for yourself, sir. But now, is it likely that Pritchard would try to climb rocks like these, so steep as they are?"

"Certainly not," I replied.

"Then how do you account for the wound, sir?" asked the man with an anxious face.

"I cannot tell you at present," I answered.

"And you and Inspector Henderson are going to spend the night in the signal-box?"

"Yes."

A horrified expression crept over the signalman's face.

"God preserve you both," he said; "I wouldn't do it—not for fifty pounds. It's not the first time I have heard tell that Felwyn Tunnel is haunted. But there, I won't say any more about that. It's a black business, and has given trouble enough. There's poor Wynne, the same thing as convicted of the murder of Pritchard; but now they say that Davidson's death will clear him. Davidson was as good a fellow as you would come across this side of the country, but for the matter of that, so was Pritchard. The whole thing is terrible—it upsets one, that it do, sir."

"I don't wonder at your feelings," I answered, "but now, see here, I want to make a most careful examination of everything. One of the theories is that Wynne crept down this rocky side and fractured Pritchard's skull. I believe such a feat to be impossible. On examining these rocks I see that a man might climb up the side of the tunnel as far as from eight to ten feet, utilising the sharp projections of rock for the purpose, but it would be out of the question for any man to come down the cutting. No; the only way Wynne could have approached Pritchard was by the line itself. But, after all, the real thing to discover is this," I continued; "what killed Davidson? Whatever caused his death is, beyond doubt, equally responsible for Pritchard's. I am now going into the tunnel."

Inspector Henderson went in with me. The place struck damp and chill. The walls were covered with green, evil-smelling fungi, and through the brickwork the moisture was oozing and had trickled down in long lines to the ground. Before us was nothing but dense darkness.

When we re-appeared the signalman was lighting the red lamp on the post, which stood about five feet from the ground just above the entrance to the tunnel.

"Is there plenty of oil?" asked the inspector.

"Yes, sir, plenty," replied the man. "Is there anything more I can do for either of you gentlemen?" he asked, pausing, and evidently dying to be off.

"Nothing," answered Henderson; "I will wish you good-evening."

"Good-evening to you both," said the man. He made his way quickly up the path and was soon lost to sight.

Henderson and I then returned to the signal-box.

By this time it was nearly dark.

"How many trains pass in the night?" I asked of the inspector.

"There's the 10.20 down express," he said, "it will pass here at about 10.40; then there's the 11.45 up, and then not another train till the 6.30 local to-morrow morning. We shan't have a very lively time," he added.

I approached the fire and bent over it, holding out my hands to try and get some warmth into them.

"It will take a good deal to persuade me to go down to the tunnel, whatever I may see there," said the man. "I don't think, Mr. Bell, I am a coward in any sense of the word, but there's something very uncanny about this place, right away from the rest of the world. I don't wonder one often hears of signalmen going mad in some of these lonely boxes. Have you any theory to account for these deaths, sir?"

"None at present," I replied.

"This second death puts the idea of Pritchard being murdered quite out of court," he continued.

"I am sure of it," I answered.

"And so am I, and that's one comfort," continued Henderson. "That poor girl, Lucy Ray, although she was to be blamed for her conduct, is much to be pitied now; and as to poor Wynne himself he protests his innocence through thick and thin. He was a wild fellow, but not the sort to take the life of a fellow-creature. I saw the doctor this afternoon while I was waiting for you at the inn, Mr. Bell, and also the police sergeant. They both say they do not know what Davidson died of. There was not the least sign of violence on the body."

"Well, I am as puzzled as the rest of you," I said. "I have one or two theories in my mind, but none of them will quite fit the situation."

The night was piercingly cold, and, although there was not a breath of wind, the keen and frosty air penetrated into the lonely signal-box. We spoke little, and both of us were doubtless absorbed by our own thoughts and speculations. As to Henderson, he looked distinctly uncomfortable, and I cannot say that my own feelings were too pleasant. Never had I been given a tougher problem to solve, and never had I been so utterly at my wits' end for a solution.

Now and then the inspector got up and went to the telegraph instrument, which intermittently clicked away in its box. As he did so he made some casual remark and then sat down again. After the 10.40 had gone through, there followed a period of silence which seemed almost oppressive. All at once the stillness was broken by the whirr of the electric bell, which sounded so sharply in our ears that we both started. Henderson rose.

"That's the 11.45 coming," he said, and, going over to the three long levers, he pulled two of them down with a loud clang. The next moment, with a rush and a scream, the express tore down the cutting, the carriage lights streamed past in a rapid flash, the ground trembled, a few sparks from the engine whirled up into the darkness, and the train plunged into the tunnel.

"And now," said Henderson, as he pushed back the levers, "not another train till daylight. My word, it is cold!"

It was intensely so. I piled some more wood on the fire and, turning up the collar of my heavy Ulster, sat down at one end of the bench and leant my back against the wall. Henderson did likewise—we were neither of us inclined to speak. As a rule, whenever I have any night work to do, I am never troubled with sleepiness, but on this occasion I felt unaccountably drowsy. I soon perceived that Henderson was in the same condition.

"Are you sleepy?" I asked of him.

"Dead with it, sir," was his answer; "but there's no fear, I won't drop off."

I got up and went to the window of the box. I felt certain that if I sat still any longer I should be in a sound sleep. This would never do. Already it was becoming a matter of torture to keep my eyes open. I began to pace up and down, I opened the door of the box and went out on the little platform.

"What's the matter, sir?" inquired Henderson, jumping up with a start.

"I cannot keep awake," I said.

"Nor can I," he answered, "and yet I have spent nights and nights of my life in signal-boxes and never was the least bit drowsy; perhaps it's the cold."

"Perhaps it is," I said; "but I have been out on as freezing nights before, and—"

The man did not reply; he had sat down again; his head was nodding.

I was just about to go up to him and shake him, when it suddenly occurred to me that I might as well let him have his sleep out. I soon heard him snoring, and he presently fell forward in a heap on the floor. By dint of walking up and down, I managed to keep from dropping off myself, and in torture which I shall never be able to describe, the night wore itself away. At last, towards morning, I awoke Henderson.

"You have had a good nap," I said, "but never mind, I have been on guard and nothing has occurred."

"Good God! have I been asleep?" cried the man.

"Sound," I answered.

"Well, I never felt anything like it," he replied. "Don't you find the air very close, sir?"

"No," I said; "it is as fresh as possible; it must be the cold."

"I'll just go and have a look at the light at the tunnel," said the man, "it will rouse me."

He went on to the little platform, whilst I bent over the fire and began to build it up. Presently he returned with a scared look on his face. I could see by the light of the oil lamp which hung on the wall that he was trembling.

"Mr. Bell," he said, "I believe there is somebody or something down at the mouth of the tunnel now." As he spoke he clutched me by the arm. "Go and look," he said; "whoever it is, it has put out the light."

"Put out the light?" I cried, "why, what's the time?"

Henderson pulled out his watch.

"Thank goodness most of the night is gone," he said; "I didn't know it was so late, it is half-past five."

"Then the local is not due for an hour yet?" I said.

"No; but who should put out the light?" cried Henderson.

I went to the door, flung it open, and looked out. The dim outline of the tunnel was just visible looming through the darkness, but the red light was out.

"What the dickens does it mean, sir?" gasped the inspector. "I know the lamp had plenty of oil in it. Can there be anyone standing in front of it, do you think?"

We waited and watched for a few moments, but nothing stirred.

"Come along," I said, "let us go down together and see what it is."

"I don't believe I can do it, sir; I really don't!"

"Nonsense," I cried. "I shall go down alone if you won't accompany me. Just hand me my stick, will you?"

"For God's sake, be careful, Mr. Bell. Don't go down whatever you do. I expect this is what happened before, and the poor fellows went down to see what it was and died there. There's some devilry at work, that's my belief."

"That is as it may be," I answered shortly, "but we certainly shall not find out by stopping here. My business is to get to the bottom of this, and I am going to do it. That there is danger of some sort I have very little doubt, but danger or not, I am going down."

"If you'll be warned by me, sir, you'll just stay quietly here."

"I must go down and see the matter out," was my answer. "Now listen to me, Henderson. I see that you are alarmed, and

I don't wonder. Just stay quietly where you are and watch, but if I call come at once. Don't delay a single instant. Remember I am putting my life into your hands. If I call 'Come', just come to me as quick as you can, for I may want help. Give me that lantern."

He unhitched it from the wall, and taking it from him, I walked cautiously down the steps on to the line. I still felt curiously, unaccountably drowsy and heavy. I wondered at this, for the moment was such a critical one as to make almost any man wide awake. Holding the lamp high above my head, I walked rapidly along the line. I hardly knew what I expected to find. Cautiously along the metals I made my way, peering right and left until I was close to the fatal spot where the bodies had been found. An uncontrollable shudder passed over me. The next moment, to my horror, without the slightest warning, the light I was carrying went out, leaving me in total darkness. I started back, and stumbling against one of the loose boulders reeled against the wall and nearly fell. What was the matter with me? I could hardly stand—I felt giddy and faint, and a horrible sensation of great tightness seized me across the chest. A loud ringing noise sounded in my ears. Struggling madly for breath, and with the fear of impending death upon me, I turned and tried to run from a danger I could neither understand nor grapple with. But before I had taken two steps my legs gave way from under me, and uttering a loud cry I fell insensible to the ground.

Out of an oblivion which, for all I knew, might have lasted for moments or centuries, a dawning consciousness came to me. I knew that I was lying on hard ground; that I was absolutely incapable of realising, nor had I the slightest inclination to discover, where I was. All I wanted was to lie quite still and undisturbed. Presently I opened my eyes.

Someone was bending over me and looking into my face.

"Thank God, he is not dead," I heard in whispered tones. Then, with a flash, memory returned to me.

"What has happened?" I asked.

"You may well ask that, sir," said the inspector gravely. "It has been touch and go with you for the last quarter of an hour—and a near thing for me too."

I sat up and looked around me. Daylight was just beginning to break, and I saw that we were at the bottom of the steps that led up to the signal-box. My teeth were chattering with the cold and I was shivering like a man with ague.

"I am better now," I said, "just give me your hand."

I took his arm, and holding the rail with the other hand staggered up into the box and sat down on the bench.

"Yes, it has been a near shave," I said, "and a big price to pay for solving a mystery."

"Do you mean to say you know what it is?" asked Henderson eagerly.

"Yes," I answered, "I think I know now—but first tell me how long was I unconscious?"

"A good bit over half an hour, sir, I should think. As soon as I heard you call out I ran down as you told me, but before I got to you I nearly fainted. I never had such a horrible sensation in my life. I felt as weak as a baby, but I just managed to seize you by the arms and drag you along the line to the steps, and that was about all I could do."

"Well, I owe you my life," I said; "just hand me that brandy flask, I shall be the better for some of its contents."

I took a long pull. Just as I was laying the flask down Henderson started from my side.

"There," he cried, "the 6.30 is coming." The electric bell at the instrument suddenly began to ring. "Ought I to let her go through, sir?" he inquired.

"Certainly," I answered. "That is exactly what we want. Oh, she will be all right."

"No danger to her, sir?"

"None, none; let her go through."

He pulled the lever and the next moment the train tore through the cutting.

"Now I think it will be safe to go down again," I said. "I believe I shall be able to get to the bottom of this business."

Henderson stared at me aghast.

"Do you mean that you are going down again to the tunnel?" he gasped.

"Yes," I said; "give me those matches. You had better come too. I don't think there will be much danger now; and there is daylight, so we can see what we are about."

The man was very loth to obey me, but at last I managed to persuade him. We went down the line, walking slowly, and at this moment we both felt our courage revived by a broad and cheerful ray of sunshine.

"We must advance cautiously," I said, "and be ready to run back at a moment's notice."

"God knows, sir, I think we are running a great risk," panted poor Henderson, "and if that devil or whatever else it is should happen to be about—why, daylight or no daylight—"

"Nonsense man," I interrupted, "if we are careful, no harm will happen to us now. Ah! and here we are!" We had reached the spot where I had fallen. "Just give me a match, Henderson."

He did so, and I immediately lit the lamp. Opening the glass of the lamp I held it close to the ground and passed it to and fro. Suddenly the flame went out.

"Don't you understand now?" I said, looking up at the inspector.

"No, I don't, sir," he replied with a bewildered expression.

Suddenly, before I could make an explanation we both heard shouts from the top of the cutting, and looking up I saw Bainbridge hurrying down the path. He had come in the dog-cart to fetch us.

"Here's the mystery," I cried as he rushed up to us, "and a deadlier scheme of Dame Nature's to frighten and murder poor humanity I have never seen."

As I spoke I lit the lamp again and held it just above a tiny fissure in the rock. It was at once extinguished.

"What is it?" said Bainbridge, panting with excitement.

"Something that nearly finished *me*," I replied. "Why, this is a natural escape of choke damp. Carbonic acid gas—the deadliest gas imaginable, because it gives no warning of its presence, and it has no smell. It must have collected here during the hours of the night when no train was passing, and gradually rising put out the signal light. The constant rushing of the trains through the cutting all day would temporarily disperse it."

As I made this explanation Bainbridge stood like one electrified, while a curious expression of mingled relief and horror swept over Henderson's face.

"An escape of carbonic acid gas is not an uncommon phenomenon in volcanic districts," I continued, "as I take this to be, but it is odd what should have started it. It has sometimes been known to follow earthquake shocks, when there is a profound disturbance of the deep strata."

"It is strange that you should have said that," said Bainbridge, when he could find his voice.

"What do you mean?"

"Why that about the earthquake. Don't you remember, Henderson," he added, turning to the inspector, "we had felt a slight shock all over South Wales about three weeks back?"

"Then that, I think, explains it," I said. "It is evident that Pritchard really did climb the rocks in a frantic attempt to escape from the gas and fell back on to these boulders. The other man was cut down at once, before he had time to fly."

"But what is to happen now?" asked Bainbridge. "Will it go on for ever?—how are we to stop it?"

"The fissure ought to be drenched with lime water, and then filled up, but all really depends on what is the size of the supply and also the depth. It is an extremely heavy gas, and would lie at the bottom of a cutting like water. I think there is more here just now than is good for us," I added.

"But how," continued Bainbridge as we moved a few steps from the fatal spot, "do you account for the interval between the first death and the second?"

"The escape must have been intermittent. If wind blew down the cutting, as probably was the case before this frost set in, it would keep the gas so diluted that its effects would not be noticed. There was enough down here this morning, before that train came through, to poison an army. Indeed, if it had not been for Henderson's promptitude, there would have been another inquest—on myself."

I then related my own experience.

"Well, this clears Wynne without doubt," said Bainbridge; "but alas! for the two poor fellows who were victims. Bell, the Lytton Vale Railway Company owe you unlimited thanks; you have doubtless saved many lives, and also the Company, for the line must have been closed if you had not made your valuable discovery. But now come home with me to breakfast. We can discuss all those matters later on."

The Dead Hand

L. T. Meade with Robert Eustace

My name is Diana Marburg. I am a palmist by profession. Occult phenomena, spiritualism, clairvoyance, and many other strange mysteries of the unseen world, have, from my earliest years, excited my keen interest.

Being blessed with abundant means, I attended in my youth many foreign schools of thought. I was a pupil of Lewis, Darling, Braid and others. I studied Reichenbach and Mesmer, and, finally, started my career as a thought reader and palmist in Maddox Street.

Now I live with a brother, five years my senior. My brother Rupert is an athletic Englishman, and also a barrister, with a rapidly growing practice. He loves and pities me—he casts over me the respectability of his presence, and wonders at what he calls my lapses from sanity. He is patient, however, and when he saw that in spite of all expostulation I meant to go my own way, he ceased to try to persuade me against my inclinations.

Gradually the success of my reading of the lines of the human hand brought me fame—my prophecies turned out correct, my intuition led me to right conclusions, and I was sought after very largely by that fashionable world which always follows anything new. I became a favourite in society, and was accounted both curious and bizarre.

On a certain evening in late July, I attended Lady Fortescue's reception in Curzon Street. I was ushered into a small ante-room which was furnished with the view of adding to the weird effect of my own appearance and words. I wore an Oriental costume, rich in colour and bespangled with sparkling gems. On my head I had twisted a Spanish scarf, my arms were bare to the elbows, and my dress open at the throat. Being tall, dark, and, I believe, graceful, my quaint dress suited me well.

Lady Fortescue saw me for a moment on my arrival, and inquired if I had everything I was likely to want. As she stood by the door she turned.

"I expect, Miss Marburg, that you will have a few strange clients to-night. My guests come from a varied and ever widening circle, and to-night all sorts and conditions of men will be present at my reception."

She left me, and soon afterwards those who wished to inquire of Fate appeared before me one by one.

Towards the close of the evening a tall, dark man was ushered into my presence. The room was shadowy, and I do not think he could see me at once, although I observed him quite distinctly. To the ordinary observer he doubtless appeared as a well set up man of the world, but to me he wore quite a different appearance. I read fear in his eyes, and irresolution, and at the same time cruelty round his lips. He glanced at me as if he meant to defy any message I might have for him, and yet at the same time was obliged to yield to an overpowering curiosity. I asked him his name, which he gave me at once.

"Philip Harman," he said; "have you ever heard of me before?"

"Never," I answered.

"I have come here because you are the fashion, Miss Marburg, and because many of Lady Fortescue's guests are flocking to this room to learn something of their future. Of course you cannot expect me to believe in your strange art, nevertheless, I shall be glad if you will look at my hand and tell me what you see there."

As he spoke he held out his hand. I noticed that it trembled. Before touching it I looked full at him.

"If you have no faith in me, why do you trouble to come here?" I asked.

"Curiosity brings me to you," he answered. "Will you grant my request or not?"

"I will look at your hand first if I may." I took it in mine. It was a long, thin hand, with a certain hardness about it. I turned the palm upward and examined it through a powerful lens. As I did so I felt my heart beat wildly and something of the fear in Philip Harman's eyes was communicated to me. I dropped the hand, shuddering inwardly as I did so.

"Well," he asked in astonishment, "what is the matter, what is my fate? Tell me at once. Why do you hesitate?"

"I would rather not tell you, Mr. Harman. You don't believe in me, go away and forget all about me."

"I cannot do that now. Your look says that you have seen something which you are afraid to speak about. Is that so?"

I nodded my head. I placed my hand on the little round table, which contained a shaded lamp, to steady myself.

"Come," he said rudely, "out with this horror—I am quite prepared."

"I have no good news for you," I answered. "I saw something very terrible in your hand."

"Speak."

"You are a ruined man," I said, taking his hand again in mine, and examining it carefully. "Yes, the marks are unmistakable. You will perpetrate a crime which will be discovered. You are about to commit a murder, and will suffer a shameful death on the scaffold."

He snatched his hand away with a violent movement and started back. His whole face was quivering with passion.

"How dare you say such infamous things!" he cried. "You go very far in your efforts to amuse, Miss Marburg."

"You asked me to tell you," was my reply.

He gave a harsh laugh, bowed low and went out of the room. I noticed his face as he did so; it was white as death.

I rang my little hand-bell to summon the next guest, and a tall and very beautiful woman between forty and fifty years of age entered. Her dress was ablaze with diamonds and she wore a diamond star of peculiar brilliancy just above her forehead. Her hair white as snow, and the glistening diamond star in the midst of the white hair, gave to her whole appearance a curious effect.

"My name is Mrs. Kenyon," she said; "you have just interviewed my nephew, Philip Harman. But what is the matter, my dear," she said suddenly, "you look ill."

"I have had a shock," was my vague reply, then I pulled myself together.

"What can I do for you?" I asked.

"I want you to tell me my future."

"Will you show me your hand?"

Mrs. Kenyon held it out, I took it in mine. The moment I glanced at it a feeling of relief passed over me. It was full of good qualities—the Mount of Jupiter well developed, the heart-line clear and unchained, a deep, long life-line, and a fate-line ascending clear upon the Mount of Saturn. I began to speak easily and rapidly, and with that fluency which often made me feel that my words were prompted by an unseen presence.

"What you tell me sounds very pleasant," said Mrs. Kenyon, "and I only hope my character is as good as you paint it. I fear it is not so, however; your words are too flattering, and you think too well of me. But you have not yet touched upon the most important point of all—the future. What is in store for me?"

I looked again very earnestly at the hand. My heart sank a trifle as I did so.

"I am sorry," I said, "I have to tell you bad news—I did not notice this at first but I see it plainly now. You are about to undergo a severe shock, a very great grief."

"Strange," answered Mrs. Kenyon. She paused for a moment, then she said suddenly: "You gave my nephew a bad report, did you not?"

I was silent. It was one of my invariable rules never to speak of one client to another.

"You need not speak," she continued, "I saw it in his face."

"I hope he will take the warning," I could not help murmuring faintly. Mrs. Kenyon overheard the words.

"And now you tell me that I am to undergo severe trouble. Will it come soon?"

"Yes," was my answer. "You will need all your strength to withstand it," and then, as if prompted by some strange impulse, I added, "I cannot tell you what that trouble may be, but I like you. If in the time of your trouble I can help you I will gladly do so."

"Thank you," answered Mrs. Kenyon, "you are kind. I do not profess to believe in you; that you should be able to foretell the future is, of course, impossible, but I also like you. I hope some day we may meet again." She held out her hand; I clasped it. A moment later she had passed outside the thick curtain which shut away the ante-room from the gay throng in the drawing-rooms.

I went home late that night. Rupert was in and waiting for me.

"Why, what is the matter, Diana?" he said the moment I appeared. "You look shockingly ill; this terrible life will kill you."

"I have seen strange things to-night" was my answer. I flung myself on the sofa, and for just a moment covered my tired eyes with my hand.

"Have some supper," said Rupert gently. He led me to the table, and helped me to wine and food.

"I have had a tiring and exciting evening at Lady Fortescue's," I said. "I shall be better when I have eaten. But where have you been this evening?"

"At the Apollo—there was plenty of gossip circulating there—two society scandals, and Philip Harman's crash. That is a big affair and likely to keep things pretty lively. But, my dear Di, what is the matter?"

I had half risen from my seat; I was gazing at my brother with fear in my eyes, my heart once again beat wildly.

"Did you say Philip Harman?" I asked.

"Yes, why? Do you know him?"

"Tell me about him at once, Rupert, I must know. What do you mean by his crash?"

"Oh, he is one of the plungers, you know. He has run through the Harman property and cannot touch the Kenyon."

"The Kenyon!" I exclaimed.

"Yes. His uncle, Walter Kenyon, was a very rich man, and has left all his estates to his young grandson, a lad of about thirteen. That boy stands between Harman and a quarter of a million. But why do you want to know?"

"Only that I saw Philip Harman to-night," was my answer.

"You did? That is curious. He asked you to prophesy with regard to his fate?"

"He did, Rupert."

"And you told him?"

"What I cannot tell you. You know I never divulge what I see in my clients' hands."

"Of course you cannot tell me, but it is easy to guess that you gave him bad news. They say he wants to marry the heiress and beauty of the season, Lady Maud Greville. If he succeeds in this he will be on his feet once more, but I doubt if she will have anything to say to him. He is an attractive man in some ways and good-looking, but the Countess of Cheddsleigh keeps a sharp look out on the future of her only daughter."

"Philip Harman must on no account marry an innocent girl," was my next impulsive remark. "Rupert, your news troubles me very much, it confirms—" I could not finish the sentence. I was overcome by what Rupert chose to consider intense nervousness.

"You must have your quinine and go to bed," he said; "come, I insist, I won't listen to another word."

A moment later I had left him, but try hard as I would I could not sleep that night. I felt that I myself was on the brink of a great catastrophe, that I personally, was mixed up in this affair. In all my experience I had never seen a hand like Philip Harman's before. There was no redeeming trait in it. The lines which denoted crime and disaster were too indelibly marked to be soon forgotten. When at last I did drop asleep that hand accompanied me into the world of dreams.

The London season came to an end. I heard nothing more about Philip Harman and his affairs, and in the excitement and interest of leaving town, was beginning more or less to forget him, when on the 25th of July, nearly a month after Lady Fortescue's party, a servant entered my consulting-room with a card. The man told me that a lady was waiting to see me, she begged for an interview at once on most urgent business. I glanced at the card. It bore the name of Mrs. Kenyon.

The moment I saw it that nervousness which had troubled me on the night when I saw Philip Harman and read his future in the ghastly lines of his hand returned. I could not speak at all for a moment; then I said, turning to the man who stood motionless waiting for my answer:

"Show the lady up immediately."

Mrs. Kenyon entered. She came hurriedly forward. When last I saw her she was a beautiful woman with great dignity of bearing and a kindly, sunshiny face. Now as she came into the room she was so changed that I should scarcely have known her. Her dress bore marks of disorder and hasty arrangement, her eyes were red with weeping.

"Pardon my coming so early, Miss Marburg," she said at once; then, without waiting for me to speak, she dropped into a chair.

"I am overcome," she gasped, "but you promised, if necessary, to help me. Do you remember my showing you my hand at Lady Fortescue's party?"

"I remember you perfectly, Mrs. Kenyon. What can I do for you?"

"You told me then that something terrible was about to happen. I did not believe it, I visited you out of curiosity and had no faith in you, but your predictions have come true, horribly true. I have come to you now for the help which you promised to give me if I needed it, for I believe it lies in your power to tell me something I wish to discover."

"I remember everything," I replied gravely; "what is it you wish me to do?"

"I want you to read a hand for me and to tell me what you see in it."

"Certainly, but will you make an appointment?"

"Can you come with me immediately to Godalming? My nephew Philip Harman has a place there."

"Philip Harman!" I muttered.

"Yes," she answered, scarcely noticing my words, "my only son and I have been staying with him. I want to take you there; can you come immediately?"

"You have not mentioned the name of the person whose hand you want me to read?"

"I would rather not do so—not yet, I mean."

"But can you not bring him or her here? I am very busy just now."

"That is impossible," replied Mrs. Kenyon. "I am afraid I must ask you to postpone all your other engagements, this thing is most imperative. I cannot bring the person whose hand I want you to read here, nor can there be any delay. You must see him if possible to-day. I implore you to come. I will give you any fee you like to demand."

"It is not a question of money," I replied, "I am interested in you. I will do what you require." I rose as I spoke. "By the way," I added, "I presume that the person whose hand you wish me to see has no objection to my doing so, otherwise my journey may be thrown away."

"There is no question about that," replied Mrs. Kenyon, "I thank you more than I can say for agreeing to come."

A few moments later we were on our way to the railway station. We caught our train, and between twelve and one o'clock arrived at Godalming. A carriage was waiting for us at the station, we drove for nearly two miles and presently found ourselves in a place with large shady grounds. We drew up beside a heavy portico, a man servant came gravely forward to help us to alight and we entered a large hall.

I noticed a curious hush about the place, and I observed that the man who admitted us did not speak, but glanced inquiringly at Mrs. Kenyon, as if for directions.

"Show Miss Marburg into the library," was her order. "I will be back again in a moment or two," she added, glancing at me.

I was ushered into a well-furnished library; there was a writing-table at one end of it on which papers of different sorts were scattered. I went forward mechanically and took up an envelope. It was addressed to Philip Harman, Esq., The Priory, Godalming. I dropped it as though I could not bear to touch it. Once again that queer nervousness seized me, and I was obliged to sit down weak and trembling. The next moment the room door was opened.

"Will you please come now, Miss Marburg?" said Mrs. Kenyon. "I will not keep you long."

We went upstairs together, and paused before a door on the first landing.

"We must enter softly," said the lady turning to me. There was something in her words and the look on her face which seemed to prepare me, but for what I could not tell. We found ourselves in a large room luxuriously furnished—the window blinds were all down, but the windows themselves were open and the blinds were gently moving to and fro in the soft summer air. In the centre of the room and drawn quite away from the wall was a small iron bedstead. I glanced towards it and a sudden irrepressible cry burst from my lips. On the bed lay a figure covered with a sheet beneath which its outline was indistinctly defined.

"What do you mean by bringing me here?" I said, turning to the elder woman and grasping her by the arm.

"You must not be frightened," she said gently, "come up to the bed. Hush, try to restrain yourself. Think of my most terrible grief; this is the hand I want you to read." As she spoke she drew aside the sheet and I found myself gazing down at the beautiful dead face of a child, a boy of about thirteen years of age.

"Dead! my only son!" said Mrs. Kenyon, "he was drowned this morning. Here is his hand; yesterday it was warm and full of life, now it is cold as marble. Will you take it, will you look at the lines? I want you to tell me if he met his death by accident or by design?"

"You say that you are living in Philip Harman's house?" I said.

"He asked us here on a visit."

"And this boy, this dead boy stood between him and the Kenyon property?" was my next inquiry.

"How can you tell? How do you know?"

"But answer me, is it true?"

"It is true."

I now went on my knees and took one of the child's small white hands in mine. I began to examine it.

"It is very strange," I said slowly, "this child has died a violent death, and it was caused by design."

"It was?" cried the mother. "Can you swear it?" She clutched me by the arm.

"I see it, but I cannot quite understand it," I answered, "there is a strong indication here that the child was murdered, and yet had I seen this hand in life I should have warned the boy against lightning, but a death by lightning would be accidental. Tell me how did the boy die?"

"By drowning. Early this morning he was bathing in the pool which adjoins a wide stream in the grounds. He did not return. We hastened to seek for him and found his body floating on the surface of the water. He was quite dead."

"Was the pool deep?"

"In one part it was ten feet deep, the rest of the pool was shallow. The doctor has been, and said that the child must have had a severe attack of cramp, but even then the pool is small, and he was a good swimmer for his age."

"Was no one with him?"

"No. His cousin, Philip Harman, often accompanied him, but he bathed alone this morning."

"Where was Mr. Harman this morning?"

"He went to town by an early train, and does not know yet. You say you think it was murder. How do you account for it?"

"The boy may have been drowned by accident, but I see something more in his hand than mere drowning, something that baffles me, yet it is plain—lightning. Is there no mark on the body?"

"Yes, there is a small blue mark just below the inner ankle of the right foot, but I think that was a bruise he must have got yesterday. The doctor said it must have been done previously and not in the pool as it would not have turned blue so quickly."

"May I see it?"

Mrs. Kenyon raised the end of the sheet and showed the mark. I looked at it long and earnestly.

"You are sure there was no thunder-storm this morning?" I asked.

"No, it was quite fine."

I rose slowly to my feet.

"I have looked at the boy's hand as you asked me," I said, "I must repeat my words—there are indications that he came by his death not by accident but design."

Mrs. Kenyon's face underwent a queer change as I spoke. She came suddenly forward, seized me by the arms and cried:

"I believe you, I believe you. I believe that my boy has been murdered in some fiendish and inexplicable way. The police have been here already, and of course there will be an inquest, but no one is suspected. Who are we to suspect?"

"Philip Harman," I could not help answering.

"Why? Why do you say that?"

"I am not at liberty to tell you. I make the suggestion."

"But it cannot be the case. The boy went to bathe alone in perfect health. Philip went to town by an earlier train than usual. I saw him off myself, I walked with him as far as the end of the avenue. It was soon afterwards that I missed my little Paul, and began to wonder why he had not returned to the house. I went with a servant to the pool and I saw, oh, I saw that which will haunt me to my dying day. He was my only son, Miss Marburg, my one great treasure. What you have suggested, what I myself, alas, believe, drives me nearly mad. But you must tell me why you suspect Philip Harman."

"Under the circumstances it may not be wrong to tell you," I said slowly. "The night I read your hand I also as you know read his. I saw in his hand that he was about to be a murderer. I told him so in as many words."

"You saw that? You told him! Oh, this is too awful! Philip has wanted money of late and has been in the strangest state. He has always been somewhat wild and given to speculation, and lately I know lost heavily with different ventures. He proposed to a young girl, a great friend of mine last week, but she would have nothing to do with him. Yes, it all seems possible. My little Paul stood between him and a great property. But how did he do it? There is not a particle of evidence against him. Your word goes for nothing, law and justice would only scout you. But we must act, Miss Marburg, and you must help me to prove the murder of my boy, to discover the murderer. I shall never rest until I have avenged him."

"Yes, I will help you," I answered.

As I descended the stairs accompanied by Mrs. Kenyon a strange thought struck me.

"I have promised to help you, and we must act at once," I said. "Will you leave this matter for the present in my hands, and will you let me send a telegram immediately to my brother? I shall need his assistance. He is a barrister and has chambers in town, but he will come to me at once. He is very clever and practical."

"Is he entirely in your confidence?"

"Absolutely. But pray tell me when do you expect Mr. Harman back?"

"He does not know anything at present, as he was going into the country for the day; he will be back as usual to-night."

"That is so much the better. May I send for my brother?"

"Do anything you please. You will find some telegraph forms in the hall and the groom can take your message at once."

I crossed the hall, found the telegraph forms on a table, sat down and filled one in as follows:

"*Come at once—I need your help most urgently. Diana.*"

I handed the telegram to a servant, who took it away at once.

"And now," I said turning to Mrs. Kenyon, "will you show me the pool? I shall go there and stay till my brother arrives."

"You will stay there, why?"

"I have my own reasons for wishing to do so. I cannot say more now. Please show me the way."

We went across the garden and into a meadow beyond. At the bottom of this meadow ran a swift-flowing stream. In the middle of the stream was the pool evidently made artificially. Beside it on the bank stood a small tent for dressing. The pool itself was a deep basin in the rock about seven yards across, surrounded by drooping willows which hung over it. At the upper end the stream fell into it in a miniature cascade—at the lower end a wire fence crossed it. This was doubtless done in order to prevent the cattle stirring the water.

I walked slowly round the pool, looking down into its silent depths without speaking. When I came back to where Mrs. Kenyon was standing I said slowly:

"I shall remain here until my brother comes. Will you send me down a few sandwiches, and bring him or send him to me directly he arrives?"

"But he cannot be with you for some hours," said Mrs. Kenyon. "I fail to understand your reason."

"I scarcely know that yet myself," was my reply, "but I am certain I am acting wisely. Will you leave me here? I wish to be alone in order to think out a problem."

Mrs. Kenyon slowly turned and went back to the house.

"I must unravel this mystery." I said to myself, "I must sift from the apparent facts of the case the awful truth which lies beneath. That sixth sense which has helped me up to the present shall help me to the end. Beyond doubt foul play has taken place. The boy met his death in this pool, but how? Beyond doubt this is the only spot where a solution can be found. I will stay here and think the matter through. If anything dangerous or fatal was put into the pool the murderer shall not remove his awful weapon without my knowledge."

So I thought and the moments flew. My head ached with the intensity of my thought, and as the afternoon advanced I was no nearer a solution than ever.

It was between four and five o'clock when to my infinite relief I saw Rupert hurrying across the meadow.

"What is the meaning of this, Diana?" he said. "Have you lost your senses? When I got your extraordinary wire I thought you must be ill."

I stood up, clasped his hands and looked into his face.

"Listen," I said. "A child has been murdered, and I want to discover the murderer. You must help me."

"Are you mad?" was his remark.

"No, I am sane," I answered; "little Paul Kenyon has been murdered. Do you remember telling me that he stood between Philip Harman and the Kenyon property? He was drowned this morning in this pool, the supposition being that the death occurred through accident. Now listen, Rupert, we have got to discover how the boy really met his death. The child was in perfect health when he entered the pool, his dead body was found floating on the water half-an-hour afterwards. The doctor said he died from drowning due to cramp. What caused such sudden and awful cramp as would drown a boy of his age within a few paces of the bank?"

"But what do you expect to find here?" said Rupert. He looked inclined to laugh at me when first he arrived, but his face was grave now, and even pale.

"Come here," I said suddenly, "I have already noticed one strange thing; it is this. Look!"

As I spoke I took his hand and approached the wire fence which protected the water from the cattle. Leaning over I said:

"Look down. Whoever designed this pool, for it was, of course, made artificially, took more precaution than is usual to prevent the water being contaminated. Do you see that fine wire netting which goes down to the bottom of the pool? That wire has been put there for some other reason than to keep cattle out. Rupert, do you think by any possibility it has been placed there to keep something in the pool?"

Rupert bent down and examined the wire carefully.

"It is curious," he said. "I see what you mean." A frown had settled on his face. Suddenly he turned to me.

"Your suggestion is too horrible, Diana. What can be in the pool? Do you mean something alive, something—" he stopped speaking, his eyes were fixed on my face with a dawning horror.

"Were there any marks on the boy?" was his next question.

"One small blue mark on the ankle. Ah! look, what is that?"

At the further end and in the deep part of the pool I suddenly saw the surface move and a slight eddying swirl appear on the water. It increased into ever widening circles and vanished.

Rupert's bronzed face was now almost as white as mine.

"We must drag the pool immediately," he said. "Harman cannot prevent us; we have seen enough to warrant what we do; I cannot let this pass. Stay here, Diana, and watch. I will bring Mrs. Kenyon with me and get her consent."

Rupert hurriedly left me and went back to the house across the meadow. It was fully an hour before he returned. The water was once more perfectly still. There was not the faintest movement of any living thing beneath its surface.

At the end of the hour I saw Mrs. Kenyon, my brother, a gardener, and another man coming across the meadow. One of the men was dragging a large net, one side of which was loaded with leaden sinkers—the other held an old-fashioned single-barrelled gun.

Rupert was now all activity. Mrs. Kenyon came and stood by my side without speaking. Rupert gave quick orders to the men. Under his directions one of them waded through the shallows just below the pool, and reaching the opposite bank, threw the net across, then the bottom of the net with the sinkers was let down into the pool.

When this was done Rupert possessed himself of the gun and stood at the upper end of the pool beside the little waterfall. He then gave the word to the men to begin to drag. Slowly and gradually they advanced, drawing the net forward, while all our eyes were fixed upon the water. Not a word was spoken; the men had not taken many steps when again was seen the swirl in the water, and a few little eddies were sucked down. A sharp cry broke from Mrs. Kenyon's lips. Rupert kept the gun in readiness.

"What is it?" cried Mrs. Kenyon, but the words had scarcely died on her lips before a dark body lashed the surface of the water and disappeared. What it was we none of us had the slightest idea; we all watched spell-bound.

Still the net moved slowly on, and now the agitation of the water became great. The creature, whatever it was, lashed and lunged to and fro, now breaking back against the net, and now attempting to spring up the smooth rock and so escape into the stream. As we caught a glimpse and yet another glimpse of the long coiling body I wondered if there was a snake in the pool.

"Come on, quicker now," shouted Rupert to the men, and they pressed forward, holding the creature in the net, and, drawing it every moment nearer the rock. The next instant

Rupert raised the gun, and leaning over the water, fired down. There was a burst of spray, and as the smoke cleared we saw that the water was stained with red blood.

Seizing the lower end of the net and exercising all their strength the men now drew the net up. In its meshes, struggling in death agony, was an enormous eel. The next moment it was on the grass coiling to and fro. The men quickly dispatched it with a stick, and then we all bent over it. It was an extraordinary-looking creature, six feet in length, yet it had none of the ordinary appearance of the eel. I had never seen anything like it before. Rupert went down on his knees to examine it carefully. He suddenly looked up. A terrible truth had struck him—his face was white.

"What is it?" gasped poor Mrs. Kenyon.

"You were right, Diana," said Rupert. "Look, Mrs. Kenyon. My sister was absolutely right. Call her power what you will, she was guided by something too wonderful for explanation. This is an electric eel, no native of these waters—it was put here by someone. This is murder. One stroke from the tail of such an eel would give a child such a dreadful shock that he would be paralysed, and would drown to a certainty."

"Then that explains the mark by lightning on the dead child's hand," I said.

"Yes," answered my brother. "The police must take the matter up."

Before that evening Mr. Harman was arrested. The sensational case which followed was in all the papers. Against my will, I was forced to attend the trial in order to give the necessary evidence. It was all too damning and conclusive. The crime was brought home to the murderer, who suffered the full penalty of the law.

The Doom

L. T. Meade with Robert Eustace

The mysterious disappearance of Mme. Koluchy was now the universal topic of conversation. Her house was deserted, her numerous satellites were not to be found. The woman herself had gone as it were from the face of the earth. Nearly every detective in London was engaged in her pursuit. Scotland Yard had never been more agog with excitement; but day after day passed, and there was not the most remote tidings of her capture. No clue to her whereabouts could be obtained. That she was alive was certain, however, and my apprehensions never slumbered. I began to see that cruel face in my dreams, and whether I went abroad or whether I stayed at home, it equally haunted me.

A few days before Christmas I had a visit from Dufrayer. He found me pacing up and down my laboratory.

"What is the matter?" he said.

"The old story," I answered.

He shook his head.

"This won't do, Norman; you must turn your attention to something else."

"That is impossible," I replied, raising haggard eyes to his face.

He came up and laid his hand on my shoulder.

"You want change, Head, and you must have it. I have come in the nick of time with an invitation which ought to suit us both. We have been asked down to Rokesby Rectory to spend Christmas with my old friend, the rector. You have often heard me talk of William Sherwood. He is one of the best fellows I know. Shall I accept the invitation for us both?"

"Where is Rokesby Rectory?" I asked.

"In Cumberland, about thirty miles from Lake Windermere, a most picturesque quarter. We shall have as much seclusion as we like at Sherwood's house, and the air is bracing. If we run down next Monday, we shall be in time for a merry Christmas. What do you say?"

I agreed to accompany Dufrayer, and the following Monday, at an early hour, we started on our journey. Nothing of any moment occurred, except that at one of the large junctions a party of gipsies got into a third-class compartment near our own. Amongst them I noticed one woman, taller than the rest, who wore a shawl so arranged over her head as to conceal her face. The unusual sight of gipsies travelling by train attracted my attention, and I remarked on it to Dufrayer. Later on I noticed, too, that they were singing, and that one voice was clear, and full, and rich. The circumstance, however, made very little impression on either of us.

At Rokesby Station the gipsies left the train, and each of them carried his or her bundle, disappearing almost immediately into a thick pine forest, which stretched away to the left of the little station.

The peculiar gait of the tall woman attracted me, and I was about to mention it to Dufrayer, when Sherwood's sudden appearance and hurried, hospitable greeting put it out of my head. Sherwood was a true specimen of a country parson; his views were broad-minded, and he was a thorough sportsman.

The vicarage was six miles from the nearest station, but the drive through the bracing air was invigorating, and I felt some of the heaviness and depression which had made my life a burden of late already leaving me.

When we reached the house we saw a slenderly-made girl standing in the porch. She held a lamp in her hand, and its bright light illuminated each feature. She had dark eyes and a pale, somewhat nervous face; she could not have been more than eighteen years of age.

"Here we are, Rosaly," called out her father, "and cold too after our journey. I hope you have seen to the fires."

"Yes, father; the house is warm and comfortable," was the reply.

The girl stepped on to the gravel, and held out her hand to Dufrayer, who was an old friend. Dufrayer turned and introduced me.

"Mr. Head, Rosaly," he said; "you have often heard me talk of him."

"Many times," she answered. "How do you do, Mr. Head? I am very glad indeed to welcome you here—you seem quite like an old friend; but come in both of you, do—you must be frozen."

She led the way into the house, and we found ourselves in a spacious and very lofty hall. It was lit by one or two standard lamps, and was in all respects on a larger and more massive scale than is usually to be found in a country rectory.

"Ah! you are noticing our hall," said the girl, observing the interest in my face. "It is quite one of the features of Rokesby; but the fact is, this is quite an old house, and was not turned into a rectory until the beginning of the present century. I will take you all over it to-morrow. Now, do come into father's smoking-room—I have had tea prepared there for you."

She turned to the left, threw open a heavy oak door, and introduced us into a room lined with cedar from floor to ceiling. Great logs were burning on the hearth, and tea had been prepared. Miss Sherwood attended to our comforts, and presently left us to enjoy our smoke.

"I have a thousand and one things to see to," she said. "With Christmas so near, you may imagine that I am very busy."

When she left the room, the rector looked after her with affection in his eyes.

"What a charming girl!" I could not help saying.

"I am glad you take to her, Mr. Head," was his reply; "I need not say that she is the light of my old eyes. Rosaly's mother died a fortnight after her birth, and the child has been as my one ewe lamb. But I am sorry to say she is sadly delicate, and I have had many hours of anxiety about her."

"Indeed," I replied; "it is true she looks pale, but I should have judged that she was healthy—rather of the wiry make."

"In body she is fairly healthy, but hers is a peculiarly nervous organism. She suffers intensely from all sorts of terrors, and her environment is not the best for her. She had a shock when young. I will tell you about it later on."

Soon afterwards Dufrayer and I went to our respective rooms, and when we met in the drawing-room half an hour later, Miss Sherwood, in a pretty dress, was standing by the hearth. Her manners were very simple and unaffected, and, although thoroughly girlish, were not wanting in dignity. She was evidently well accustomed to receiving her father's guests, and also to making them thoroughly at home. When we entered the dining-room we had already engaged in a brisk conversation, and her young voice and soft, dark-brown eyes added much to the attractiveness of the pleasant scene.

Towards the end of the meal I alluded once again to the old house.

"I suppose it is very old," I said; "it has certainly taken me by surprise—you must tell me its history."

I looked full at my young hostess as I spoke. To my surprise a shadow immediately flitted over her expressive face; she hesitated, then said, slowly:—

"Everyone remarks the house, and little wonder. I believe in parts it is over three hundred years old. Of course, some of the rooms are more modern. Father thinks we were in great luck when it was turned into a rectory, but"—here she dropped her voice, and a faint sigh escaped her lips.

I looked at her again with curiosity.

"The place was spoiled by the last rector," she went on. "He and his family committed many acts of vandalism, but father has done his best to restore the house to its ancient appearance. You shall see it to-morrow, if you are really interested."

"I take a deep interest in old houses," I answered; "and this, from the little I have seen of it, is quite to my mind. Doubtless you have many old legends in connection with it, and if you have a real ghost it will complete the charm."

I smiled as I spoke, but the next instant the smile died on my lips. A sudden flame of colour had rushed into Miss Sherwood's face, leaving it far paler than was natural. She dropped her napkin, and stooped to pick it up. As she did so, I observed that the rector was looking at her anxiously. He immediately burst into conversation, completely turning the subject into what I considered a trivial channel.

A few moments later the young girl rose and left us to our wine.

As soon as we were alone, Sherwood asked us to draw our chairs to the fire and began to speak.

"I heard what you said to Rosaly, Mr. Head," he began; "and I am sorry now that I did not warn you. There is a painful legend connected with this old house, and the ghost whom you so laughingly alluded to exists, as far as my child is concerned, to a painful degree."

"Indeed," I answered.

"I do not believe in the ghost myself," he continued; "but I do believe in the influence of a very strong, nervous terror over Rosaly. If you like, I will tell you the story."

"Nothing could please me better," I answered.

The rector opened a fresh box of cigars, handed them to us, and began.

"The man who was my predecessor here had a scapegrace son, who got into serious trouble with a peasant girl in this forest. He took the girl to London, and then deserted her. She drowned herself. The boy's father vowed he would never see the lad again, but the mother pleaded for him, and there was a sort of patched-up reconciliation. He came down to spend Christmas in the house, having faithfully promised to turn over a new leaf. There were festivities and high mirth.

"On Christmas night the whole family retired to bed as usual, but soon afterwards a scream was heard issuing from the room where the young man slept—the West Room it is called. By the way, it is the one you are to occupy, Dufrayer. The rector rushed into the room, and, to his horror and surprise, found the unfortunate young man dead, stabbed to the heart. There was, naturally, great excitement and alarm, more particularly when it was discovered that a well-known herb-woman, the mother of the girl whom the young man had decoyed to London, had been seen haunting the place. Rumour went so far as to say that she had entered the house by means of a secret passage known only to herself. Her name was Mother Heriot, and she was regarded by the villagers as a sort of witch. This woman was arrested on suspicion; but nothing was definitely proved against her, and no trial took place. Six weeks later she was found dead in her hut, on Grey Tor, and since then the rumour is that she haunts the rectory on each Christmas night—entering the house through the secret passage which we none of us can discover. This story is rife in the house, and I suppose Rosaly heard it from her old nurse. Certain it is that, when she was about eight years old, she was found on Christmas night screaming violently, and declaring that she had seen the herb-woman, who entered her room and bent down over her. Since then her nerves have never been the same. Each Christmas as it comes round is a time of mental terror to her, although she tries hard to struggle against her fears. On her account I shall be glad when Christmas is over. I do my best to make it cheerful, but I can see that she dreads it terribly."

"What about the secret passage?" I interrupted.

"Ah! I have something curious to tell you about that," said the old rector, rising as he spoke. "There is not the least doubt that it exists. It is said to have been made at the time of the Monmouth Rebellion, and is supposed to be connected with the churchyard, about two hundred yards away; but although we have searched, and have even had experts down to look into the matter, we have never been able to get the slightest clue to its whereabouts. My impression is that it was bricked up long ago, and that whoever committed the murder entered the house by some other means. Be that as it may, the passage cannot be found, and we have long ceased to trouble ourselves about it."

"But have you no clue whatever to its whereabouts?" I asked.

"Nothing which I can call a clue. My belief is that we shall have to pull down the old pile before we find the passage."

"I should like to search for it," I said, impulsively; "these sorts of things interest me immensely."

"I could give you a sort of key, Head, if that would be any use," said Sherwood; "it is in an old black-letter book." As he spoke he crossed the room, took a book bound in vellum, with silver clasps, from a locked bookcase, and, opening it, laid it before me.

"This book contains a history of Rokesby," he continued. "Can you read black-letter?"

I replied that I could.

He then turned a page, and pointed to some rhymed words. "More than one expert has puzzled over these lines," he continued. "Read for yourself."

I read aloud, slowly:—

When the Yew and Star combine,
Draw it twenty cubits line;
Wait until the saintly lips
Shall the belfry spire eclipse.
Cubits eight across the first,
There shall lie the tomb accurst.

"And you have never succeeded in solving this?" I continued.

"We have often tried, but never with success. The legend runs that the passage goes into the churchyard, and has a connection with one of the old vaults, but I know nothing more. Shall we join Rosaly in the drawing-room?"

"May I copy this old rhyme first?" I asked.

My host looked at me curiously; then he nodded. I took a memorandum-book from my pocket and scribbled down the words. Mr. Sherwood then locked up the book in its accustomed place, and we left the subject of the secret passage and the ghost, to enjoy the rest of the evening in a more everyday manner.

The next morning, Christmas Eve, was damp and chill, for a thaw had set in during the night. Miss Sherwood asked Dufrayer and me to help her with the church decorations, and we spent a busy morning in the very old Norman church just at the back of the vicarage. When we left it, on our way home to lunch, I could not help looking round the churchyard with interest. Where was the tomb accurst into which the secret passage ran? As I could not talk, however, on the subject with Miss Sherwood, I resolved, at least for the present, to banish it from my mind. A sense of strong depression was still hanging over me, and Mme. Koluchy, herself, seemed to pervade the air. Yet, surely, no place could be farther from her accustomed haunts than this secluded rectory at the base of the Cumberland Hills.

"The day is brightening," said Rosaly, turning her eyes on my face, as we were entering the house; "suppose we go for a walk after lunch? If you like, we could go up Grey Tor and pay a visit to Mother Heriot."

"Mother Heriot?" I repeated, in astonishment.

"Yes—the herb-woman—but do you know about her?"

"Your father spoke about a woman of the name last night."

"Oh, I know," replied Miss Sherwood, hastily; "but he alluded to the mother—the dreadful ghost which is said to haunt Rokesby. This is the daughter. When the mother died a long time ago, after committing a terrible murder, the daughter took her name and trade. She is a very curious person, and I should like you to see her. She is much looked up to by the neighbours, although they also fear her. She is said to have a panacea against every sort of illness: she knows the property of each herb that grows in the neighbourhood, and has certainly performed marvellous cures."

"Does she deal in witchcraft and fortune-telling?" I asked.

"A little of the latter, beyond doubt," replied the girl, laughing; "she shall tell your fortune this afternoon. What fun it will be! We must hurry with lunch, for the days are so short now."

Soon after the mid-day meal we set off, taking the road for a mile or two, and then, turning sharply to the right, we began to ascend Grey Tor. Our path led through a wood of dark pine and larches, which clothed the side of the summit of the hill. The air was still very chilly, and it struck damp as we entered the pine forest. Wreaths of white mist clung to the dripping branches of the trees, the earth was soft and yielding, with fallen pine leaves and dead fern.

"Mother Heriot's hut is just beyond the wood," said Rosaly; "you will see it as soon as we emerge. Ah! there it is," she cried.

I looked upward and saw a hut made of stone and mud, which seemed to cling to the bare side of the mountain.

We walked quickly up a winding path, that grew narrower as we proceeded. Suddenly we emerged on to a little plateau on the mountain side. It was grass covered and strewn with grey granite boulders. Here stood the rude hut. From the chimney some smoke was going straight up like a thin, blue ribbon. As we approached close, we saw that the door of the hut was shut. From the eaves under the roof were hanging several small bunches of dried herbs. I stepped forward and struck upon the door with my stick. It was immediately opened by a thin, middle-aged woman, with a singularly lined and withered face. I asked her if we might come in. She gave me a keen glance from out of her beady-black eyes, then seeing Rosaly, her face brightened, she made a rapid motion with her hand, and then, to my astonishment, began to speak on her fingers.

"She can hear all right, but she is quite dumb—has been so since she was a child," said the rector's daughter to me. "She does not use the ordinary deaf and dumb language, but she taught me her peculiar signs long ago, and I often run up here to have a chat with her."

"Now, look here, mother," continued the girl, going up close to the dame, "I have brought two gentlemen to see you: we want you to tell us our fortunes. It is lucky to have the fortune told on Christmas Eve, is it not?"

The herb-woman nodded, then pointed inside the hut. She then spoke quickly on her fingers. Rosaly turned to us.

"We are in great luck," said the girl, excitedly. "A curious thing has happened. Mother Heriot has a visitor staying with her, no less a person than the greatest fortune-teller in England, the Queen of the Gipsies; she is spending a couple of nights in the hut. Mother Heriot suggests that the Queen of the Gipsies shall tell us our fortunes. It will be quite magnificent."

"I wonder if the woman she alludes to is one of the gipsies who arrived at Rokesby Station yesterday," I said, turning to Dufrayer.

"Very possibly," he answered, just raising his brows.

Rosaly continued to speak, in great excitement.

"You consent, don't you?" she said to us both.

"Certainly," said Dufrayer, with a smile.

"All right, mother," cried Miss Sherwood, turning once again to the herb-woman; "we will have our fortunes told, and your gipsy friend shall tell them. Will she come out to us here, or shall we go in to her?"

Again there was a quick pantomime of fingers and hands. Rosaly began to interpret.

"Mother Heriot says that she will speak to her first. She seems to stand in considerable awe of her."

The herb-woman vanished inside the hut. We continued to stand on the threshold.

I looked at Dufrayer, who gave me an answering glance of amusement. Our position was ridiculous, and yet, ridiculous as it seemed, there was a curiously tense feeling at my heart, and my depression grew greater than ever. I felt myself to be standing on the brink of a great catastrophe, and could not understand my own sensations.

The herb-woman returned, and Miss Sherwood eagerly interpreted.

"How queer!" she exclaimed. "The gipsy will only see me alone. I am to meet her in the hut. Shall I go?"

"I should advise you to have nothing to do with the matter," said Dufrayer.

"Oh, but I am curious. I should like to," she answered.

"Well, we will wait for you; but don't put faith in her silly words."

The girl's face slightly paled. She entered the hut; we remained outside.

"Knowing her peculiar idiosyncrasy, I wonder if we did right to let her go in?" I said to my friend.

"Why not?" said Dufrayer.

"With such a disposition she ought not to be indulged in ridiculous superstitions," I said.

"She cannot take such nonsense seriously," was his reply. He was leaning up against the lintel of the little hut, his arms folded, his eyes looking straight before him. I had never seen his face look keener or more matter-of-fact.

A moment later Miss Sherwood re-appeared. There was a marked, and quite terrible, change in her face—it was absolutely white. She avoided our eyes, slipped a piece of silver into Mother Heriot's hand, and said, quickly:—

"Let us hurry home; it is turning very cold."

"Now, what is it?" said Dufrayer, as we began to descend the mountain; "you look as if you had heard bad news."

"The Queen of the Gipsies was very mysterious," said the girl.

"What sort of person was she?" I asked.

"I cannot tell you, Mr. Head; I saw very little of her. She was in a dark part of the hut, and was in complete shadow. She took my hand and looked at it, and said what I am not allowed to repeat."

"I am sorry you saw her," I answered, "but surely you don't believe her? You are too much a girl of the latter end of the nineteenth century to place your faith in fortune-tellers."

"But that is just it," she answered; "I am not a girl of the nineteenth century at all, and I do most fully believe in fortune-telling and all kinds of superstitions. I wish we hadn't gone. What I have heard does affect me strangely, strangely. I wish we had not gone."

We were now descending the hill, but as we walked Miss Sherwood kept glancing behind her as if afraid of someone or something following us. Suddenly she stopped, turned round and clutched my arm.

"Hark! Who is that?" she whispered, pointing her hand towards a dark shadow beneath the trees. "There is someone coming after us, I am certain there is. Don't you see a figure behind that clump? Who can it be? Listen."

We waited and stood silent for a moment, gazing towards the spot which the girl had indicated. The sharp snap of a dead twig followed by the rustling noise of rapidly retreating footsteps sounded through the stillness. I felt Miss Sherwood's hand tremble on my arm.

"There certainly was someone there," said Dufrayer; "but why should not there be?"

"Why, indeed?" I echoed. "There is nothing to be frightened about, Miss Sherwood. It is doubtless one of Mother Heriot's bucolic patients."

"They never venture near her at this hour," she answered. "They believe in her, but they are also a good deal afraid. No one ever goes to see Mother Heriot after dark. Let us get quickly home."

I could see that she was much troubled, and thought it best to humour her. We hurried forward. Just as we entered the pine wood I looked back. On the summit of the little ridge which contained Mother Heriot's hut I saw dimly through the mist a tall figure. The moment my eyes rested on it, it vanished. There was something in its height and gait which made my heart stand still. It resembled the tall gipsy whom I had noticed yesterday, and it also bore—God in Heaven, yes—an intangible and yet very real resemblance to Mme. Koluchy. Mme. Koluchy here! Impossible! My brain must be playing me a trick. I laughed at my own nervousness. Surely here at least we were safe from that woman's machinations.

We reached home, and I mentioned my vague suspicion to Dufrayer.

"A wild idea has occurred to me," I said.

"What?" he answered.

"It has flashed through my brain that there is just a remote possibility that the gipsy fortune-teller in Mother Heriot's hut is Madame herself."

He looked thoughtful for a moment.

"We never can tell where and how Madame may reappear," he said; "but I think in this case, Head, you may banish the suspicion from your mind. Beyond doubt, the woman has left England long ago."

The evening passed away. I noticed that Rosaly was silent and preoccupied; her nervousness was now quite apparent to everyone, and her father, who could not but remark it, was especially tender to her.

Christmas Day went by quietly. In the morning we all attended service in the little church, and at night some guests arrived for the usual festivities. We passed a merry evening, but now and then I glanced with a certain apprehension at Miss Sherwood. She was in white, with holly berries in her belt and dark hair. She was certainly a very pretty girl, but the uneasiness plainly manifested in her watchful eyes and trembling lips marred her beauty. There was a want of quiet about her, too, which infected me uncomfortably. Suddenly I determined to ask for her confidence. What had the mysterious gipsy said to her? This was the night when, according to old tradition, the ghost of the herb-woman appeared. If Miss Sherwood could relieve her mind before retiring to rest, it would be all the better for her. We were standing near each other, and as she stooped to pick up a bunch of berries which had fallen from her belt, I bent towards her.

"You are troubled about something," I said.

"Oh, I am a very silly girl," she replied.

"Will you not tell me about it?" I continued. "I will respect your confidence, and give you my sympathy."

"I ought not to encourage my nervous fears," she replied. "By the way, did father tell you about the legend connected with this house?"

"He did."

"This is the night when the herb-woman appears."

"My dear child, you don't suppose that a spirit from the other world really comes back in that fashion! Dismiss it from your mind—there is nothing in it."

"So you say," she answered, "but you never saw"—she began to tremble, and raising her hand brushed it across her eyes. "I feel a ghostly influence in the air," she said; "I know that something dreadful will happen to-night."

"You think that, because the fortune-teller frightened you yesterday."

She gave me a startled and wide-awake glance.

"What do you mean?"

"I judge from your face and manner. If you will take courage and unburden your mind, I may, doubtless, be able to dispel your fears."

"But she told me what she did under the promise of secrecy; dare I break my word?"

"Under the circumstances, yes," I answered, quickly.

"Very well, I will tell you. I don't feel as if I could keep it to myself another moment. But you on your part must faithfully promise that it shall go no farther."

"I will make the promise," I said.

She looked me full in the face.

"Come into the conservatory," she said. She took my hand, and led me out of the long, low drawing-room into a great conservatory at the farther end. It was lit with many Chinese lanterns, which gave a dim, and yet bright, effect. We went and stood under a large lemon tree, and Miss Sherwood took one of my hands in both her own.

"I shall never forget that scene yesterday," she said. "I could scarcely see the face of the gipsy, but her great, brilliant eyes pierced the gloom, and the feel of her hand thrilled me when it touched mine. She asked me to kneel by her, and her voice was very full, and deep, and of great power; it was not like that of an uneducated woman. She spoke very slowly, with a pause between each word.

" 'I pity you, for you are close to death,' she began.

"I felt myself quite incapable of replying, and she continued:—

" 'Not your own death, nor even that of your father, but all the same you are very close to death. Death will soon touch you, and it will be cold, and mysterious, and awful, and try as you may, you cannot guard against it, for it will come from a very unlooked-for source, and be instant and swift in its work. Now ask me no more—go!'

" 'But what about the fortunes of the two gentlemen who are waiting outside?' I said.

" 'I have told you the fortunes of those men,' she answered; 'go!'

"She waved me away with her hand, and I went out. That is all, Mr. Head. I do not know what it means, but you can understand that to a nervous girl like me it has come as a shock."

"I can, truly," I replied; "and now you must make up your mind not to think of it any more. The gipsy saw that you were nervous, and she thought she would heighten the impression by words of awful portent, which doubtless mean nothing at all."

Rosaly tried to smile, and I think my words comforted her. She little guessed the battle I was having with my own heart. The unaccountable depression which had assailed me of late now gathered thick like a pall.

Late that evening I went to Dufrayer's room. I had promised Miss Sherwood that I would not betray her confidence, but the words of the gipsy in the herb-woman's hut kept returning to me again and again.

"*I pity you, for you are close to death. You cannot guard against it, for it will come from an unlooked-for source, and be instant and swift in its work.*"

"What is the matter?" said Dufrayer, glancing into my face.

"I am depressed," I replied; "the ghostly legend belonging to this house is affecting me."

He smiled.

"And by the way," I added, "you are sleeping in the room where the murder was committed."

He smiled again, and gave me a glance of amused commiseration.

"Really, Head," he cried, "this sort of thing is unlike you. Surely old wives' fables ought not to give you a moment's serious thought. The fact that an unfortunate lad was murdered in this room cannot affect my nerves some twenty years afterwards. Do go to bed, my dear fellow; you need a long sleep."

He bade me good-night. I had no excuse to linger, and I left him.

Just as I had reached the door, he called after me.

"Good-night, old man; sleep well."

I turned and looked at him. He was standing by the window, his face was towards me, and he still wore that inscrutable smile which was one of his special characteristics. I left him. I little guessed . . .

I retired to my room; my brain was on fire; it was impossible for me to rest. What was yesterday but a vague suspicion was now assuming the form of a certainty. Only one person could have uttered the words which Miss Sherwood had heard. Beyond doubt, Madame Koluchy had known of our proposed visit to Rokesby. Beyond doubt, she, in company with some gipsies, had joined our train, and when we arrived at Rokesby, she alighted there also. With her knowledge of the gipsies, an acquaintanceship with Mother Heriot would be easily made. To take refuge in her hut would be a likely contingency. Why had she done so? What mischief could she do to us from such a vantage point? Suddenly, like a vivid flash, the memory of the secret passage, which none of the inmates of the house could discover, returned to me. In all probability this passage was well known to Mother Heriot, for had not her mother committed the murder which had taken place in this very house, and did not the legend say that she had entered the house, and quitted it again, through the secret passage?

I quickly made up my mind. I must act, and act at once. I would go straight to the hut; I would confront Madame; I would meet her alone. In open combat I had nothing to fear. Anything was better than this wearing and agonizing suspense.

I waited in my room until the steps of the old rector retiring for the night were heard, and then went swiftly downstairs. I took the key of the hall door from its hook on the wall, opened it, locked it behind me, went to the stables, secured a lantern, and then began my ascent of Grey Tor.

The night was clear and starlit, the moon had not yet risen, but the stars made sufficient light for me to see my way. After a little over an hour's hard walking, I reached the herb-woman's hut. I thundered on the door with my stick, and in a minute the dame appeared. Suddenly I remembered that she was dumb, but she could hear. I spoke to her.

"I have a word to say to the stranger who was here yesterday," I began. "Is she within? I must see her at once."

The herb-woman shook her head.

"I do not believe you," I said; "stand aside, I must search the hut."

She stood aside, and I entered. There was no one else present. The hut was small, a glance showed me each corner—the herb-woman's guest had departed.

Without even apologizing for my abrupt intrusion, I quickly ran down the mountain, and, as I did so, the queer rhyme which contained the key to the secret passage occurred to my memory. I had my memorandum-book with me; I opened it now, and read the words:—

> When the Yew and Star combine,
> Draw it twenty cubits line;
> Wait until the saintly lips
> Shall the belfry spire eclipse.
> Cubits eight across the first,
> There shall lie the tomb accurst.

Gibberish doubtless, and yet gibberish with a possible meaning. I pondered over the enigmatical words.

"There is a yew tree in the churchyard," I said to myself, "but the rest seems unfathomable."

There was a short cut home through the churchyard—I resolved to take it. I went there and walked straight to the yew tree.

"When the Yew and Star combine," I said, speaking aloud. "Surely there is only one star which remains immovable—the Pole, or North Star."

I looked up at the sky—the Pole star was shining down upon me. I became excited and much interested. Moving about, I presently got the trunk of the old yew tree and the star in a line. Then I again examined my key.

"Draw it twenty cubits line."

Twenty cubits meant thirty feet. I walked on in a straight line that distance, and then perceived in the moonlight, for the moon had now risen, that standing here, and looking at the church spire, the lips of the stone carving of a saint just covered the spire itself from view. Surely the meaning of the second couplet was plain:—

> Wait until the saintly lips
> Shall the belfry spire eclipse.

The third and last couplet ran as follows:—

Cubits eight across the first,
There shall lie the tomb accurst.

My heart beating hard, I quickly measured eight cubits, namely twelve feet, and then started back with a cry of horror, for I had come to a large vault, which stood open. The entrance-stone had been moved aside. Without an instant's hesitation I ran down some steps. The tomb was a large one, and was quite empty; never coffin of man had lain here, but a passage wound away to the left, a tortuous passage, down which I quickly walked. My lantern threw light on the ghastly place, and the air was sufficiently good to prevent the candle going out.

Why was the tomb open? What was happening? Fear itself seemed to walk by my side. Never before had I so felt its ghastly presence. I hurried my steps, and soon perceived a dim light at the farther end. The next instant I had entered the hall of the old house. I had done so through a panel which had been slipped aside. Had anyone gone in before me? If so, who! Who had opened the tomb? Who had traversed the passage? Who had gone into the house by this fearful and long-closed door?

I was just about to rush upstairs, when a piercing scream fell on my ears; it came from just above me. With two or three bounds I cleared the stairs, and the next instant my eyes fell upon a huddled-up heap on the landing. I bent over it; it was Rosaly. Her features were twitching in a horrible manner, and her dilated eyes stared at me without any recognition. Her lips were murmuring, "Catch her! catch her!"

The next moment the rector appeared hurrying down the passage in his dressing-gown.

"What is wrong?" he cried; "what has happened?"

The girl clung to my arm, and now sent up scream after scream. The entire house was aroused, and the servants with scared faces came running to the spot. Rosaly's terror now found vent in fresh words.

"The herb-woman," she sobbed, "the ghost of the herb-woman. I heard a noise and ran on to the landing. I met her—she was coming from Mr. Dufrayer's room—she was making straight for yours, Mr. Head. Suddenly she saw me, uttered a cry, and fled downstairs. Oh, catch her, the ghost! the ghost!"

"Did you say the woman was coming from Dufrayer's room?" I asked. A sudden maddening fear clutched at my heart. Where was Dufrayer? Surely he must have heard this uproar. I went to his room, opened the door, and dashed in. Inside all was darkness.

"Wake up," I said to him, "something dreadful has happened—did you not hear Rosaly scream? Wake up!"

There was no answer. I returned to the landing to fetch a light. The rector now accompanied me into the room. We both went up to the silent figure in the bed. I bent over him and shook him by the shoulder. Still he did not stir. I bent lower, and observed on his neck, just behind the ear, a slight mark, the mark which a hypodermic syringe would make. Good God! what had happened?

"*You are close to death. You cannot guard against it, try as you may, for it will come from an unlooked-for source, and be instant and swift in its work.*"

The words echoed mockingly in my ears. I flung down the bed-clothes, and, in an access of agony, laid my hand on the heart of the man I loved best on earth. He was dead!

I staggered back, faint and giddy, against the bed-post.

"See," I said to the old clergyman, "her work, the fiend; she has been in this house. She has entered by the secret passage. Come at once; there is not an instant to lose. As there is a God in Heaven, she shall pay the price for this crime."

Sherwood gazed at me, as if he thought me bereft of my senses. He could not believe that Dufrayer was really dead. I pointed to the small wound on his neck, and asked him to feel where the heart no longer beat.

"But who has done it?" he said. "What fiend do you allude to?"

"Mme. Koluchy; let us follow her."

I rushed from the room and downstairs. The panel in the hall had been slammed to, but my memory could not play me false; I knew its position. I found what had been so long searched for in vain, touched a spring, and opened it. Sherwood and I hurried down the winding passage. Just at the entrance to the tomb we came upon a gipsy woman's bonnet and cloak. They had been dropped there, doubtless, by Madame when she had flown after committing her deadly work. We entered the empty tomb. On the floor lay a small hypodermic syringe. I picked it up—it was broken. To its sides clung a whitish-grey substance. I guessed what it afterwards proved to be—trinitrin, or nitro-glycerine in strong solution. The effect of such a terrible poison would be instantaneous.

Sherwood and I returned to the house—the place was in an uproar of excitement. The local police were called in. I told my strange tale, and my strong suspicions, to which they listened with breathless interest.

Rosaly was very ill, going from one strong hysterical fit into another. The doctor was summoned to attend her. The fact of Dufrayer's death was carefully kept from the sick girl. Her father was so distracted about her that he could give no attention to anyone else.

Meanwhile I was alone, utterly alone, with my anguish and horror. The friend of my life had fallen by the hand of Mme. Koluchy. A fire was burning in my brain, which grew hotter each instant. Never was man more pursued with a deadly thirst for vengeance. The thought that Madame was moment by moment putting a greater distance between herself and me drove me mad. Towards morning I could stand inaction no longer, and determined to walk to the station. When I got there I learned that no train left before nine o'clock. This was more than I could bear; my restlessness increased. The junction which connected with the main line was a distance of fifteen miles off. There was no carriage to be obtained. Nevertheless, I resolved to walk the distance. I had overestimated my own strength. I was already faint and giddy. The shock had told on me more than I dared to own. I had not gone half the distance before I was seized with a queer giddiness, my eyes grew dim, the earth seemed to reel away from me, I staggered forward a few steps, and then all was lost in darkness. I must have stumbled and fallen by the wayside, and my fit of unconsciousness must have been long, for when I came to myself the sun was high in the heavens. A rough-looking man, dressed as a workman, was bending over me.

"You have been real bad," he said, the moment my eyes met his. "The lady said to throw cold water on you and you'd be better."

The man's words roused me as no ordinary restorative could do. I sat up, and the next moment had tottered to my feet.

"The lady?" I said. "Did you mention a lady? What lady?"

"A tall lady," was the reply, "a stranger in these parts. She was bending over you when I come along. She had black eyes, and I thought she was giving you something to bring you round. When she saw me she said, 'You dash cold water over him, and he'll come to.' "

"But where is the lady now?" I gasped.

"There by yonder hill, just going over the brow, don't you see?"

"I do, and I know who she is. I must overtake her. Good-bye, my man, I am all right."

So I was: the sudden stimulus had renewed my faltering strength. I recognised that figure. With that grace, inimitable and perfect, which never at any moment deserted it, it was moving from my view. Yes, I knew it. Mme. Koluchy had doubtless found me by the wayside, and had meant to complete the work which she had begun last night. Had she still possessed her syringe I should now have been a dead man. Where was she going? Doubtless to catch the very train to which I was hurrying. If so, we should meet almost immediately. I hurried forward. Once again I caught sight of the figure in the far distance. I could not get up to it, and suddenly I felt that I did not want to. I should meet her in London to-night. That was my thought of thoughts.

As I approached the great junction I heard the whistle of a coming train. It was the express. It dashed into the station just as I reached it. I was barely in time. Without waiting for a ticket I stumbled almost in a fainting condition into the first carriage I could reach. The train moved on. I felt a sudden sense of satisfaction. Mme. Koluchy was also on board.

How that awful journey was passed is difficult for me to remember. Beyond the thought of thoughts that Madame and I were rushing to London by the same train, that we should beyond doubt meet soon, I had little feeling of any sort. Her hour was close at hand—my hour of vengeance was nigh.

At the first junction I handed two telegrams to a porter and desired him to send them off immediately. They were to Tyler and Ford.

When between eight and nine o'clock that night we reached Euston, the detectives were waiting for me.

"Mme. Koluchy is in the train," I said to them; "you can apprehend her if you are quick—there is not an instant to lose."

The men in wild excitement began to search along the platform. I followed them. Surely Madame could not have already escaped. She had not the faintest idea that I was in the train; she would take things leisurely when she reached Euston. So I had hoped, but my hopes were falsified. Nowhere could we get even a glimpse of the face for which we sought.

"Never mind," said Ford, "I also have news, and I believe that our success is near. We will go straight to her house. I learned not an hour ago that a fresh staff of servants had been secured, and the house is brightly lit up. Our detectives who surround the place are under the impression that she will be in her old quarters to-night. I have a carriage in waiting: we will start immediately."

Without a word I entered it, and we drove off. We made no plans beyond the intention in each man's breast that Madame should be taken either alive or dead.

As the carriage drew up at the house I noticed that the hall was brilliantly lighted. The moment Ford touched the bell a flunkey threw the door open, as if he were waiting for us.

"My mistress is in her laboratory," was his reply to our inquiries. "She has just returned after a journey. I think she expects you, gentlemen. Will you go to her there?—you know the way."

We rapidly crossed the hall and began to descend the stone steps. As we did so the muffled hum of machinery in rapid motion fell on our ears. Just as we reached the laboratory door Ford, who had been leading the way, stopped and turned round. His face was very pale, but he spoke firmly and quietly.

"There is not the least doubt," he said, in a semi-whisper, "that we are going into great danger. Madame would not receive us like this if she had not made a plan for our destruction which only she could devise. It is impossible to tell what may happen. That it will be a terrible encounter, and that it will need all our strength and presence of mind, is certain, for we are now about to enter the very sanctuary of her fiendish arts and appliances. I will go first. The moment

I see her I shall cover her, and if she stirs will shoot her dead on the spot."

He turned the handle of the door, and we slipped silently into the laboratory.

It was like entering a furnace, the heat was stifling. A single incandescent burner shed a subdued light over the place, revealing the outline of the stone roof and dim recesses in the walls. At the farther end stood Madame. As we entered, she turned slowly and faced us; her face was quiet, her lips closed, her eyes alone expressed emotion.

"Hands up, or I fire!" rang out from Ford, who stepped forward and immediately covered her with his revolver.

She instantly obeyed, raising both her arms; her eyes now met mine, and the faintest of smiles played round her lips.

The next instant, as if wrenched from his grasp by some unseen power, the weapon leapt from Ford's hands, and dashed itself with terrific force against the poles of an enormous electro-magnet beside him. Every loose piece of iron started and sprang towards it with a deafening crash. Madame must have made the current by pressing a key on the floor with her foot. For a moment we stood rooted to the spot, thunder-struck by the sudden and unforeseen method by which we had been disarmed.

Mme. Koluchy still continued to gaze at us, but now her smile grew broader, and soon it rang out in a scornful laugh.

"It is my turn to dictate terms," she said, in a steady, even voice. "Advance one step towards me, and we die together. Norman Head, this is your supposed hour of victory, but know that you will never take me either alive or dead."

As she spoke her hand moved to a small lever on the bench beside her. She drew herself up to her full, majestic height, and stood rigid as a figure carved in marble. I glanced at Ford: his lips were firmly compressed, drops of sweat gleamed upon his face, he began to breathe quickly through distended nostrils, then with a sudden spring he bounded forward, and simultaneously there leapt up, straight before our eyes, what seemed like one huge sheet of white flame. So fearfully bright and dazzling was it that it struck us like a blow, and Tyler and I fell. We were blinded by a heat that seemed to sear our very eyeballs. The next moment all was darkness.

When I came to myself a cool draught of air was blowing upon my face, and Tyler's voice sounded in my ears. I rose, staggering. Before my eyes there still seemed to dance a thousand sparks and whirling wheels of fire. The servants were running about wildly, and one of the men had brought a lamp from the hall—it lit up the wild and haggard face of my companion.

"We dare not go back," he whispered, pointing to the laboratory door, trembling and almost gibbering as he did so.

"But what has happened?" I said.

I made a rush towards the laboratory. Two of the men held me back forcibly.

"It's not safe, sir," one of them said; "the room within is a furnace. You would die if you entered."

By main force I was kept from rushing to my own destruction.

It was an hour later when we entered. Even then the heat was almost past bearing. Slowly and cautiously Tyler and I approached the spot where we had last seen Mme. Koluchy. Upon the stone flags lay the body of the detective, so terribly burnt as to be almost unrecognisable, and a few yards farther was the mouth of a big hole, from which still radiated a fierce heat. By degrees it cooled sufficiently to allow us to examine it. It was about eight feet deep and circular in shape. From its walls jutted innumerable jets. Their use was evident to me at once, for upon the floor beside us stood an enormous iron cylinder, such as are used for compressed gases. These had presumably been used before to create by means of the jets one vast oxyhydrogen flame to give the intensest heat known, a heat computed by scientists at the enormous temperature of 2,400 degrees centigrade.

It was evident what had happened. As Ford sprang forward Madame must have released the iron trap and descended through a column of this fearful flame, not only causing instantaneous death, but simultaneously also an absolute annihilation.

At the bottom of the well lay a small heap of smouldering ashes. These were all the earthly remains of the brain that had conceived and the body that had executed some of the most malignant designs against mankind that the history of the world has ever shown.

The Woman with the Hood

It was late in the October of a certain year when I was asked to become "*locum tenens*" to a country practitioner in one of the midland counties. He was taken ill and obliged to leave home hastily. I therefore entered on my duties without having any indication of the sort of patients whom I was to visit. I was a young man at the time, and a great enthusiast with regard to the medical profession. I believed in personal influence and the magnetism of a strong personality as being all-conducive to the furtherance of the curative art. I had no experience, however, to guide me with regard to country patients, my work hitherto having been amongst the large population of a manufacturing town. On the very night of my arrival my first experience as a country doctor began. I had just got into bed, and was dozing off into a sound sleep, when the night bell which hung in my room rang pretty sharply. I jumped up and went to the tube, calling down to ask what was the matter.

"Are you the new doctor?" asked the voice.

"Yes, my name is Bruce; who wants me?"

"Mrs. Frayling of Garth Hall. The young lady is very bad. I have got a trap here; how soon can you be ready?"

"In a couple of minutes," I answered. I hastily got into my clothes, and in less than five minutes had mounted beside a rough-looking man, into a high gig. He touched his horse, who bounded off, at a great speed, and I found myself rattling through the country in the dead of night.

"How far off is the Hall?" I asked.

"A matter of two miles," was the reply.

"Do you know anything of the nature of the young lady's illness?"

"Yes I do; it is the old thing."

"Can you not enlighten me?" I asked, seeing that the man had shut up his lips and employed himself flicking his horse with the end of his long whip. The beast flew faster and faster, the man turned and fixed his eyes full upon me in the moonlight.

"They'll tell you when you get there," he said. "All I can say is that you will do no good, no one can, the matter ain't in our province. We are turning into the avenue now; you will soon know for yourself."

We dashed down a long avenue, and drew up in a couple of moments at a door sheltered by a big porch. I saw a tall lady in evening dress standing in the brightly lighted hall within.

"Have you brought the doctor, Thompson?" I heard her say to the man who had driven me.

"Yes, ma'am," was the reply. "The new doctor, Doctor Bruce."

"Oh! Then Dr. Mackenzie has really left?"

"He left this morning, ma'am, I told you so."

I heard her utter a slight sigh of disappointment.

"Come this way, Dr. Bruce," she said. "I am sorry to have troubled you."

She led me as she spoke across the hall and into a drawing-room of lofty dimensions, beautifully furnished in modern style. It was now between one and two in the morning, but the whole house was lit up as if the night were several hours younger. Mrs. Frayling wore a black evening dress, low to the neck and with demi sleeves. She had dark eyes and a beautiful, kindly face. It looked haggard now and alarmed.

"The fact is," she said, "I have sent for you on a most extraordinary mission. I do not know that I should have troubled a strange doctor, but I hoped that Dr. Mackenzie had not yet left."

"He left this morning," I said. "He was very ill; a case of nervous breakdown. He could not even wait to give me instructions with regard to my patients."

"Ah, yes," she said averting her eyes from mine as she spoke. "Our doctor used to be as hale a man as could be found in the country round. Nervous breakdown; I think I understand. I hope, Dr. Bruce, that you are not troubled by nerves."

"Certainly not," I answered. "As far as I am concerned they don't exist. Now what can I do for you, Mrs. Frayling?"

"I want you to see my daughter. I want you to try and quiet her terrors. Dr. Mackenzie used to be able to do so, but of late—"

"Her terrors!" I said. "I must ask you to explain further."

"I am going to do so. My daughter, Lucy, she is my only child, is sorely troubled by the appearance of an apparition."

I could scarcely forbear from smiling.

"Your daughter wants change," I said, "change of scene and air."

"That is the queer thing," said Mrs. Frayling; "she will not take change, nothing will induce her to leave Garth Hall; and yet living here is slowly but surely bringing her either to her grave or to a worse fate, that of a lunatic asylum. She went to bed to-night as usual, but an hour afterwards I was awakened by her screams; I ran to her room and found her sitting up in bed, trembling violently. Her eyes were fixed on a certain part of the room; they were wide open, and had a look of the most horrified agony in them which I have never seen in the human face. She did not see me when I went into the room, but when I touched her hand she clasped it tightly.

" 'Tell her to go away, mother,' she said, 'she won't stir for me; I cannot speak to her, I have not the courage, and she is waiting for me to speak; tell her to go away, mother—tell her to cease to trouble me—tell her to go.'

"I could see nothing, Dr. Bruce, but she continued to stare just towards the foot of her bed, and described the terrible thing which was troubling her.

" 'Can't you see her yourself?' she said. 'She is a dead woman, and she comes here night after night—see her yellow face—oh, mother, tell her to go—tell her to go!'

"I did what I could for my poor child, but no words of mine could soothe or reassure her. The room was bright with firelight, and there were several candles burning, I could not see a soul. At last the poor girl fainted off with terror. I then sent a messenger for Dr. Mackenzie. She now lies moaning in her bed, our old nurse is sitting with her. She is terribly weak, and drops of agony are standing on her forehead. She cannot long continue this awful strain."

"It must be a case of delusion," I said. "You say you saw nothing in the room?"

"Nothing; but it is only right to tell you that the house is haunted."

I smiled, and fidgeted in my chair.

"Ah! I know," said Mrs. Frayling, "that you naturally do not believe in ghosts and apparitions, but perhaps you would change your mind if you lived long at Garth Hall. I have lived here for the last twelve years, and can certainly testify to the fact of having heard most unaccountable sounds, but I have never seen anything. My daughter, Lucy, has been educated abroad, and did not come to Garth Hall to live until three months ago; it was soon after this that the apparition began to appear to her. Now it is her nightly torment, and it is simply killing her, and yet she refuses to go. Every day she says to me, 'I know, mother, that that awful spirit is in fearful trouble, and perhaps to-night I may have the courage to speak to it,' but night after night much the same thing takes place; the poor child endures the agony until she faints right off, and each day her nerves are weaker and her whole strength more completely shattered."

"Well, I will go up now and see the patient," I said. "It is of course nothing whatever but a case of strong delusion, and against her will, Mrs. Frayling, it is your duty to remove your daughter from this house immediately."

"You will tell a different story after you have seen her," said the mother.

She rose as she spoke and conducted me up some shallow bright-looking stairs. She then led me into a large bedroom on the first landing. The fire burned brightly in the grate, and four or five candles stood about in different directions. Their light fell full upon the form of a very young and extremely beautiful girl.

Her face was as white as the pillow on which it rested; her eyes were shut, and the dark fringe of her long eyelashes rested on her cheeks; her hair was tossed over the pillow; her hands, thin to emaciation, lay outside the coverlet; now and then her fingers worked convulsively.

Bending gently forward I took her wrist between my finger and thumb. The pulse was very faint and slow. As I was feeling it she opened her eyes.

"Who are you?" she asked, looking at me without any alarm, and with only a very languid curiosity in her tone.

"I am the new doctor who has come in Dr. Mackenzie's place," I answered. "My name is Bruce."

She gave me just the ghost of a smile.

"Mine is not a case for the doctor," she said. "Has mother told you what troubles me?"

"Yes," I answered. "You are very nervous and must not be alone. I will sit with you for a little."

"It makes no difference whether you are here or not," she said. "She will come back again in about an hour. You may or may not see her. She will certainly come, and then my awful terrors will begin again."

"Well, we will wait for her together," I said, as cheerfully as I could.

I moved a chair forward as I spoke and sat down by the bedside.

Miss Frayling shut her eyes with a little impatient gesture. I motioned to Mrs. Frayling to seat herself not far away; and going deliberately to some of the candles put them out. The light no longer fell strongly on the bed—the patient was in shadow. I hoped she might fall into really deep slumber and not awaken till the morning light had banished ghostly terrors. She certainly seemed to have sunk into gentle and calm sleep; the expression of her face seemed to smooth out, her brow was no longer corrugated with anxious wrinkles—gentle smiles played about her lips. She looked like the child she was. I guessed as I watched her that her years could not number more than seventeen or eighteen.

"She is better," said Mrs. Frayling. "She may not have another attack to-night." As she spoke she rose, and telling me she would return in a few minutes, left the room. She and I were the only watchers by the sick girl, the servants having retired to bed. Mrs. Frayling went to fetch something. She had scarcely done so before I was conscious of a complete change in the aspect of the room—it had felt home-like, warm, and comfortable up to this moment; now I was distinctly conscious of a sense of chill. I could not account for my sensations, but most undoubtedly my heart began to beat more quickly than was quite agreeable; I felt a creeping sensation down my back—the cold seemed to grow greater.

I said to myself, "The fire wants replenishing," but I had an unaccountable aversion to stirring; I did not even want to turn my head. At the same moment Miss Frayling, who had been sleeping so peacefully, began evidently to dream; her face worked with agitation; she suddenly opened her eyes and uttered a sharp, piercing cry.

"Keep her back," she said, flinging out her arms, as if she wanted to push something from her.

I started up instantly, and went to the bedside.

At this moment Mrs. Frayling came into the room. The moment she did so the sense of chill and unaccountable horror left me; the room became once more warm and home-like. I looked at the fire, it was piled up high in the grate and was burning merrily. Miss Frayling, however, did not share my pleasanter sensations.

"I said she would come back," she exclaimed, pointing with her finger to the foot of the bed.

I looked in that direction but could see nothing.

"Can't you see her? Oh, I wish you could see her," she cried. "She stands there at the foot of the bed; she wears a hood, and her face is yellow. She has been dead a long time, and I know she wants to say something. I cannot speak to her. Oh, tell her to go away; tell her to go away."

"Shut your eyes, Miss Frayling; do not look," I said.

Then I turned and boldly faced the empty space where the excited girl had seen the apparition.

"Whoever you are, leave us now," I said in an authoritative voice. "We are not prepared for you to-night. Leave us now."

To my surprise Miss Frayling gave a gleeful laugh.

"Why, she has gone," she exclaimed in a voice of relief. "She walked out of the door—I saw her go. I don't believe she will come back at present. How queer! Then you did see her, Dr. Bruce?"

"No," I answered; "I saw nothing."

"But she heard you; she nodded her head once and then went. She will come back again, of course; but perhaps not to-night. I don't feel frightened any longer. I believe I shall sleep."

She snuggled down under the bedclothes.

"Have some of this beef-tea, Lucy," said her mother, bringing a cup to the bedside. It was steaming hot, she had gone away to warm it.

"Yes, I feel faint and hungry," replied the girl; she raised her pretty head and allowed her mother to feed and pet her.

"I am much better," she said. "I know she won't come back again to-night; you need not stay with me any longer, Dr. Bruce."

"I will stay with her, Doctor; you must lie down in another room," said the mother.

I consented to go as far as the ante-room. There was a comfortable sofa there, and I had scarcely laid my head upon it before I fell into a sound slumber.

When I awakened it was broad daylight and Mrs. Frayling was standing over me.

"Lucy is much better and is getting up," she said. "She looks almost herself. What an extraordinary effect your words had, Dr. Bruce."

"They came as a sort of inspiration," I said; "I did not mean them to be anything special."

"Then you do not believe that she really saw the apparition?"

"Certainly not; her brain is very much excited and overwrought. You ought to take her away to-day."

"That is the queer thing," said Mrs. Frayling. "I told you that she would not consent to leave the house, believing, poor child, that her mission was to try and comfort this awful ghost, in case she could summon courage to speak to it. She told me this morning, however, that she was quite willing to go and suggested that we should sleep at the Metropole in town to-night."

"The best thing possible," I said. "Take her away immediately. Give her plenty of occupation and variety, and let her see heaps of cheerful people. She will doubtless soon get over her terrors."

"It is very strange," repeated Mrs. Frayling. "Her attitude of mind seems completely altered. She wishes to see you for a moment before you leave us. I will meet you in the breakfast-room in a quarter of an hour, Dr. Bruce."

I made a hasty toilet and followed Mrs. Frayling downstairs. We ate breakfast almost in silence, and just before the meal was over Miss Frayling made her appearance. She was a very slightly-built girl, tall and graceful as a reed. She came straight up to me.

"I don't know how to thank you," she said, holding out her hand.

"Why?" I asked in astonishment. "I am glad I was able to relieve you, but I am rather puzzled to know what great thing I really did."

"Why, don't you know?" she answered. "Can't you guess? She will come to you now. I don't believe she will trouble me any more."

"Well, I am stronger to receive her than you are," I said, smiling and trying to humour the girl's fancy.

Soon afterwards I took my leave and returned to Dr. Mackenzie's house. I spent the day without anything special occurring, and in the evening, being dead tired, went to bed as usual. Dr. Mackenzie's house was an essentially modern one. Anything less ghostly than the squarely-built cheerful rooms could scarcely be imagined. I was alone in the house with the exception of his servants. I went to bed, and had scarcely laid my head on the pillow before I was sound asleep. I was suddenly awakened out of my first slumbers by someone calling to me through the speaking-tube.

"Yes, I will come immediately," I answered.

I sprang out of bed and applied my ear to the tube. "You are wanted at Garth Hall," said the voice.

"But surely there is no one ill there to-night?" I said.

"You are wanted immediately; come without delay," was the reply.

"I will be with you in a minute," I answered.

I felt almost annoyed, but there was no help for it. I hurried into my clothes and went downstairs.

"How very silly of Mrs. Frayling not to have taken her daughter away—shall I have to go through a repetition of last night's scene over again?" I thought.

I opened the hall door, expecting to see a horse and gig, and the man who had driven me the night before. To my astonishment there was not a soul in sight.

"What can this mean?" I said to myself. "Has the messenger been careless enough not to bring a trap—it will be very troublesome if I have to get my own horse out at this hour—where can the man be?"

I looked to right and left—the night was a moonlit one—there was not a soul in sight. Very much provoked, but never for a moment doubting that I was really summoned, I went off to the stables, saddled Dr. Mackenzie's horse, Rover, and mounting, rode off to Garth Hall. The hour was quite late, between twelve and one o'clock. When I drew up at the door the house was in total darkness.

"What can this mean?" I said to myself. I rang a bell fiercely, and after a long time a servant put her head out of an upper window.

"Who is there?" she asked.

"I—Dr. Bruce," I cried. "I have been sent for in a hurry to see Miss Frayling."

"Good Lord!" I heard the woman exclaim. "Wait a minute, sir, and I will come down to you," she shouted.

In a couple of minutes the great hall door was unchained and unlocked, and a respectable middle-aged woman stood on the steps.

"Miss Frayling has gone to London with her mother, sir," she said. "You are quite certain you were sent for?"

"Quite," I answered. "Your man—the man who came last night—"

"Not Thompson!" she cried.

"Yes, the same man called for me through the speaking-tube to come here at once—he said Miss Frayling was ill, and wanted me."

"It must have been a hoax, sir," said the housekeeper, but I noticed a troubled and perplexed look on her face. "I am very sorry indeed, but Miss Frayling is not here—we do not expect the ladies back for some weeks," she added.

"I am sorry I troubled you," I answered; I turned my horse's head and went home again.

The next day I set enquiries on foot with regard to the hoax which had been played upon me. Whoever had done the trick, no one was ready to own to it, and I noticed that the servants looked mysterious and nodded their heads when I said it was to Garth Hall I had been summoned.

The next night the same thing occurred. My night bell was rung and a voice shouted to me through the speaking-tube to come immediately to Garth Hall. I took no notice whatever of the trick, but determined to lay a trap for the impertinent intruder on my repose for the following night. I had a very savage dog, and I tied him outside the house. My housekeeper also agreed to sit up. Between twelve and one o'clock I was called again. I flew to my window and looked out. There was not a soul in sight, but a queer sense of indescribable chill and unaccountable horror took sudden possession of me. The dog was crouching down on the ground with his face hidden in his paws; he was moaning feebly. I dressed, went downstairs, unchained him and brought him up to my room. He crept on to my bed and lay there trembling; I will own to the fact that his master shared the unaccountable horror. What was the matter? I dared not answer this question even to myself. Mrs. Marks, my housekeeper, looked very solemn and grave the next morning.

"Sir," she said, when she brought in breakfast, "if I were you, I would go away from here. There is something very queer at the Hall and it seems to me—but there, I cannot speak of it."

"There are some things best not spoken of," I said shortly; "whoever is playing me a hoax has not chosen to reveal himself or herself. We can best tire the unlucky individual out by taking no notice."

"Yes, sir, perhaps that is best. Now I have got some news for you."

"What is that?" I asked.

"Mrs. and Miss Frayling returned to the Hall this morning."

"This morning!" I exclaimed, in astonishment, "but it is not yet nine o'clock."

"True, sir, but early as the hour is they passed this house not half-an-hour ago in the closed brougham. Miss Frayling looked very white, and the good lady, her mother, full of anxiety. I caught a glimpse of them as I was cleaning the steps; I doubt not, sir, but you will be summoned to the Hall to-day."

"Perhaps so," I answered briefly.

Mrs. Marks looked at me as if she would say something further, but refrained, and to my relief soon afterwards left me alone.

I finished my breakfast and went out about my daily rounds. I do not think myself destitute of pluck but I cannot pretend that I liked the present position. What was the mystery? What horrible dark joke was being played? With my healthy bringing up I could not really ascribe the thing to supernatural agency. A trick there was, of course. I vowed that I would find it out before I was much older, but then I remembered the chill and the terror which had assailed me when sitting up with Miss Frayling. The same chill and terror had come over me when I suddenly opened my window the night before.

"The best thing I can do is not to think of this," I commented, and then I absorbed myself with my patients.

Nothing occurred of any moment that day, nor was I summoned to attend the ladies at Garth Hall. About ten o'clock that night I had to go out to attend a farmer's wife who was suddenly taken ill. I sat with her for a little time and did not return till about half-past eleven. I then went straight up to my room and went to bed. I had scarcely fallen into my first slumber when I was aroused by the sharp ringing of my night bell. I felt inclined for a moment not to pay the least attention to it, but as it rang again with a quick imperative sound, I got up, more from the force of habit than anything else, and calling through the speaking-tube, applied my ear to it.

"Dr. Bruce, will you come at once to Garth Hall?" called a voice.

"No, I will not," I called back in reply.

There was a pause below, evidently of astonishment—and then the voice called again.

"I don't think you quite understand, sir. Mrs. Frayling wants you to visit Miss Frayling immediately; the young lady is very ill."

I was about to put the cap on the tube and return to my bed when I distinctly heard the crunch of wheels beneath my window and the pawing of an impatient horse. I crossed the room, threw open the window and looked out. A horse and gig were now standing under the window, and the man, Thompson, who had summoned me on the first night, was staring up at me.

"For God's sake, come, sir," he said. "The young lady is mortal bad."

"I will be with you in a minute," I said. I dressed myself trembling.

In an incredibly short space of time Thompson and I arrived at the Hall. Through our entire drive the man never spoke, but when we drew up at the great porch he uttered a heavy sigh of relief and muttered the words: "The devil is in this business. I don't pretend to understand it."

I looked at him, but resolved to take no notice of his queer remark. Mrs. Frayling met me on the steps.

"Come in at once," she said. She took both my hands in hers and drew me into the house. We entered her cheerful drawing-room. The poor lady's face was ghastly, her eyes full not only of trouble, but of horror.

"Now, Dr. Bruce," she said, "you must do your best."

"In what way?" I said.

"I fear my poor girl is mad. Unless you can manage to relieve her mind, she certainly will be by morning."

"Tell me what has happened since I last saw you, as briefly as possible," I said.

"I will do so," she replied. "Acting on your instructions, Lucy and I went to the Metropole. She was quite happy on the first day, but in the middle of the night grew very much disturbed. She and I were sleeping together. She awakened me and told me that the apparition at Garth Hall was pulling her—that the woman in the hood was imperatively demanding her presence.

" 'I know what has happened.' said Lucy. 'Dr. Bruce has refused to help her. She has gone to him but he won't respond to her efforts to bring him on the scene. How cruel he is!'

"I soothed the poor child as best I could, and towards morning she dropped off asleep. The next night she was in a still greater state of terror, again assuring me that the lady in the hood was drawing her, and that you, Dr. Bruce, were turning a deaf ear to her entreaties. On the third night she became almost frantic.

" 'I must go back,' she said. 'My spirit is being torn out of my body. If I am not back at Garth Hall early in the morning I shall die.'

"Her distress and horror were so extreme that I had to humour her. We took the very earliest train from London, and arrived at the Hall at nine o'clock. During the day Lucy was gentle and subdued; she seemed relieved at being back again, told me that she would go early to bed and that she hoped that she might have a good night. About an hour ago I heard her screaming violently, and, rushing to her room, found her in almost a state of collapse from horror—she kept pointing in a certain direction, but could not speak. I sent Thompson off in a hurry for you. As soon as ever I said I would do so she became a little better, and said she would dress herself. It is her intention now to ask you to spend the night with us, and, if possible, speak again to the horrible thing which is driving my child into a madhouse."

"I will tell you something strange," I said, when Mrs. Frayling paused, "I was undoubtedly called during the last three nights. A voice shouted through my speaking-tube, desiring me to come to Garth Hall. On the first night I went, feeling sure that I was really summoned; since then I have believed that it was a hoax."

"Oh, this is awful," said Mrs. Frayling, trembling excessively; she turned and asked me to follow her upstairs. We entered the same spacious and cheerful bedroom; Lucy Frayling was now pacing up and down in front of the fireplace; she did not notice either of us when we came in; the expression on her face was almost that of an insane person. The pupils of her eyes were widely dilated.

"Lucy," said her mother, "Here is Dr. Bruce."

She paused when my name was mentioned and looked at me fixedly. Her eyes grew dark with anger—she clenched her hand.

"You were faithless," she said; "she wanted you, and you would not accept the burden; you told me when last I saw you that you were glad she turned to you, for you are stronger than me, but you are a coward."

"Come, come," I said, trying to speak cheerfully. "I am here now, and will do anything you wish."

"I will prove you," said Miss Frayling, in an eager voice. "She will come again presently; when she comes, will you speak to her?"

"Certainly," I replied, "but remember I may not see her."

"I will tell you when she appears; I will point with my hand—I may not have power to utter words—but I will point to where she stands. When I do, speak to her; ask her why she troubles us—promise—you spoke once, speak again."

"I promise," I replied, and my voice sounded solemn and intense.

Miss Frayling heaved a deep sigh of relief, she went and stood by the mantelpiece with her back to the fire. I sat down on the nearest chair, and Mrs. Frayling followed my example. The clock ticked loudly on the mantelpiece, the candles burned with a steady gleam, the fire threw out cheerful flames, all was silent in the chamber. There was not a stir, not a sound. The minutes flew on. Miss Frayling stood as quiet as if she were turned into stone; suddenly she spoke,

"There is an adverse influence here," she said. "Mother, will you go into the ante-room. You can leave the door open, but will you stay in the ante-room for a little?"

Mrs. Frayling glanced at me; I nodded to her to comply. She left the room, going into a pretty little boudoir out of which the bedroom opened. I could see her from where I sat. Lucy now slightly altered her position. I saw that her eyes were fixed in the direction of another door, which opened from the outside corridor into the room. I tried to speak, to say something cheerful, but she held up her finger to stop me.

"She is coming," she said, in a stifled voice. "I feel the first stirring of the indescribable agony which always heralds her approach. Oh, my God, help me to endure. Was ever girl tortured as I am, before?"

She wrung her slight hands, her brows were knit, I saw the perspiration standing in great drops on her brow. I thought she would faint, and was about to rise to administer some restorative, when in the far distance I distinctly heard a sound; it was the sound of a woman's footsteps. It came along, softly tapping on the floor as it came; I heard the swish of a dress, the sound came nearer, the handle of the door was turned, I started and looked round. I did not see anybody, but immediately the room was filled with that sense of cold and chill which I had twice before experienced. My heart beat to suffocation, I felt my tongue cleave to the roof of my mouth. I was so overpowered by my own sensations that I had no time to watch Miss Frayling. Suddenly I heard her utter a low groan. I made a violent effort and turned my face in her direction. The poor girl was staring straight before her as if she were turned into stone. Her eyes were fixed in the direction of the door.

She raised her hand slowly and tremblingly, and pointed in the direction where her eyes were fixed. I looked across the room. Was it fancy, or was I conscious of a faint blue mist where no mist ought to be? I am not certain on that point, but I know at the same moment the horror which had almost overbalanced my reason suddenly left me. I found my voice.

"What do you want?" I said. "Why do you trouble us? What is the matter?"

The words had scarcely passed my lips before Miss Frayling's face underwent a queer change; she was also relieved from the agony of terror which was overmastering her.

"She is beckoning," she said; "come quickly."

She sprang across the room as she spoke, and seized a candle.

"Come at once," she said in a breathless voice, "she is beckoning—come."

Miss Frayling ran out of the room; I followed her, and Mrs. Frayling, who had come to the door while this strange scene was going on, accompanied us. Miss Frayling still taking the lead, we went downstairs. The whole house was full of strange unaccountable chill. We entered the upper hall, and then turning to our left, went down some steep stairs which led into a cellar.

"Where are you going now?" asked Mrs. Frayling.

"Come on, mother, come on," called Lucy, "she will tell us what to do."

We turned at the foot of the stairs into a low arched room with one tiny window. There was a heavy buttress of wall here which bulged out in unaccountable manner. The moment we entered this room, Lucy turned and faced us.

"She has gone in there," she said—"right into the wall."

"Well," I said, "now that we have followed her, let us go back—it is cold in the cellar."

Miss Frayling laughed hysterically.

"Do you think," she said, "that I will go back now? We must have this opened—can you do it, Dr. Bruce? Can you do it now, this moment? Mother, are there tools anywhere?"

"Not now, dear, not to-night," said the mother.

"Yes, to-night, this moment," exclaimed the girl. "Let Thompson be called—we have not a moment to lose. She went in right through this wall and smiled at me as she went. Poor, poor ghost! I believe her sad wanderings are nearly over."

"What are we to do?" said Mrs. Frayling, turning to me.

"We will open the wall at once," I said. "It will not be difficult to remove a few bricks. If you will kindly tell me where Thompson is I will fetch him."

"No, I will go for him myself," said Mrs. Frayling.

She left the cellar, returning in the space of a few minutes with the man. He brought a crowbar and other tools with him. He and I quickly removed some bricks. As soon as we had done so we found an empty space inside, into which we could thrust our hands. We made it a little larger and then were able to insert a candle. Lying on the floor within this space was a human skeleton.

I cried out at the awful discovery we had made, but Miss Frayling showed neither surprise nor terror.

"Poor ghost!" repeated the girl; "she will rest now. It was worth all this fearful suffering to bring her rest at last."

The discovery of the skeleton was the topic of the neighbourhood. It was given a Christian burial in due course, and from that hour to this the ghost at Garth Hall has never appeared.

I cannot pretend to account for this story in any way—no one has ever found out why those human bones were built into the old wall. The whole thing is queer and uncomfortable, a phenomenon which will not be explained on this side of Eternity.

Followed

L. T. Meade with Robert Eustace

I am David Ross's wife. I was married to him a month ago. I have lived through the peril and escaped the danger. What I have lived through, how it happened, and why it happened, this story tells.

My maiden name was Flower Dalrymple. I spent my early days on the Continent, travelling about from place to place and learning much of Bohemian life and Bohemian ways. When I was eighteen years of age my father got an appointment in London. We went to live there—my father, my mother, two brothers, a sister, and myself. Before I was twenty I was engaged to David Ross. David was a landed proprietor. He had good means, and was in my eyes the finest fellow in the world. In appearance he was stalwart and broad-shouldered, with a complexion as dark as a gipsy. He had a passionate and almost wild look in his eyes, and his wooing of me was very determined, and I might almost say stormy.

When first he proposed to me I refused him from a curious and unaccountable sense of fear, but that night I was miserable, and when two days after he repeated his offer, I accepted him, for I discovered that, whatever his character, he was the man I could alone love in all the world.

He told me something of his history. His father had died when he was a baby, and he had spent all the intervening years, except when at school and the University, with his mother. His mother's name was Lady Sarah Ross. On her own mother's side she was of Spanish extraction, but she was the daughter of Earl Reighley. She was a great recluse, and David gave me to understand that her character and ways of life were peculiar.

"You must be prepared for eccentricities in connection with my mother," he said. "I see her, perhaps, through rose-coloured spectacles, for she is to me the finest and the most interesting woman, with the exception of yourself, in the world. Her love for me is a very strange and a very deep passion. She has always opposed the idea of my marrying. Until I met you, I have yielded to her very marked wishes in this respect. I can do so no longer. All the same, I am almost afraid to tell her that we are engaged."

"Your account of your mother is rather alarming," I could not help saying. "Must I live with her after we are married, David?"

"Certainly not," he answered, with some abruptness. "You and I live at my place, Longmore; she goes to the Dower House."

"She will feel being deposed from her throne very acutely," I said.

"It will be our object in life, Flower, not to let her feel it," he answered. "I look forward with the deepest interest to your conquering her, to your winning her love. When you once win it, it is yours for ever."

All the time David was speaking I felt that he was hiding something. He was holding himself in check. With all his pluck and dash and daring, there was a weight on his mind, something which caused him, although he would not admit it, a curious sensation of uneasiness.

We had been engaged for a fortnight when he wrote to Lady Sarah apprising her of the fact. His letter received no answer. After a week, by his request, I wrote to her, but neither did she notice my letter.

At last, a month after our letters were written, I received a very cordial invitation from Lady Sarah. She invited me to spend Christmas with David and herself at Longmore. She apologised for her apparent rudeness in not writing sooner, but said she had not been well. She would give me, she said, a very hearty welcome, and hoped I would visit the old place in the second week in December and remain over Christmas.

"You will have a quiet time," she wrote, "not dull, for you will be with David; but if you are accustomed to London and the ways of society, you must not expect to find them at Longmore."

Of course I accepted her invitation. Our wedding was to take place on the 10th of January. My trousseau was well under way, and I started for Longmore on a certain snowy afternoon, determined to enjoy myself and to like Lady Sarah in spite of her eccentricities.

Longmore was a rambling old place situated on the borders of Salisbury Plain. The house was built in the form of a cross. The roof was turreted, and there was a tower at one end. The new rooms were in a distant wing. The centre of the cross, forming the body of the house, was very old, dating back many hundreds of years.

David came to meet me at Salisbury. He drove a mail phaeton, and I clambered up to my seat by his side. A pair of thoroughbred black horses were harnessed to the carriage. David touched the arched neck of one of his favourites with his whip, and we flew through the air.

It was a moonlight night, and I looked at David once or twice. I had never regarded him as faultless, but I now saw something in his appearance which surprised me. It was arbitrary and haughty. He had a fierce way of speaking to the man who sat behind. I could guess that his temper was overbearing. Never mind! No girl could care for David Ross a little. She must love him with all her heart, and soul, and strength, or hate him. I cared for him all the more because of his faults. He was human, interesting, very tender when he chose, and he loved me with a great love.

We arrived at Longmore within an hour, and found Lady Sarah standing on the steps of the old house to welcome us. She was a tall and very stately woman, with black eyes and a swarthy complexion—a complexion unnaturally dark. Notwithstanding the grace of her appearance I noticed from the very first that there was something wild and uncanny about her. Her eyes were long and almond-shaped. Their usual expression was somewhat languid, but they had a habit of lighting up suddenly at the smallest provocation with a fierce and almost unholy fire. Her hair was abundant and white as snow, and her very black eyes, narrow-arched brows, and dark complexion were brought out into sharper contrast by this wealth of silvery hair.

She wore black velvet and some very fine Brussels lace, and as she came to meet me I saw the diamonds glittering on her fingers. Whatever her faults, few girls could desire a more picturesque mother-in-law.

Without uttering a word she held out both her hands and drew me into the great central hall. Then she turned me round and looked me all over in the firelight.

"Fair and *petite*," she said. "Blue eyes, lips indifferent red, rest of the features ordinary. An English girl by descent, by education, by appearance. Look me full in the face, Flower!"

I did what I was bid. She gazed from her superior height into my eyes. As my eyes met hers I was suddenly overpowered by the most extraordinary feeling which had ever visited me. All through my frame there ran a thrill of ghastly and overmastering fear. I shrank away from her, and I believe my face turned white. She drew me to her side again, stooped, and kissed me. Then she said, abruptly:—

"Don't be nervous"—and then she turned to her son.

"You have had a cold drive," she said. "I hope you have not taken a chill?"

"Dear me, no, mother. Why should I?" he replied, somewhat testily. "Flower and I enjoyed our rush through the air."

He was rubbing his hands and warming himself by the log fire as he spoke—now he came to me and drew me towards its genial blaze. Lady Sarah glanced at us both. I saw her lips quiver and her black brows meet across her forehead. A very strange expression narrowed her eyes, a vindictive look, from which I turned away.

She swept, rather than walked, across the hall and rang a bell. A neatly dressed, pleasant-looking girl appeared.

"Take Miss Dalrymple to her room, Jessie, and attend on her," said Lady Sarah.

I was conducted up some low stairs and down a passage to a pretty, modern-looking room.

"Longmore is very old, miss," said Jessie, "and some of it is even tumbling to pieces, but Lady Sarah is never one for repairs. You won't find anything old, however, in this room, miss, for it has not been built more than ten years. You will have a lovely view of Salisbury Plain from here in the morning. I am glad, very glad, Miss Dalrymple, that you are not put into one of the rooms in the other wing."

I did not ask Jessie the meaning of her words. I thought she looked at me in an expressive way, but I would not meet her glance.

When I was ready Jessie conducted me to the drawing-room, where I found David standing on the rug in front of a log fire.

"Where is your mother?" I asked.

"She will be down presently. I say, what a pretty little girl it is," he cried, and he opened his big arms and folded me in a close embrace.

Just at that moment I heard the rustle of a silk dress, and, turning, saw Lady Sarah.

She wore a rich ruby gown, which rustled and glistened every time she moved. I tore myself from David's arms and faced her. There was a flush on my cheeks, and my eyes, I am sure, were suspiciously bright. She called me to her side and began to talk in a gentle and pleasant way.

Suddenly she broke off.

"Dinner is late," she said. "Ring the bell, David."

David's summons was answered by a black servant: a man with the most peculiar and, I must add, forbidding face I had ever seen.

"Is dinner served, Sambo?" inquired his mistress.

"It is on the table, missis," he replied, in excellent English.

Lady Sarah got up.

"David," she said, "will you take Flower to her place at the dinner-table?"

David led the way with me; Lady Sarah followed. David took the foot of the table, his mother the head. I sat at Lady Sarah's left hand.

During the meal which followed she seemed to forget all about me. She talked incessantly, on matters relating to the estate, to her son. I perceived that she was a first-rate business woman, and I noticed that David listened to her with respect and interest. Her eyes never raised themselves to meet his without a softened and extraordinary expression filling them. It was a look of devouring and overmastering love. His eyes, as he looked into hers, had very much the same expression. Even at me he had never looked quite like this. It was as if two kindred souls, absolutely kindred in all particulars, were holding converse one with the other, and as if I, David's affianced wife, only held the post of interloper.

Sambo, the black servant, stood behind Lady Sarah's chair. He made a striking figure. He was dressed in the long, soft, full trousers which Easterns wear. I learnt afterwards that Sambo was an aborigine from Australia, but Lady Sarah had a fancy to dress him as though he hailed from the Far East. The colour of his silken garments was a rich deep yellow. His short jacket was much embroidered in silver, and he had a yellow turban twisted round his swarthy head.

His waiting was the perfection of the art. He attended to your slightest wants, and never made any sound as he glided about the apartment. I did not like him, however; I felt nearly as uncomfortable in his presence as I did in that of Lady Sarah.

We lingered for some little time when the meal was over; then Lady Sarah rose.

"Come, Flower," she said.

She took my hand in one of hers.

"You will join us, David, when you have had your smoke," she continued, and she laid her shapely hand across her son's broad forehead.

He smiled at her.

"All right, madre," he said, "I shall not be long."

His black eyes fell from his mother's face to mine, and he smiled at me—a smile of such heart-whole devotion that my momentary depression vanished.

Lady Sarah took me into the drawing-room. There she made me seat myself in a low chair by her side, and began to talk.

"Has David never told you of my peculiar tastes, my peculiar recreations?"

"No," I replied; "all he has really told me about you, his mother, is that you love him with a very great love, and that he feared our marriage would pain you."

"Tut!" she replied. "Do you imagine that a little creature like you can put a woman like me out? But we won't talk personal things to-night. I want you to see the great charm of my present life. You must know that I have for several years eschewed society. David has mingled with his kind, but I have stayed at home with my faithful servant Sambo and—my pets."

"Your pets!" I said; "dogs, horses?"

"Neither."

"Cats then, and perhaps birds?"

"I detest cats, and always poison any stray animals of that breed that come to Longmore. It is true I keep a few pigeons, but they are for a special use. I also keep rabbits for the same purpose."

"Then what kind of pets have you?" I asked.

"Reptiles," she said, shortly. "Would you like to see them?"

I longed to say to Lady Sarah that nothing would induce me to look at her horrible pets, but I was afraid. She gazed full at me, and I nodded my head. Her face was white, and her lips had taken on once more that hard, straight line which terrified me.

She rose from her seat, took my hand, and led me across the drawing-room into the hall. We crossed the hall to the left. Here she opened a baize door and motioned to me to follow her. We went down some stairs—they were narrow and winding. At the bottom of the stairs was a door. Lady Sarah took a key from her pocket, fitted it into the lock, and opened the door.

A blast of wintry air blew on my face, and some scattered, newly-fallen snow wetted my feet.

"I forgot about the snow," she said. "The reptile-house is only just across the yard. It is warm there; but if you are afraid of wetting your feet, say so."

"I am not afraid," I replied.

"That is good. Then come with me."

She held up her ruby-coloured silk dress, and I caught a glimpse of her neat ankles and shapely feet.

At the other side of the stone yard was a building standing by itself and completely surrounded with a high fence of closely meshed wire netting. Lady Sarah opened a door in the fence with another key, then she locked it carefully behind her. With a third key she unfastened the door of the building itself. When she opened this door the air from within, hot and moist, struck on my face.

She pushed me in before her, and I stood just within the entrance while she lit a lantern. As the candle caught the flame I uttered a sudden cry, for against my arm, with only the glass between, I saw a huge mottled snake, which, startled by the sudden light, was coiling to and fro. Its black forked tongue flickered about its lips as if it were angry at being disturbed in its slumbers.

I drew back from the glass quickly, and caught Lady Sarah's eyes fixed upon me with a strange smile.

"My pets are here," she said, "and this is one. I was a great traveller in my youth, as was my father before me. After my husband died I again went abroad. When David's education was finished he went with me. I inherit my father's taste for snakes and reptiles. I have lived for my pets for many long years now, and I fancy I possess the most superb private collection in the kingdom. Look for yourself, Flower. This is the *Vipera nascicornis*, or in our English language the African nose-horned snake. Pray notice his flat head. He is a fine specimen, just nine feet long. I caught him myself on the Gold Coast, with my friend Jane Ashley."

"Is he—venomous?" I asked. My lips trembled so that I could scarcely get out the words.

"Four hours for a man," was the laconic reply. "We count the degree of poison of a snake by the time a man lives after he is bitten. This fellow is, therefore, comparatively harmless. But see, here is the *Pseudechis porphyriacus*—the black snake of Tasmania and Australia. His time is six minutes. Wake up, Darkey!" and she tapped the glass with her knuckles.

An enormous glistening coil, polished as ebony, moved, reared its head, and disappeared into the shadow of the wall.

I gave a visible shudder. Lady Sarah took no notice. She walked slowly between the cases, explaining various attributes and particulars with regard to her favourites.

"Here are puff adders," she said; "here are ring snakes; in this cage are whip snakes. Ah! here is the dreaded moccasin from Florida—here are black vipers from the South African mountains and copper-heads from the Peruvian swamps. I have a pet name for each," she continued; "they are as my younger children."

As she said the words it flashed across my mind, for the first time, that, perhaps, Lady Sarah was not in her right senses. The next instant her calm and dignified voice dispelled my suspicions.

"I have shown you my treasures," she said; "I hope you think it a great honour. My father, the late Lord Reighley, had a passion for reptiles almost equal to my own. The one thing I regret about David is that he has not inherited it."

"But are you not afraid to keep your collection here?" I asked. "Do you not dread some of them escaping?"

"I take precautions," she said, shortly; "and as to any personal fear, I do not know the meaning of the word. My favourites know me, and after their fashion they love me."

As she spoke she slid back one of the iron doors and, reaching in her hand, took out a huge snake and deliberately whipped the creature round her neck.

"This is my dear old carpet snake," she said; "quite harmless. You can come close to him and touch him, if you like."

"No, thank you," I replied.

She put the snake back again and locked the door.

We returned to the drawing-room. I went and stood by the fire. I was trembling all over, but not altogether from the coldness of the atmosphere.

"You are nervous," said Lady Sarah. "I thought you brave a few minutes ago. The sight of my beauties has shocked you. Will you oblige me by not telling David to-night that I showed them to you?"

I bowed my head, and just at that moment David himself entered the room.

He went to the piano, and almost without prelude began to sing. He had a magnificent voice, like a great organ. Lady Sarah joined him. He and she sang together, the wildest, weirdest, most extraordinary songs I had ever listened to. They were mostly Spanish. Suddenly Lady Sarah took out her guitar and began to play—David accompanying her on the piano.

The music lasted for about an hour. Then Lady Sarah shut the piano.

"The little white English girl is very tired," she said. "Flower, you must go to bed immediately. Good-night."

When I reached my room I found Jessie waiting to attend on me. She asked me at once if I had seen the reptiles.

"Yes," I said.

"And aren't you nearly dead with terror of them, miss?"

"I am a little afraid of them," I said. "Is there any fear of their escaping?"

"Law, no, miss! Who would stay in the house if there were? You need not be frightened. But this is a queer house, very queer, all the same."

The next day after breakfast David asked me if I had seen his mother's pets.

"I have," I replied, "but she asked me not to mention the fact to you last night. David, I am afraid of them. Must they stay here when I come to live at Longmore?"

"The madre goes, and her darlings with her," he answered, and he gave a sigh, and a shadow crossed his face.

"You are sorry to part with your mother?" I said.

"I shall miss her," he replied. "Even you, Flower, cannot take the place my mother occupies in my heart. But I shall see her daily, and you are worth sacrificing something for, my little white English blossom."

"Why do you speak of me as if I were so essentially English?" I said.

"You look the part. You are very much like a flower of the field. Your pretty name, and your pretty ways, and your fair complexion foster the idea. Mother admires you; she thinks you very sweet to look at. Now come into the morning-room and talk to her."

That day, after lunch, it rained heavily. We were all in the morning-room, a somewhat dismal apartment, when David turned to his mother.

"By the way, madre," he said, "I want to have the jewels re-set for Flower."

"What do you say?" inquired his mother.

"I mean to have the diamonds and the other jewels re-set for my wife," he replied, slowly.

"I don't think it matters," said Lady Sarah.

"Matters!" cried David; "I don't understand you. Flower must have the jewels made up to suit her *petite* appearance. I should like her to see them. Will you give me the key of the safe and I will bring them into this room?"

"You can show them, of course," said Lady Sarah. She spoke in a careless tone.

He looked at her, shrugged his shoulders, and I was surprised to see an angry light leap into his eyes. He took the key without a word and left the room.

I sat down on the nearest window-ledge—a small, slight, very fair girl. No one could feel more uncomfortable and out of place.

David returned with several morocco cases. He put them on the table, then he opened them one by one. The treasures within were magnificent. There were necklets and bracelets and rings and tiaras innumerable. David fingered them, and Lady Sarah stood close by.

"This tiara is too heavy for you, Flower," said David, suddenly.

As he spoke, he picked up a magnificent circlet of flashing diamonds and laid them against my golden head. The next moment the ornament was rudely snatched away by Lady Sarah. She walked to a glass which stood between two windows and fitted the tiara over her own head.

"Too heavy for Flower, and it suits you, mother," said the young man, his eyes flashing with a sudden genuine admiration.

She laid the tiara on the table.

"Leave the things as they are for the present," she said. "It is not necessary to have them altered. You are marrying a flower, remember, and flowers of the field do not need this sort of adornment."

She tried to speak quietly, but her lips trembled and her words came in jerks.

"And I don't want to wear them," I cried. "I don't like them."

"That is speaking in a very childish way," said Lady Sarah.

"You must wear them when you are presented, dear," remarked David. "But there is time enough; I will put the things away for the present."

The jewels were returned to the safe, and I breathed a sigh of relief.

That night I was tired out and slept well, and as the next morning was a glorious one, more like spring than mid-winter, David proposed that he and I should spend the day driving about Salisbury Plain and seeing the celebrated stones.

He went to the stables to order the dog-cart to be got ready, and I ran up to my room to put on my hat and warm jacket.

When I came back to the hall my future mother-in-law was standing there. Her face was calm and her expression mild and genial. She kissed me almost affectionately, and I went off with David in high spirits, my fears lulled to slumber.

He knew every inch of the famous Stonehenge, and told me many of the legends about its origin. There was one stone in particular which we spent some time in observing. It was inside the circle, a flat, broad stone, with a depression in the middle.

"This," said David, "is called the 'Slaughter Stone'. On this stone the Druids killed their victims."

"How interesting and how horrible!" I cried.

"It is true," he answered. "These stones, dating back into the ages of the past, have always had a queer fascination for me. I love them almost as much as my mother does. She often comes here when her nerves are not at their best and wanders about this magic circle for hours."

David told me many other legends. We lunched and had tea in the small town of Wilton, and did not return home until time for late dinner.

I went to my room, and saw nothing of Lady Sarah until I entered the drawing-room. I there found David and his mother in earnest conversation. His face looked full of annoyance.

"I am sorry," said Lady Sarah; "I am afraid, Flower, you will have to make up your mind to having a dull day alone with me to-morrow."

"But why dull?" interrupted David. "Flower will enjoy a day by herself with you, mother. She wants to know you, she wants to love you, as I trust you will soon love her."

Lady Sarah made no answer. After a pause, during which an expression of annoyance and displeasure visited her thin lips, she said:—

"An urgent telegram has arrived from our lawyers for David. He must go to town by the first train in the morning."

"I will come back to-morrow night, little girl," he said.

He patted me on my hand as he spoke, and I did not attempt to raise any objection. A moment later we went into the dining-room.

During the meal I was much disturbed by the persistent way in which Sambo watched me. Without exception, Sambo had the ugliest face I had ever seen. His eyes were far apart, and wildly staring out of his head. His features were twisted, he had very thick lips, and the whole of the lower part of his face was in undue prominence. But, ugly as he was in feature, there was a certain dignity about him. His very upright carriage, his very graceful movements, his very picturesque dress, could not but impress me, although, perhaps, in a measure they added to the uneasiness with which I regarded him. I tried to avoid his gaze, but whenever I raised my eyes I encountered his, and, in consequence, I had very little appetite for dinner.

The evening passed quickly, and again that night I slept well. When I awoke it was broad daylight, and Jessie was pouring hot water into a bath for me.

"Mr. Ross went off more than two hours ago, miss," she said. "He left a message that I was to be very attentive to you, so if you want anything I hope you will ask me."

"Certainly I will," I replied.

Jessie was a pretty girl, with a rosy face and bright, pleasant eyes. I saw her fix these eyes now upon my face—she came close to me.

"I am very glad you are going to marry Mr. Ross," she said, "and I am very glad that you will be mistress here, for if there was not to be a change soon, I could not stay."

"What do you mean?" I said.

She shrugged her shoulders significantly.

"This is a queer house," she said—"there are queer people in it, and there are queer things done in it, and—*there are the reptiles*!"

I gave an involuntary shiver.

"There are the reptiles," she repeated. "Lady Sarah and Sambo play tricks with them at times. Sambo has got a stuff that drives them nearly mad. When Lady Sarah is at her wildest he uses it. I have watched them when they didn't know I was looking: half-a-dozen of the snakes following Sambo as if they were demented, and Lady Sarah looking on and laughing! He puts the thing on his boots. I do not know what it is. They never hurt him. He flings the boots at them and they are quiet. Yes, it is a queer house, and I am afraid of the reptiles. By the way, miss, would you not like *me* to clean your boots for you?"

"Why so?" I asked. My face had turned white and my teeth were chattering. Her words unnerved me considerably.

"I will, if you like," she said. "Sambo sha'n't have them. Now, miss, I think you have everything you want."

She left me, and I dressed as quickly as I could. As I did so my eyes fell upon a little pair of brown boots, for which I had a special affection. They were polished up brightly; no boots could be more beautifully cleaned. What did Jessie mean? What did she mean, too, by speaking of Lady Sarah's wild fits?

I went downstairs, to find Lady Sarah in a genial humour. She was smiling and quite agreeable. Sambo did not wait at breakfast, and in consequence we had a pleasant meal. When it was over she took my hand and led me into her morning-room.

"Come here," she said, "I want to speak to you. So you are David's choice! Now listen. The aim and object of my life ever since I lost my husband has been to keep David single."

"What do you mean?" I asked.

"What I say. I love my son with a passion which you, you little white creature, cannot comprehend. I want him for myself *entirely*. You have dared to step in—you have dared to take him from me. But listen: even if you do marry him, you won't keep him long. You would like to know why—I will tell you. Because his love for you is only the passion which a man may experience for a pair of blue eyes, and a white skin, and childish figure. It is as water unto wine compared to the love he feels for me. He will soon return to me. Be warned in time. Give him up."

"I cannot," I said.

"You won't be happy here. The life is not your life. The man is not the right sort of man for you. In some ways he is half a savage. He has been much in wild countries, in lands uninhabited by civilised people. He is not the man for you, nor am I the mother-in-law for you. Give him up. Here is paper and here is a pen. Write him a letter. Write it now, and the carriage shall be at the door and you will be taken to Wilton—from there you can get a train to London, and you will be safe, little girl, quite safe."

"You ask the impossible," I replied; "I love your son."

She had spoken with earnestness, the colour flaming into her cheeks, her eyes very bright. Now her face grew cold and almost leaden in hue.

"I have given you your choice and a way of escape," she said. "If you don't take the offer, it is not my fault." She walked out of the room.

What did she mean? I stayed where she had left me. I was trembling all over. Terrors of the most overmastering and unreasoning sort visited me. All I had lived through since I came to Longmore now flooded my imagination and made me weak with nervous fears. The reptile-house—Lady Sarah—Sambo's strange behaviour—Sambo's wicked glance—Jessie's words. Oh, why had I come? Why had David left me alone in this terrible place?

I got up, left the room, and strode into the grounds. The grounds were beautiful, but I could find no pleasure in them. Over and over the desire to run away visited me. I only restrained my nervous longing for David's sake. He would never forgive me if I left Longmore because I feared his mother.

The gong sounded for lunch, and I went into the house. Lady Sarah was seated at the table; Sambo was absent.

"I have had a busy morning," she said. "Darkey is ill."

"Darkey!" I exclaimed.

"Yes, the black snake whose bite kills in six minutes. Sambo is with him; he and I have been giving him some medicine. I trust he will be better soon. He is my favourite reptile—a magnificent creature."

I made no remark.

"I am afraid you must amuse yourself as best you can this afternoon," she continued, "for Sambo and I will be engaged with the snake. I am sorry I cannot offer to send you for a drive, but two of the horses are out and the bay mare is lame."

I said I would amuse myself, and that I should not require the use of any of the horses, and she left me.

I did not trouble to go on the Plain. I resumed my restless wanderings about the place. I wondered, as I did so, if Longmore could ever be a real home to me. As the moments flew past I looked at my watch, counting the hours to David's return. When he was back, surely the intangible danger which I could not but feel surrounded me would be over.

At four o'clock Sambo brought tea for one into the drawing-room. He laid it down, with a peculiar expression.

"You will be sorry to hear, missie," he said, "that Missah Ross not coming back to-night." The man spoke in a queer kind of broken English.

I sprang to my feet, my heart beating violently.

"Sorry, missie, business keep him—telegram to missis; not coming back till morning. Yah, missie, why you stay?"

"What do you mean?" I asked.

The man had a hazel wand in his hand. I had noticed it without curiosity up to the present. Now he took it and pointed it at me. As he did so he uttered the curious word "*Ullinka*." The evil glitter in his eyes frightened me so much that I shrank up against the wall.

"What are you doing that for?" I cried. He snapped the stick in two and flung it behind him.

"Missie, you take Sambo's word and go right away to-night. Missis no well—Darkey no well—Sambo no well. No place for missie with blue eyes and fair hair. I say 'Ullinka', and 'Ullinka' means *dead*—this fellah magic stick. Missie run to Wilton, take train from Wilton to London. Short track 'cross Plain—missie go quick. Old Sambo open wicket-gate and let her go. Missie go soon."

"Do you mean it?" I said.

"*Yowi*—yes."

"I will go," I said. "You terrify me. Can I have a carriage?"

"No time, missie. Old missis find out. Old missis no wish it—missie go quick 'cross Plain short track to Wilton. Moon come up short time."

"I will go," I whispered.

"Missie take tea first and then get ready," he continued. "Sambo wait till missie come downstairs."

I did not want the tea, but the man brought me a cup ready poured out.

"One cup strengthen missie, then short track 'cross Plain straight ahead to Wilton. Moon in sky. Missie safe then from old missis, from Darkey, and from Sambo."

I drank the tea, but did not touch the cake and bread and butter. I went to my room, fear at my heels. In my terror I forgot to remark, although I remembered it well afterwards, that for some extraordinary reason most of my boots and shoes had disappeared. My little favourite pair of brown boots alone was waiting for me. I put them on, buttoned them quickly, put on my fur coat and cap, and with my purse in my pocket ran downstairs. No matter what David thought of me now.

There was something terrible in this house—an unknown and indescribable *fear*—I must get away from Longmore at any cost.

Sambo conducted me without a word down the garden and out on to the Plain through the wicket-gate.

"Quick, missie," he said, and then he vanished from view, shutting and locking the gate behind him.

It was a perfect evening, still and cold. The sun was near the horizon and would soon set, and a full moon was just rising. I determined to walk briskly. I was strong and active, and the distance between Longmore and Wilton did not frighten me. I could cross the Plain direct from Longmore, and within two hours at longest would reach Wilton. My walk would lead past Stonehenge.

The Plain looked weird in the moonlight. It looked unfathomable: it seemed to stretch into space as if it knew no ending. Walking fast, running at intervals, pausing now and then to take breath, I continued my fearful journey.

Was Lady Sarah mad, was Sambo mad, and what ailed Darkey, the awful black snake whose bite caused death in six minutes? As the thought of Darkey came to me, making my heart throb until I thought it would stop, I felt a strange and unknown sensation of fatigue creeping over me: my feet began to lag. I could not account for this. I took out my watch and looked at it. I felt so tired that to go on without a short rest was impossible. There was a stone near. I sat on it for a moment or two. While resting I tried to collect my scattered thoughts. I wondered what sort of story I should tell David: how I would appease his anger and satisfy him that I did right in flying like a runaway from the home which was soon to be my own. As these thoughts came to me I closed my eyes; I felt my head nodding. Then all was lost in unconsciousness.

I awoke after what seemed a moment's sleep to find that I had been sitting on the stone for over half an hour. I felt refreshed by my slumber, and started now to continue my walk rapidly. I went lightly over the springy turf. I knew my bearings well, for David had explained everything to me on our long expedition yesterday.

I must have gone over a mile right on to the bare Plain when I began once again to experience that queer and unaccountable sensation of weakness. My pace slowed down and I longed again to rest. I resolved to resist the sensation and continued my way, but more slowly now and with a heavily beating heart. My heart laboured in a most unnatural way. I could not account for my own sensations.

Suddenly I paused and looked back. I fancied that I heard a noise, very slight and faint and different from that which the wind made as it sighed over the vast, billowy undulations of the Plain. Now, as I looked back, I saw something about fifty yards away, something which moved swiftly over the short grass. Whatever the thing was, it came towards me, and as it came it glistened now and then in the moonlight. What could it be? I raised my hand to shade my eyes from the bright light of the moon. I wondered if I was the subject of an hallucination. But, no; whatever that was which was now approaching me, it was a reality, no dream. It was making straight in my direction. The next instant every fibre in my body was tingling with terror, for gliding towards me, in great curves, with head raised, was an enormous black snake!

For one moment I gazed, in sickened horror, and then I ran—ran as one runs in a nightmare, with thumping heart and clogged feet and knees that were turned to water. There could be no doubt of what had happened: the great black snake, Darkey, had escaped from Longmore and was following me. Why had it escaped? How had it escaped? Was its escape premeditated? Was it meant to follow me? Was I the victim of a pre-arranged and ghastly death? Was it—was it?—

my head reeled, my knees tottered. There was not a tree or a house in sight. The bare, open plain surrounded me for miles. As I reeled, however, to the crest of the rise I saw, lying in the moonlight, not a quarter of a mile away, the broken ring of Stonehenge. I reached it in time to clamber on to one of the stones. I might be saved. It was my only chance.

Summoning all my energies I made for the ruined temple. For the first hundred yards I felt that I was gaining on the brute, though I could hear, close on my track, its low, continuous hiss. Then the deadly faintness for which I could not account once more seized me. I fancied I heard someone calling me in a dim voice, which sounded miles away.

Making a last frantic effort, I plunged into the circle of stones and madly clambered on to the great "Slaughter Stone". Once more there came a cry, a figure flashed past me, a loud report rang in my ears, and a great darkness came over me.

"Drink this, Flower."

I was lying on my back. Lady Sarah was bending over me. The moonlight was shining, and it dazzled my eyes when I first opened them. In the moonlight I could see that Lady Sarah's face was very white. There was a peculiar expression about it. She put her hand gently and deftly under my head, and held something to my lips. I drank a hot and fiery mixture, and was revived.

"Where am I—what has happened?" I asked.

"You are on the great 'Slaughter Stone' on Salisbury Plain. You have had a narrow escape. Don't speak. I am going to take you home."

"Not back to Longmore?"

"Yes, back to Longmore, your future home. Don't be silly."

"But the snake, Darkey, the black snake?" I said. I cowered, and pressed my hand to my face. "He followed me, he followed me," I whispered.

"He is dead," she answered; "I shot him with my own hands. You have nothing to fear from me or from Darkey any more. Come!"

I was too weak to resist her. She did not look unkind. There was no madness in her eyes. At that moment Sambo appeared in view. Sambo lifted me from the stone and carried me to a dogcart which stood on the Plain. Lady Sarah seated herself by my side, took the reins, and we drove swiftly away.

Once again we entered the house. Lady Sarah took me to the morning-room. She shut the door, but did not lock it. There was a basin of hot soup on the table.

"Drink, and be quick," she said, in an imperious voice.

I obeyed her; I was afraid to do otherwise.

"Better?" she asked.

"Yes," I replied, in a semi-whisper.

"Then listen."

I tried to rise, but she motioned me to stay seated.

"The peril is past," she said. "You have lived through it. You are a plucky girl, and I respect you. Now hear what I have to say."

I tried to do so and to keep down my trembling. She fixed her eyes on me and she spoke.

"Long ago I made a vow," she said. "I solemnly vowed before Almighty God that as long as I lived I would never allow my only son to marry. He knew that I had made this vow, and for a long time he respected it, but he met you and became engaged to you in defiance of his mother's vow and his mother's wish. When I heard the tidings I lost my senses. I became wild with jealousy, rage, and real madness. I would not write to you nor would I write to him."

"Why did you write at last—why did you ask me here?" I said then.

"Because the jealousy passed, as it always does, and for a time I was sane."

"Sane!" I cried.

"Yes, little girl; yes, *sane*! But listen. Some years ago, when on the coast of Guinea, I was the victim of a very severe sunstroke. From that time I have had fits of madness. Any shock, any excitement, brings them on.

"I had such a fit of madness when my son wrote to say that he was engaged to you. It passed, and I was myself again. You were not in the house an hour, however, before I felt it returning. There is only one person who can manage me at these times; there is only one person whom I fear and respect—my black servant Sambo. Sambo manages me, and yet at the same time I manage him. He loves me after his blind and heathen fashion. He has no fear; he has no conscience; to commit a crime is nothing to him. He loves me, and he passionately loves the reptiles. To please me and to carry out my wishes are the sole objects of his life.

"With madness in my veins I watched you and David during the last two days, and the wild desire to crush you to the very earth came over me. David went to London, and I thought the opportunity had come. I spoke to Sambo about it, and Sambo made a suggestion. I listened to him. My brain was on fire. I agreed to do what he suggested. My snake Darkey was to be the weapon to take your life. I felt neither remorse nor pity. Sambo is a black from Australia, an aborigine from that distant country. He knows the secrets of the blacks. There is a certain substance extracted from an herb which the blacks know, and which, when applied to any part of the dress or the person of an enemy, will induce each snake which comes across his path to turn and follow him. The substance drives the snake mad, and he will follow and kill his victim. Sambo possessed the stuff, and from time to time, to amuse me, he has tried its power on my reptiles. He has put it on his own boots, but he himself has never been bitten, for he has flung the boots to the snakes at the last moment. This afternoon he put it on the brown boots which you are now wearing. He then terrified you, and induced you to run away across Salisbury Plain. He put something into your tea to deprive you of strength, and when you were absent about three-quarters of an hour he let Darkey loose. Darkey followed you as a needle will follow a magnet. Sambo called me to the wicket-gate and showed me the glistening creature gliding over the Plain in your direction. As I looked, a veil fell from my eyes. The madness left me, and I became sane. I saw the awful thing that I had done. I repented with agony. In a flash I ordered the dogcart, and with Sambo by my side I followed you. I was just in time. I shot my favourite reptile. You were saved."

Lady Sarah wiped the drops of perspiration from her forehead.

"You are quite safe," she said, after a pause, "and I am sane. What I did, I did when I was not accountable. Are you going to tell David?"

"How can I keep it from him?"

"It seems hard to you now, but I ask you to do it. I promise not to oppose your marriage. I go meekly to the Dower House. I am tired of the reptiles—my favourite is dead, and the others are nothing to me. They shall be sent as a gift to the Zoological Gardens. Now will you tell David? If you do, I shall shoot myself to-night. Think for an hour, then tell me your decision." She left the room.

How I endured that hour I do not know! At the end of it I went to seek her. She was pacing up and down the great hall. I ran to her. I tried to take her hand, but she held her hands behind her.

"He will love you, he will worship you, and I, his old mother, will be nothing to him. What are you going to do?" she said then.

"I will never tell him," I whispered.

She looked hard at me, and her great black eyes softened.

"You are worthy to be his wife," she said, in a hoarse voice, and she left me.

I am David's wife, and David does not know. He will never know. We are still on our honeymoon, but David is in trouble, for by the very last post news reached him of Lady Sarah's sudden death. He was absent from her when she breathed her last. He shall never know the worst. He shall always treasure her memory in his heart.

The Man Who Disappeared

L. T. Meade with Robert Eustace

I am a lawyer by profession, and have a snug set of chambers in Chancery Lane. My name is Charles Pleydell. I have many clients, and can already pronounce myself a rich man.

On a certain morning towards the end of September in the year 1897 I received the following letter:—

> SIR,—I have been asked to call on you by a mutual friend, General Cornwallis, who accompanied my step-daughter and myself on board the *Osprey* to England. Availing myself of the General's introduction, I hope to call to see you or to send a representative about eleven o'clock to-day.
>
> The General says that he thinks you can give me advice on a matter of some importance.
>
> I am a Spanish lady. My home is in Brazil, and I know nothing of England or of English ways. I wish, however, to take a house near London and to settle down. This house must be situated in the neighbourhood of a large moor or common. It must have grounds surrounding it, and must have extensive cellars or basements, as my wish is to furnish a laboratory in order to carry on scientific research. I am willing to pay any sum in reason for a desirable

habitation, but one thing is essential: the house must be as near London as is possible under the above conditions.—Yours obediently, STELLA SCAIFFE.

This letter was dated from the Carlton Hotel.

Now, it so happened that a client of mine had asked me a few months before to try and let his house—an old-fashioned and somewhat gruesome mansion, situated on a lonely part of Hampstead Heath. It occurred to me that this house would exactly suit the lady whose letter I had just read.

At eleven o'clock one of my clerks brought me in a card. On it were written the words, "Miss Muriel Scaiffe". I desired the man to show the lady in, and a moment later a slight, fair-haired English girl entered the room.

"Mrs. Scaiffe is not quite well and has sent me in her stead. You have received a letter from my step-mother, have you not, Mr. Pleydell?"

"I have," I replied. "Will you sit down, Miss Scaiffe?"

She did so. I looked at her attentively. She was young and pretty. She also looked good, and although there was a certain anxiety about her face which she could not quite repress, her smile was very sweet.

"Your step-mother," I said, "requires a house with somewhat peculiar conditions?"

"Oh, yes," the girl answered. "She is very anxious on the subject. We want to be settled within a week."

"That is a very short time in which to take and furnish a house," I could not help remarking.

"Yes," she said, again. "But, all the same, in our case it is essential. My step-mother says that anything can be done if there is enough money."

"That is true in a sense," I replied, smilingly. "If I can help you I shall be pleased. You want a house on a common?"

"On a common or moor."

"It so happens, Miss Scaiffe, that there is a place called The Rosary at Hampstead which may suit you. Here are the particulars. Read them over for yourself and tell me if there is any use in my giving you an order to view."

She read the description eagerly, then she said:—

"I am sure Mrs. Scaiffe would like to see this house. When can we go?"

"To-day, if you like, and if you particularly wish it I can meet you at The Rosary at three o'clock."

"That will do nicely," she answered.

Soon afterwards she left me.

The rest of the morning passed as usual, and at the appointed hour I presented myself at the gates of The Rosary. A carriage was already drawn up there, and as I approached a tall lady with very dark eyes stepped out of it.

A glance showed me that the young lady had not accompanied her.

"You are Mr. Pleydell?" she said, holding out her hand to me, and speaking in excellent English.

"Yes," I answered.

"You saw my step-daughter this morning?"

"Yes," I said again.

"I have called to see the house," she continued. "Muriel tells me that it is likely to suit my requirements. Will you show it to me?"

I opened the gates, and we entered a wide carriage-drive. The Rosary had been unlet for some months, and weeds partly covered the avenue. The grounds had a desolate and gloomy appearance, leaves were falling thickly from the trees, and altogether the entire place looked undesirable and neglected.

The Spanish lady, however, seemed delighted with everything. She looked around her with sparkling glances. Flashing her dark eyes into my face, she praised the trees and avenue, the house, and all that the house contained.

She remarked that the rooms were spacious, the lobbies wide; above all things, the cellars numerous.

"I am particular about the cellars, Mr. Pleydell," she said.

"Indeed!" I answered. "At all events, there are plenty of them."

"Oh, yes! And this one is so large. It will quite suit our purpose. We will turn it into a laboratory.

"My brother and I—Oh, I have not told you about my brother. He is a Spaniard—Señor Merello—he joins us here next week. He and I are scientists, and I hope scientists of no mean order. We have come to England for the purpose of experimenting. In this land of the free we can do what we please. We feel, Mr. Pleydell—you look so sympathising that I cannot help confiding in you—we feel that we are on the verge of a very great—a very astounding discovery, at which the world, yes, the whole world will wonder. This house is the one of all others for our purpose. When can we take possession, Mr. Pleydell?"

I asked several questions, which were all answered to my satisfaction, and finally returned to town, prepared to draw up a lease by which the house and grounds known as The Rosary, Hampstead Heath, were to be handed over at a very high rent to Mrs. Scaiffe.

I felt pleased at the good stroke of business which I had done for a client, and had no apprehensions of any sort. Little did I guess what that afternoon's work would mean to me and still more to one whom I had ever been proud to call my greatest friend.

Everything went off without a hitch. The Rosary passed into the hands of Mrs. Scaiffe, and also into the hands of her brother, Señor Merello, a tall, dark, very handsome man bearing all over him the well-known characteristics of a Spanish don.

A week or two went by and the affair had well-nigh passed my memory, when one afternoon I heard eager, excited words in my clerks' room, and the next moment my head clerk entered, followed by the fair-haired English-looking girl who had called herself Muriel Scaiffe.

"I want to speak to you, Mr. Pleydell," she said, in great agitation. "Can I see you alone, and at once?"

"Certainly," I answered. I motioned to the clerk to leave us and helped the young lady to a chair.

"I cannot stay a moment," she began. "Even now I am followed. Mr. Pleydell, he has told me that he knows you; it was on that account I persuaded my step-mother to come to you about a house. You are his greatest friend, for he has said it."

"Of whom are you talking?" I asked, in a bewildered tone.

"Of Oscar Digby!" she replied. "The great traveller, the great discoverer, the greatest, most single-minded, the grandest man of his age. You know him? Yes—yes."

She paused for breath. Her eyes were full of tears.

"Indeed, I do know him," I answered. "He is my very oldest friend. Where is he? What is he doing? Tell me all about him."

She had risen. Her hands were clasped tightly together, her face was white as death.

"He is on his way to England," she answered. "Even now he may have landed. He brings great news, and the moment he sets foot in London he is in danger."

"What do you mean?"

"I cannot tell you what I mean. I dare not. He is your friend, and it is your province to save him."

"But from what, Miss Scaiffe? You have no right to come here and make ambiguous statements. If you come to me at all you ought to be more explicit."

She trembled and now, as though she could not stand any longer, dropped into a chair.

"I am not brave enough to explain things more fully," she said. "I can only repeat my words, 'Your friend is in danger.'

Tell him—if you can, if you will—to have nothing to do with *us*. Keep him, at all risks, away from *us*. If he mentions us pretend that you do not know anything about us. I would not speak like this if I had not cause—the gravest. When we took The Rosary I did not believe that matters were so awful; indeed, then I was unaware that Mr. Digby was returning to London. But last night I overheard . . . Oh! Mr. Pleydell, I can tell you no more. Pity me and do not question me. Keep Oscar Digby away from The Rosary and, if possible, do not betray me; but if in no other way you can insure his leaving us alone, tell him that I—yes, I, Muriel Scaiffe—wish it. There, I cannot do more."

She was trembling more terribly than ever. She took out her handkerchief to wipe the moisture from her brow.

"I must fly," she said. "If this visit is discovered my life is worth very little."

After she had gone I sat in absolute amazement. My first sensation was that the girl must be mad. Her pallor, her trembling, her vague innuendoes pointed surely to a condition of nerves the reverse of sane. But although the madness of Muriel Scaiffe seemed the most possible solution of her strange visit, I could not cast the thing from my memory. I felt almost needlessly disturbed by it. All day her extraordinary words haunted me, and when, on the next day, Digby, whom I had not seen for years, unexpectedly called, I remembered Miss Scaiffe's visit with a queer and ever-increasing sense of apprehension.

Digby had been away from London for several years. Before he went he and I had shared the same rooms, had gone about together, and had been chums in the fullest sense of the word. It was delightful to see him once again. His hearty, loud laugh fell refreshingly on my ears, and one or two glances into his face removed my fears. After all, it was impossible to associate danger with one so big, so burly, with such immense physical strength. His broad forehead, his keen, frank blue eyes, his smiling mouth, his strong and muscular hands, all denoted strength of mind and body. He looked as if he were muscle all over.

"Well," he said, "here I am, and I have a good deal to tell you. I want your help also, old man. It is your business to introduce me to the most promising and most enterprising financier of the day. I have it in my power, Pleydell, to make his fortune, and yours, and my own, and half-a-dozen other people's as well."

"Tell me all about it," I said. I sat back in my chair, prepared to enjoy myself.

Oscar was a very noted traveller and thought much of by the Geographical Society.

He came nearer to me and dropped his voice a trifle.

"I have made an amazing discovery," he said, "and that is one reason why I have hurried back to London. I do not know whether you are sufficiently conversant with extraordinary and out-of-the-way places on our globe. But anyhow, I may as well tell you that there is a wonderful region, as yet very little known, which lies on the watershed of the Essequibo and Amazon rivers. In that region are situated the old Montes de Cristæs or Crystal Mountains, the disputed boundary between British Guiana and Brazil. There also, according to the legend, was supposed to be the wonderful lost city of Manos. Many expeditions were sent out to discover it in the seventeenth century, and it was the Eldorado of Sir Walter Raleigh's famous expedition in 1615, the failure of which cost him his head."

I could not help laughing.

"This sounds like an old geography lesson. What have you to do with this *terra incognita*?"

He leant forward and dropped his voice.

"Do not think me mad," he said, "for I speak in all sanity. I have found the lost Eldorado!"

"Nonsense!" I cried.

"It is true. I do not mean to say that I have found the mythical city of gold; that, of course, does not exist. But what I have discovered is a spot close to Lake Amacu that is simply laden with gold. The estimates computed on my specimens and reports make it out to be the richest place in the world. The whole thing is, as yet, a close secret, and I have come to London now to put it into the hands of a big financier. A company must be formed with a capital of something like ten millions to work it."

"By Jove!" I cried. "You astonish me."

"The thing will create an enormous sensation," he went on, "and I shall be a millionaire; that is, if the secret does not leak out."

"The secret," I cried.

"Yes, the secret of its exact locality."

"Have you charts?"

"Yes; but those I would rather not disclose, even to you, old man, just yet."

I was silent for a moment, then I said:—"Horace Lancaster is the biggest financier in the whole of London. He is undoubtedly your man. If you can satisfy him with your reports, charts, and specimens he can float the company. You must see him, Digby."

"Yes, that is what I want," he cried.

"I will telephone to his office at once."

I rang the bell for my clerk and gave him directions.

He left the room. In a few moments he returned with the information that Lancaster was in Paris.

"He won't be back for a week, sir," said the clerk.

He left the room, and I looked at Digby.

"Are you prepared to wait?" I asked.

He shrugged his great shoulders.

"I must, I suppose," he said. "But it is provoking. At any moment another may forestall me. Not that it is likely; but there is always the possibility. Shall we talk over matters to-night, Pleydell? Will you dine with me at my club?"

"With a heart and a half," I answered.

"By the way," continued Digby, "some friends of mine—Brazilians—ought to be in London now: a lady of the name of Scaiffe, with her pretty little step-daughter, an English girl. I should like to introduce you to them. They are remarkably nice people. I had a letter from Mrs. Scaiffe just as I was leaving Brazil telling me that they were *en route* for England and asking me to look her up in town. I wonder where they are? Her brother, too, Señor Merello, is a most charming man. Why, Pleydell, what is the matter?"

I was silent for a moment; then I said: "If I were you I would have nothing to do with these people. I happen to know their whereabouts, and—"

"Well?" he said, opening his eyes in amazement.

"The little girl does not want you to call on them, Digby. Take her advice. She looked true and good." To my astonishment I saw that the big fellow seemed quite upset at my remarks.

"True!" he said, beginning to pace the room. "Of course the little thing is true. I tell you, Pleydell, I am fond of her. Not engaged, or anything of that sort, but I like her. I was looking forward to meeting them. The mother—the step-mother, I mean—is a magnificent woman. I am great friends with her. I was staying at their Quinta last winter. I also know the brother, Señor Merello. Has little Muriel lost her head?"

"She is anxious and frightened. The whole thing seems absurd, of course, but she certainly did beg of me to keep you away from her step-mother, and I half promised to respect her secret and not to tell you the name of the locality where Mrs. Scaiffe and Señor Merello are at present living."

He tried not to look annoyed, but he evidently was so. A few moments later he left me.

That evening Digby and I dined together. We afterwards went exhaustively into the great subject of his discovery. He showed me his specimens and reports, and, in short, so completely fired my enthusiasm that I was all impatience for Lancaster's return. The thing was a big thing, one worth fighting for. We said no more about Mrs. Scaiffe, and I hoped that my friend would not fall into the hands of a woman who, I began to fear, was little better than an adventuress.

Three or four days passed. Lancaster was still detained in Paris, and Digby was evidently eating his heart out with impatience at the unavoidable delay in getting his great scheme floated.

One afternoon he burst noisily into my presence.

"Well," he cried. "The little girl has discovered herself. Talk of women and their pranks! She came to see me at my hotel. She declared that she could not keep away. I just took the little thing in my arms and hugged her. We are going to have a honeymoon when the company is floated, and this evening, Pleydell, I dine at The Rosary. Ha! ha! my friend. I know all about the secret retreat of the Scaiffes by this time. Little Muriel told me herself. I dine there to-night, and they want you to come, too."

I was about to refuse when, as if in a vision, the strange, entreating, suffering face of Muriel Scaiffe, as I had seen it the day she implored me to save my friend, rose up before my eyes. Whatever her present inexplicable conduct might mean, I would go with Digby to-night.

We arrived at The Rosary between seven and eight o'clock. Mrs. Scaiffe received us in Oriental splendour. Her dress was a wonder of magnificence. Diamonds flashed in her raven black hair and glittered round her shapely neck. She was certainly one of the most splendid-looking women I had ever seen, and Digby was not many moments in her company before he was completely subjugated by her charms.

The pale little Muriel looked washed-out and insignificant beside this gorgeous creature. Señor Merello was a masculine edition of his handsome sister: his presence and his wonderful courtly grace of manner seemed but to enhance and accentuate her charms.

At dinner we were served by Spanish servants, and a repulsive-looking negro of the name of Samson stood behind Mrs. Scaiffe's chair.

She was in high spirits, drank freely of champagne, and openly alluded to the great discovery.

"You must show us the chart, my friend," she said.

"No!" he answered, in an emphatic voice. He smiled as he spoke and showed his strong, white teeth.

She bent towards him and whispered something. He glanced at Muriel, whose face was deadly white. Then he rose abruptly.

"As regards anything else, command me," he said; "but not the chart."

Mrs. Scaiffe did not press him further. The ladies went into the drawing-room, and by-and-by Digby and I found ourselves returning to London.

During the journey I mentioned to him that Lancaster had wired to say that he would be at his office and prepared for a meeting on Friday. This was Monday night.

"I am glad to hear that the thing will not be delayed much longer," he answered. "I may as well confess that I am devoured by impatience."

"Your mind will soon be at rest," I replied. "And now, one thing more, old man. I must talk frankly. I do not like Mrs. Scaiffe—I do not like Señor Merello. As you value all your future, keep that chart out of the hands of those people."

"Am I mad?" he questioned. "The chart is seen by no living soul until I place it in Lancaster's hands. But all the same, Pleydell," he added, "you are prejudiced. Mrs. Scaiffe is one of the best of women."

"Think her so, if you will," I replied; "but, whatever you do, keep your knowledge of your Eldorado to yourself. Remember that on Friday the whole thing will be safe in Lancaster's keeping."

He promised, and I left him.

On Tuesday I saw nothing of Digby.

On Wednesday evening, when I returned home late, I received the following letter:—

> I am not mad. I have heavily bribed the kitchen-maid, the only English woman in the whole house, to post this for me. I was forced to call on Mr. Digby and to engage myself to him at any cost. I am now strictly confined to my room under pretence of illness. In reality I am quite well, but a close prisoner. Mr. Digby dined here again last night and, under the influence of a certain drug introduced into his wine, has given away the whole of his discovery *except* the exact locality.
>
> He is to take supper here late to-morrow night (Thursday) and to bring the chart. If he does, he will never leave The Rosary alive. All is prepared. *I speak who know*. Don't betray me, but save him.

The letter fell from my hands. What did it mean? Was Digby's life in danger, or had the girl who wrote to me really gone mad? The letter was without date, without any heading, and without signature. Nevertheless, as I picked it up and read it carefully over again, I was absolutely convinced beyond a shadow of doubt of its truth. Muriel Scaiffe was not mad. She was a victim, to how great an extent I did not dare to think. Another victim, one in even greater danger, was Oscar Digby. I must save him. I must do what the unhappy girl who was a prisoner in that awful house implored of me.

It was late, nearly midnight, but I knew that I had not a moment to lose. I had a friend, a certain Dr. Garland, who had been police surgeon for the Westminster Division for several years. I went immediately to his house in Eaton Square. As I had expected, he was up, and without any preamble I told him the whole long story of the last few weeks.

Finally, I showed him the letter. He heard me without once interrupting. He read the letter without comment. When he folded it up and returned it to me I saw that his keen, clean-shaven face was full of interest. He was silent for several minutes, then he said:—

"I am glad you came to me. This story of yours may mean a very big thing. We have four *primâ-facie* points. *One:* Your friend has this enormously valuable secret about the place in Guiana or on its boundary; a secret which may be worth anything. *Two:* He is very intimate with Mrs. Scaiffe, her step-daughter, and her brother. The intimacy started in Brazil. *Three:* He is engaged to the step-daughter, who evidently is being used as a sort of tool, and is herself in a state of absolute terror, and, so far as one can make out, is not specially in love with Digby nor Digby with her. *Four:* Mrs. Scaiffe and her brother are determined, at any risk, to secure the chart which Digby is to hand to them to-morrow evening. The girl thinks this so important that she has practically risked her life to give you due warning. By the way, when did you say Lancaster would return? Has he made an appointment to see Digby and yourself?"

"Yes; at eleven o'clock on Friday morning."

"Doubtless Mrs. Scaiffe and her brother know of this."

"Probably," I answered. "As far as I can make out they have such power over Digby that he confides everything to them."

"Just so. They have power over him, and they are not scrupulous as to the means they use to force his confidence. If Digby goes to The Rosary to-morrow evening the interview with Lancaster will, in all probability, never take place."

"What do you mean?" I cried, in horror.

"Why, this. Mrs. Scaiffe and Señor Merello are determined to learn Digby's secret. It is necessary for their purpose that they should know the secret and also that they should be the *sole possessors* of it. You see why they want Digby to call on them? They must get his secret from him *before* he sees Lancaster. The chances are that if he gives it up he will never leave the house alive."

"Then, what are we to do?" I asked, for Garland's meaning stunned me, and I felt incapable of thought or of any mode of action.

"Leave this matter in my hands. I am going immediately to see Inspector Frost. I will communicate with you directly anything serious occurs."

The next morning I called upon Digby and found him breakfasting at his club. He looked worried, and, when I came in, his greeting was scarcely cordial.

"What a solemn face, Pleydell!" he said. "Is anything wrong?" He motioned me to a seat near. I sank into it.

"I want you to come out of town with me," I said. "I can take a day off. Shall we both run down to Brighton? We can return in time for our interview with Lancaster to-morrow."

"It is impossible," he answered. "I should like to come with you, but I have an engagement for to-night."

"Are you going to The Rosary?" I asked.

"I am," he replied, after a moment's pause. "Why, what is the matter?" he added. "I suppose I may consider myself a free agent." There was marked irritation in his tone.

"I wish you would not go," I said.

"Why not?"

"I do not trust the people."

"Folly, Pleydell. In the old days you used not to be so prejudiced."

"I had not the same cause. Digby, if ever people are trying

to get you into their hands, they are those people. Have you not already imparted your secret to them?"

"How do you know?" he exclaimed, springing up and turning crimson.

"Well, can you deny it?"

His face paled.

"I don't know that I want to," he said. "Mrs. Scaiffe and Merello will join me in this matter. There is no reason why things should be kept dark from them."

"But is this fair or honourable to Lancaster? Remember, I have already written fully to him. Do, I beg of you, be careful."

"Lancaster cannot object to possible wealthy shareholders," was Digby's answer. "Anyhow," he added, laughing uneasily, "I object to being interfered with. Pray understand that, old man, if we are to continue friends; and now by-bye for the present. We meet at eleven o'clock to-morrow at Lancaster's."

His manner gave me no pretext for remaining longer with him, and I returned to my own work. About five o'clock on that same day a telegram was handed to me which ran as follows:—

Come here at once.—GARLAND.

I left the house, hailed a hansom, and in a quarter of an hour was shown into Garland's study. He was not alone. A rather tall, grey-haired, grey-moustached, middle-aged man was with him. This man was introduced to me as Inspector Frost.

"Now, Pleydell," said Garland, in his quick, incisive way, "listen to me carefully. The time is short. Inspector Frost and I have not ceased our inquiries since you called on me last night. I must tell you that we believe the affair to be of the most serious kind. Time is too pressing now to enter into all details, but the thing amounts to this. There is the gravest suspicion that Mrs. Scaiffe and her brother, Señor Merello, are employed by a notorious gang in Brazil to force Digby to disclose the exact position of the gold mine. We also know for certain that Mrs. Scaiffe is in constant and close communication with some very suspicious people both in London and in Brazil.

"Now, listen. The crisis is to be to-night. Digby is to take supper at The Rosary, and there to give himself absolutely away. He will take his chart with him; that is the scheme. Digby must not go—that is, if we can possibly prevent him. We expect you to do what you can under the circumstances, but as the case is so serious, and as it is more than probable that Digby will not be persuaded, Inspector Frost and myself and a number of men of his division will surround the house as soon as it becomes dark, and if Digby should insist on going in every protection in case of difficulty will be given him. The presence of the police will also insure the capture of Mrs. Scaiffe and her brother."

"You mean," I said, "that you will, if necessary, search the house?"

"Yes."

"But how can you do so without a warrant?"

"We have thought of that," said Garland, with a smile. "A magistrate living at Hampstead has been already communicated with. If necessary, one of our men will ride over to his house and procure the requisite instrument to enforce our entrance."

"Very well," I answered; "then I will go at once to Digby's, but I may as well tell you plainly that I have very little hope of dissuading him."

I drove as fast as I could to my friend's rooms, but was greeted with the information that he had already left and was not expected back until late that evening. This was an unlooked-for blow.

I went to his club—he was not there. I then returned to Dr. Garland.

"I failed to find him," I said. "What can be done? Is it possible that he has already gone to his fate?"

"That is scarcely likely," replied Garland, after a pause. "He was invited to supper at The Rosary, and according to your poor young friend's letter the time named was late. There is nothing for it but to waylay him on the grounds before he goes in. You will come with us to-night, will you not, Pleydell?"

"Certainly," I answered.

Garland and I dined together. At half-past nine we left Eaton Square and, punctually at ten o'clock, the hansom we had taken put us down at one of the roads on the north side of the Heath. The large house which I knew so well loomed black in the moonlight.

The night was cold and fresh. The moon was in its second quarter and was shining brightly. Garland and I passed down the dimly-lit lane beside the wall. A tall, dark figure loomed from the darkness and, as it came forward, I saw that it was Inspector Frost.

"Mr. Digby has not arrived yet," he said. "Perhaps, sir," he added, looking at me, "you can even now dissuade him, for it is a bad business. All my men are ready," he continued, "and at a signal the house will be surrounded; but we must have one last try to prevent his entering it. Come this way, please, sir," he added, beckoning to me to follow him.

We passed out into the road.

"I am absolutely bewildered, inspector," I said to him. "Do you mean to say there is really great danger?"

"The worst I ever knew," was his answer. "You cannot stop a man entering a house if he wishes to; but I can tell you, Mr. Pleydell, I do not believe his life is worth that if he goes in." And the inspector snapped his fingers.

He had scarcely ceased speaking when the jingling of the bells of a hansom sounded behind us. The cab drew up at the gates and Oscar Digby alighted close to us.

Inspector Frost touched him on the shoulder.

He swung round and recognised me.

"Halloa! Pleydell," he said, in no very cordial accents. "What in the name of Heaven are you doing here? What does this mean? Who is this man?"

"I am a police-officer, Mr. Digby, and I want to speak to you. Mr. Pleydell has asked you not to go into that house. You are, of course, free to do as you like, but I must tell you that you are running into great danger. Be advised by me and go away."

For answer Digby thrust his hand into his breast-pocket. He pulled out a note which he gave me.

"Read that, Pleydell," he said; "and receive my answer." I tore the letter from its envelope and read in the moonlight:—

> Come to me. I am in danger and suffering. Do not fail me.—MURIEL.

"A hoax! A forgery!" I could not help crying. "For God's sake, Digby, don't be mad."

"Mad or sane, I go into that house," he said. His bright blue eyes flashed with passion and his breath came quickly.

"Hands off, sir. Don't keep me."

He swung himself away from me.

"One word," called the inspector after him. "How long do you expect to remain?"

"Perhaps an hour. I shall be home by midnight."

"And now, sir, please listen. You can be assured, in case of any trouble, that we are here, and I may further tell you that if you are not out of the house by one o'clock, we shall enter with a search warrant."

Digby stood still for a moment, then he turned to me.

"I cannot but resent your interference, but I believe you mean well. Good-bye!" He wrung my hand and walked quickly up the drive.

We watched him ring the bell. The door was opened at once by the negro servant. Digby entered. The door closed silently. Inspector Frost gave a low whistle.

"I would not be that man for a good deal," he said.

Garland came up to us both.

"Is the house entirely surrounded, Frost?" I heard him whisper. Frost smiled, and I saw his white teeth gleam in the darkness. He waved his hand.

"There is not a space of six feet between man and man," I heard him say; "and now we have nothing to do but to wait and hope for at least an hour and a half. If in an hour's time Mr. Digby does not reappear I shall send a man for the warrant. At one o'clock we enter the house."

Garland and I stood beneath a large fir tree in a dense shade and within the inclosed garden. The minutes seemed to crawl. Our conversation was limited to low whispers at long intervals.

Eleven o'clock chimed on the church clock near by; then half-past sounded on the night air. My ears were strained to catch the expected click of the front door-latch, but it did not come. The house remained wrapt in silence. Once Garland whispered:—

"Hark!" We listened closely. It certainly seemed to me that a dull, muffled sound, as of pounding or hammering, was just audible; but whether it came from the house or not it was impossible to tell.

At a quarter to twelve the one remaining lighted window on the first floor became suddenly dark. Still there was no sign of Digby. Midnight chimed.

Frost said a word to Garland and disappeared, treading softly. He was absent for more than half an hour. When he returned I heard him say:—

"I have got it," and he touched his pocket with his hand as he spoke.

The remaining moments went by in intense anxiety, and, just as the deep boom of one o'clock was heard the inspector laid his hand on my shoulder.

"Come along quietly," he whispered.

Some sign, conveyed by a low whistle, passed from him to his men, and I heard the bushes rustle around us.

The next moment we had ascended the steps, and we could hear the deep whirr of the front door bell as Frost pressed the button.

In less time than we had expected we heard the bolts shot back. The door was opened on a chain and a black face appeared, at the slit.

"Who are you and what do you want?" said a voice.

"I have called for Mr. Digby," said Frost. "Go and tell him that his friend, Mr. Pleydell, and also Doctor Garland want to see him immediately."

A look of blank surprise came over the negro's face.

"But no one of the name of Digby lives here," he said.

"Mrs. Scaiffe lives here," replied the inspector, "and also a Spanish gentleman of the name of Señor Merello. Tell them that I wish to see them immediately, and that I am a police-officer."

A short conversation was evidently taking place within. The next moment the door was flung open, electric lights sprang into being, and my eyes fell upon Mrs. Scaiffe.

She was dressed with her usual magnificence. She came forward with a stately calm and stood silently before us. Her large black eyes were gleaming.

"Well, Mr. Pleydell," she said, speaking in an easy voice, "what is the reason of this midnight disturbance? I am always glad to welcome you to my house, but is not the hour a little late?"

Her words were interrupted by Inspector Frost, who held up his hand.

"Your attitude, madam," he said, "is hopeless. We have all come here with a definite object. Mr. Oscar Digby entered this house at a quarter past ten to-night. From that moment the house has been closely surrounded. He is therefore still here."

"Where is your authority for this unwarrantable intrusion?" she said. Her manner changed, her face grew hard as iron. Her whole attitude was one of insolence and defiance.

The inspector immediately produced his warrant.

She glanced over it and uttered a shrill laugh.

"Mr. Digby is not in the house," she said.

She had scarcely spoken before an adjoining door was opened, and Señor Merello, looking gaunt and very white about the face, approached. She looked up at him and smiled, then she said, carelessly:—

"Gentlemen, this is my brother, Señor Merello."

The Señor bowed slightly, but did not speak.

"Once more," said Frost, "where is Mr. Digby?"

"I repeat once more," said Mrs. Scaiffe, "that Mr. Digby is not in this house."

"But we saw him enter at a quarter past ten."

She shrugged her shoulders.

"He is not here now."

"He could not have gone, for the house has been surrounded."

Again she gave her shoulders a shrug. "You have your warrant, gentlemen," she said; "you can look for yourselves."

Frost came up to her.

"I regret to say, madam, that you, this gentleman, and all your servants must consider yourselves under arrest until we find Mr. Oscar Digby."

"That will be for ever, then," she replied; "but please yourselves."

My heart beat with an unwonted sense of terror. What could the woman mean? Digby, either dead or alive, must be in the house.

The operations which followed were conducted rapidly. The establishment, consisting of Mrs. Scaiffe, her brother, two Spanish men-servants, two maids, one of Spanish extraction, and the negro who had opened the door to us, were summoned and placed in the charge of a police-sergeant.

Muriel Scaiffe was nowhere to be seen.

Then our search of the house began. The rooms on the ground-floor, consisting of the drawing-room, dining-room, and two other big rooms, were fitted up in quite an everyday manner. We did not take much time going through them.

In the basement, the large cellar which had attracted Mrs. Scaiffe's pleased surprise on the day when I took her to see The Rosary had now been fitted up as a laboratory. I gazed at it in astonishment. It was evidently intended for the manufacture of chemicals on an almost commercial scale. All the latest chemical and electrical apparatus were to be found there, as well as several large machines, the purposes of which were not evident. One in particular I specially noticed. It was a big tank with a complicated equipment for the manufacture of liquid air in large quantities.

We had no time to give many thoughts to the laboratory just then. A foreboding sense of ever-increasing fear was upon each and all of us. It was sufficient to see that Digby was not there.

Our search in the upper regions was equally unsuccessful. We were just going down stairs again when Frost drew my attention to a door which we had not yet opened. We went to it and found it locked. Putting our strength to work, Garland and I between us burst it open. Within, we found a girl crouching by the bed. She was only partly dressed, and her head was buried in her hands. We went up to her. She turned, saw my face, and suddenly clung to me.

"Have you found him? Is he safe?"

"I do not know, my dear," I answered, trying to soothe her. "We are looking for him. God grant us success."

"Did he come to the house? I have been locked in here all day and heavily drugged. I have only just recovered consciousness and scarcely know what I am doing. Is he in the house?"

"He came in. We are searching for him; we hope to find him."

"That you will never do!" She gave a piercing cry and fell unconscious on the floor.

We placed the unhappy girl on the bed. Garland produced brandy and gave her a few drops; she came to in a couple of minutes and began to moan feebly. We left her, promising to return. We had no time to attend to her just then.

When we reached the hall Frost stood still.

"The man is not here," he muttered.

"But he is here," was Garland's incisive answer. "Inspector, you have got to tear the place to pieces."

The latter nodded.

The inspector's orders were given rapidly, and dawn was just breaking when ten policemen, ordered in from outside, began their systematic search of the entire house from roof to basement.

Pick and crowbar were ruthlessly applied, and never have I seen a house in such a mess. Floorings were torn up and rafters cut through. Broken plaster littered the rooms and lay about on the sumptuous furniture. Walls were pierced and bored through. Closets and cupboards were ransacked. The backs of the fireplaces were torn out and the chimneys explored.

Very little was said as our investigation proceeded, and room after room was checked off.

Finally, an exhaustive examination of the basement and cellars completed our search.

"Well, Dr. Garland, are you satisfied?" asked the inspector.

We had gone back to the garden, and Garland was leaning against a tree, his hands thrust in his pockets and his eyes fixed on the ground. Frost pulled his long moustache and breathed quickly.

"Are you satisfied?" he repeated.

"We must talk sense or we shall all go mad," was Garland's answer. "The thing is absurd, you know. Men don't disappear. Let us work this thing out logically. There are only three planes in space and we know matter is indestructible. If Digby left this house he went up, down, or horizontally. *Up is out of the question.* If he disappeared in a balloon or was shot off the roof he must have been seen by us, for the house was surrounded. He certainly did not pass through the cordon of men. *He did not go down*, for every cubic foot of basement and cellar has been accounted for, as well as every cubic foot of space in the house.

"So we come to the chemical change of matter, dissipation into gas by heat. There are no furnaces, no ashes, no gas cylinders, nor dynamos, nor carbon points. The time when we lost sight of him to the time of entrance was exactly two hours and three-quarters. There is no way out of it. He is still there."

"He is not there," was the quiet retort of the inspector. "I have sent for the Assistant Commissioner to Scotland Yard, and will ask him to take over the case. It is too much for me."

The tension in all our minds had now reached such a state of strain that we began to fear our own shadows.

Oscar Digby, standing, as it were, on the threshold of a very great future, the hero of a legend worthy of old romance, had suddenly and inexplicably vanished. I could not get my reason to believe that he was not still in the house, for there was not the least doubt that he had not come out. What would happen in the next few hours?

"Is there no secret chamber or secret passage that we have overlooked?" I said, turning to the inspector.

"The walls have been tapped," he replied. "There is not the slightest indication of a hollow. There are no underground passages. The man is not within these walls."

He now spoke with a certain degree of irritation in his voice which the mystery of the case had evidently awakened in his mind. A few moments later the sound of approaching wheels caused us to turn our heads. A cab drew up at the gates, out of which alighted the well-known form of Sir George Freer.

Garland had already entered the house, and on Sir George appearing on the scene he and I followed him.

We had just advanced across the hall to the room where the members of the household, with the exception of poor Muriel Scaiffe, were still detained, when, to our utter amazement, a long, strange peal of laughter sounded from below. This was followed by another, and again by another. The laughter came from the lips of Garland. We glanced at each other. What on earth did it mean? Together we darted down the stone steps, but before we reached the laboratory another laugh rang out. All hope in me was suddenly changed to a chilling fear, for the laugh was not natural. It had a clanging, metallic sound, without any mirth.

In the centre of the room stood Garland. His mouth was twitching and his breath jerked in and out convulsively.

"What is it? What is the matter?" I cried.

He made no reply, but, pointing to a machine with steel blocks, once more broke into a choking, gurgling laugh which made my flesh creep.

Had he gone mad? Sir George moved swiftly across to him and laid his hand on his shoulder.

"Come, what is all this, Garland?" he said, sternly, though his own face was full of fear.

I knew Garland to be a man of extraordinary self-control, and I could see that he was now holding himself in with all the force at his command.

"It is no use—I cannot tell you," he burst out.

"What—you know what has become of him?"

"Yes."

"You can prove it?"

"Yes."

"Speak out, man."

"He is not here," said Garland.

"Then where is he?"

He flung his hand out towards the Heath, and I saw that the fit was taking him again, but once more he controlled himself. Then he said, in a clear, level voice:—

"He is dead, Sir George, and you can never see his body. You cannot hold an inquest, for there is nothing to hold it on. The winds have taken him and scattered him in dust on the Heath. Don't look at me like that, Pleydell. I am sane, although it is a wonder we are not all mad over this business. Look and listen."

He pointed to the great metal tank.

"I arrived at my present conclusion by a process of elimination," he began. "Into that tank which contained liquid air Digby, gagged and bound, must have been placed violently, probably after he had given away the chart. Death would have been instantaneous, and he would have been frozen into complete solidity in something like forty minutes. The ordinary laboratory experiment is to freeze a rabbit, which can then be powdered into mortar like any other friable stone. The operation here has been the same. It is only a question of size. Remember, we are dealing with 312 degrees below zero Fahrenheit, and then—well, look at this and these."

He pointed to a large machine with steel blocks and to a bench littered with saws, chisels, pestles, and mortars.

"That machine is a stone-breaker," he said. "On the dust adhering to these blocks I found this."

He held up a test tube containing a blue liquid.

"The Guiacum test," he said. "In other words, blood. This fact taken with the facts we already know, that Digby never left the house; that the only other agent of destruction of a body, fire, is out of the question; that this tank is the receptacle of that enormous machine for making liquid air in very large quantities; and, above all, the practical possibility of the operation being conducted by the men who are at present in the house, afford me absolutely conclusive proof beyond a possibility of doubt as to what has happened. The body of that unfortunate man is as if it had never been, without a fragment of pin-point size for identification or evidence. It is beyond the annals of all the crimes that I have ever heard of. What law can help us? Can you hold an inquest on nothing? Can you charge a person with murder where no victim or trace of a victim can be produced?"

A sickly feeling came over me. Garland's words carried their own conviction, and we knew that we stood in the presence of a horror without a name. Nevertheless, to the police mind horror *per se* does not exist. To them there is always a mystery, a crime and a solution. That is all. The men beside me were police once more. Sentiment might come later.

"Are there any reporters here?" asked Sir George.

"None," answered Frost.

"Good. Mr. Oscar Digby has disappeared. There is no doubt how. There can, of course, be no arrest, as Dr. Garland has just said. Our official position is this. We suspect that Mr. Digby has been murdered, but the search for the discovery of the body has failed. That is our position."

Before I left that awful house I made arrangements to have Muriel Scaiffe conveyed to a London hospital. I did not consult Mrs. Scaiffe on the subject. I could not get myself to say another word to the woman. In the hospital a private ward was secured for the unhappy girl, and there for many weeks she hovered between life and death.

Meanwhile, Mrs. Scaiffe and her brother were detained at The Rosary. They were closely watched by the police, and although they made many efforts to escape they found it impossible. Our hope was that when Muriel recovered strength she would be able to substantiate a case against them. But, alas! this hope was unfounded, for, as the girl recovered, there remained a blank in her memory which no efforts on our part could fill. She had absolutely and completely forgotten Oscar Digby, and the house on Hampstead Heath was to her as though it had never existed. In all other respects she was well. Under these circumstances we were forced to allow the Spaniard and his sister to return to their own country, our one most earnest hope being that we might never see or hear of them again.

Meanwhile, Muriel grew better. I was interested in her from the first. When she was well enough I placed her with some friends of my own. A year ago she became my wife. I think she is happy. A past which is forgotten cannot trouble her. I have long ago come to regard her as the best and truest woman living.

Eyes of Terror

The strange story which I am about to tell happened just when the late war in South Africa was at its height. I was in a very nervous condition at the time, having lost my dear father, who was killed in action shortly before the taking of Pretoria. The news of my father's death reached us on a certain evening in May, just when the days were approaching their longest, and summer, with all its beauties, was about to visit the land. It was immediately afterwards that the visitations which I am about to describe took place. They were of a very alarming character, and so much did they upset my mental equilibrium that I determined to put my case into the hands of a certain Professor Ellicott, who was not only a physician and surgeon in the ordinary sense, but was also a man of great learning and keen original research.

I had met the Professor once at the house of a neighbour, and on that occasion had admired him, not only for his intellectual appearance, but also for the massive strength of his face and the calmness of his bearing. I knew that a strong man, who was also sympathetic and tactful, would not laugh at a girl's fears, however unreasonable he might consider them, and had not the least doubt that I should receive a patient hearing when I told him my story.

My name is Nora Dallas. I am twenty-one years of age. I have lived all my life in a beautiful old place about a mile and a half from the town of Ashingford. Professor Ellicott lived in the High Street, and I was fortunate enough to find him at home.

I sent in my card and was immediately admitted into his presence. He was a man of about thirty, with resolute grey eyes and a determined chin. He gave me a quick glance when I entered the room; then, without uttering a word, pointed to a chair.

"I am called Nora Dallas," I said.

"I know," he replied, in a gentle voice. "You are the daughter of that Colonel Dallas whose gallant action, when he sacrificed his life for his country on the march to Pretoria, is the talk and admiration of the country."

My eyes filled with tears.

"It is only three weeks since I heard of my father's death," I said. "You will forgive me, sir, but I cannot bear any sympathetic reference to the subject, at least for the present."

"I understand," he replied, his hard face softening. "And now, what can I do for you?"

"I want to consult you as a doctor."

"But I am not a consultant—I mean that I do not practise medicine in the ordinary sense."

"I am aware of that fact," I answered. "And just for that very reason, Professor Ellicott, I have been compelled to come to you."

"I do not quite understand."

He looked at me with the dawn of a smile on his lips.

"I think you will give me a frank opinion, and be unbiased by the red-tapism which causes many medical men to hide the truth from their patients."

"Ah, you think well of me," he said, with a smile, "and I perceive that you are a brave woman. Nevertheless, I must inform you that I am scarcely qualified to enter into your case. My work lies altogether in the regions of original research."

"May I at least tell you my story?" I insisted. "You can make up your mind afterwards whether you will help me or not."

His reply to this was to get up and pace the room, stopping once or twice to look at me, then continuing his slow, measured tread up and down. I did not interrupt him. I sat as still as though carved in marble.

"You must forgive my apparent rudeness, Miss Dallas," he said, "but I was endeavouring to recall what I had already heard about you. I remember everything now. I met you a month ago at Sir John Newcome's. You live at Courtlands, one of the finest places in the neighbourhood. You are an only child. Doubtless, now that your father is dead, you are wealthy. You have lived at Courtlands almost all your life. Of course, Miss Dallas, you have your own family physician?"

"Yes," I answered.

"Will you not consult him?"

"No; for he is not the man for my purpose."

He smiled.

"You think that I am?"

"If anyone can help me, you can."

"How like a woman!" he said, somewhat impatiently. "And yet you know nothing about me. As I said just now, I am not a consultant. I have come to Ashingford for quiet, and for the opportunity to examine into the length and breadth of a problem which, if I can bring it to a successful issue, will mean health and happiness to millions. And yet a girl, little more than a child, wants to interrupt my train of thought. Do you think you are fair to me?"

"I don't know anything about that," I replied, with vehemence. "I only know that I want help. Will you give it to me?"

My voice broke.

"Of course I will," he said, cordially, and his whole manner completely altered. "I only said what I did to test you. Now we will preamble no more. Tell me your story."

"I was twenty-one last March," I began, immediately, "and now that my dear father is dead am absolutely my own mistress. With the exception of my Aunt Sophia, my father's sister, who lives with me, and my two cousins, I am without relations. It is about these cousins that I wish specially to speak. They are the sons of my father's younger brother, who has long been dead. My father adopted them in their infancy, brought them up, sent them to school, and gave them all they required. They are twins and are now five-and-twenty years of age. Rudolf has been called to the Bar and Lionel is a solicitor. Professor Ellicott, I must be truthful—I must be truthful even at the risk of failing in charity. My cousins are not good men. I have nothing absolutely to say against them—I have no means at present of proving my words—nevertheless, instinct tells me that I am right. Rudolf is the sort of man who imposes on people. I have seen him rhapsodise over poetry or a sunset, and his friends then imagine that he has a great love for the beautiful. But I know better. The only love in his wicked heart is the love of money. Lionel is his weak shadow—his dupe and tool."

"Surely you are hard on your cousins?"

"You would naturally think so; and yet I hope to convince you that I have read their characters aright.

"My father, before he went to South Africa, made a will, the contents of which he fully explained to me. In the event of his death I was to inherit the house and estate and also the bulk of his money, with the exception of a sum of sixty thousand pounds, which was to be divided between my two cousins. He fully explained all that he wanted to tell me with regard to his last will, and gave me directions as to certain affairs which he wished to be specially attended to. My dear father then continued to say some words which astonished and distressed me very much. He declared that it was the darling wish of his heart that Rudolf and I should marry. My father said that he had the highest opinion of my cousin, and assured me that nothing would make him happier than such a marriage. Rudolf had told him of his attachment to me—an attachment which I knew well did not exist.

"I heard my father in silence. Then I gave an emphatic negative to the whole proposal. My father listened in amazement. I said that I neither liked nor trusted my cousin, and that nothing—no words, no conditions—would make me accept him. After a pause my father said that my feelings must be my guide, but he continued:—

" 'I cannot agree with your opinion, and I sincerely hope that time may alter it.'

"From the hour of his departure there began for me a detestable period, during which I was persecuted by Rudolf's odious attentions. As he and Lionel practically lived in our house, you can imagine that it was impossible for me to escape altogether from his presence. But at last it became so intolerable that I wrote to my father on the subject. I told Rudolf quite frankly that I was doing so, and even made him acquainted with the greater part of my letter. In that letter I told my father that he did not rightly gauge his nephew's character, that he was not what he believed him to be, and, in order to prove my words, I mentioned a few instances which, unconvincing to a stranger like yourself, might have the effect of opening his eyes.

"That letter was posted two months ago. Up to the present I have had no reply to it, but am even now waiting and hoping to hear my father's views on the subject. Important letters must be on the road from South Africa for me. I have only received the news of my dear father's death by cablegram."

My voice broke. I paused, struggling with emotion; then I continued:—

"I am sorry to trouble you, Professor Ellicott, with this long preamble. I am now approaching that strange thing about which I wish to consult you.

"We received the cablegram acquainting us with the news of my father's death on a certain morning towards the end of last month. On the evening of that same day another long cablegram from South Africa was put into Rudolf's hands. He was sitting with my aunt and me in the drawing-room when he received it. He opened it, was evidently very much upset, but refused to divulge its contents. He called Lionel to his side, and they left the room together. I saw them pacing up and down in the shrubbery, evidently consulting with regard to the contents of the cablegram, but never from that hour till now have I heard the slightest inkling of what it was about.

"Three days later my father's will was read and my cousins heard of the large sums of money which would fall to their share. They fully expected to be remembered in my father's will, but not to such a generous extent, and their satisfaction was very great. As to Rudolf, his face quite beamed with delight, and they were both in feverish haste to possess themselves of the money. Mr. Brewster, our family lawyer, however, said that it would be impossible for them to receive their legacies for several weeks, as probate would have to be taken and other preliminaries attended to. Finally he made the remark:—

" 'Nothing can really be done until Colonel Dallas's letters and papers arrive from South Africa. This can scarcely be expected until a month from the present date.'

"On that very evening my elder cousin came to me again and once more implored me to become his wife. He spoke of my father and his well-known wishes on the subject, and pleaded with such power that had I not known him well I might have been touched into a semblance of kindness by his manner. I did know my cousin, however, and told him so in unmistakable terms. He seemed to struggle with emotion for a minute; then he said, rising as he spoke:—

" 'All right, Nora, I see I must accept your verdict. You may be sure that I will not trouble you on this subject again. It would be brutal to do so,' he added, 'for you are looking very ill. I see it in your eyes.'

" 'I am not exactly ill,' I answered. 'I am naturally in very great trouble, but I am no more really ill than you are.'

" 'I am all right,' he said, with a shrug of his shoulders. 'But your nerves, poor Nora, are in a sad condition. You have received a most serious shock, and it is telling on you. You ought to be exceedingly careful. I mean it is your duty to be much more careful than most women.'

" 'I don't understand you,' I answered. 'And I wish,' I added, 'that you would leave me now.'

" 'I will in a minute,' he said, and then he approached quite close to my side.

" 'One word before I go,' he went on, and he fixed his great, strong, dark eyes on mine. 'Whether you like me or whether you hate me we are cousins, Nora. Our family history is well known to each of us. I in particular, however, have studied medicine, and am therefore in a position to speak. I only gave up medicine for the Bar because I thought I saw a more speedy way of earning money in that profession. Now, Nora, listen. Raise your eyes to mine. Don't shrink, child. If you encourage the morbid fancies which are now filling your brain you will share the fate of poor Aunt Ethel. I know what I am talking about. The pupils of your eyes point to a disordered brain.'

"He left me. I sat still for a minute, feeling more nervous and disturbed than I cared to own. Then I went to Aunt Sophia.

" 'What is the matter, Nora?' she said, when I found her. 'You are trembling all over and looking so ill. What is wrong, child?'

" 'I want to ask you a straight question,' I replied. 'Who was, or who is, Aunt Ethel? I have never heard of her.'

"Aunt Sophia looked startled. She did not speak for a minute; then she said, with considerable reluctance:—

" 'It doesn't matter about your Aunt Ethel. She has been long in her grave. Let her memory rest in peace.'

" 'But what about her?' I said. 'I *will* know,' I continued, and then I repeated what Rudolf had told me.

"Aunt Sophia looked very queer. After a further pause she said:—

" 'Rudolf has done wrong, but as you know so much you may as well know all. Your Aunt Ethel was your father's eldest sister. She went mad when about your age, and eventually ended her days by suicide.'

" 'And I was never told,' I said, turning white.

" 'Why should you be told?'

" 'But there must be insanity in our family.'

" 'Hers was the only case. Don't think about it again, child. Busy yourself with those active employments which a woman in your position has naturally so much to do with.'

"I left Aunt Sophia and returned to my room. There was a moon in the sky. My bedroom windows were open. I lit a pair of candles at each side of the long mirror at one end of the room, and deliberately studied my face. I had always known that my eyes were somewhat peculiar, my pupils being more dilated than those of most women."

"That fact merely betokens a high degree of nervous sensibility," said the Professor.

"I examined my eyes that night," I continued, "and it did seem to me that they had a wild and startled glance. I called my courage to my aid, however, and determined not to be fanciful, and to try to forget my cousin's words. That was easily said, but very difficult to act upon. My courage certainly did ebb as night went on. I found that my thoughts dwelt on Aunt Ethel and her horrible fate, and also found that I could turn them in no other direction. Presently I went to the window and looked out into the beautiful night. The moonlight was falling across the grass and causing black shadows under the trees.

"Suddenly I uttered a scream and fell back, too startled to keep my self-control. For gazing at me fixedly out of the deep mass of foliage were two very bright, luminous eyes, eyes full of a strange and terrifying gleam. I saw them as distinctly as I now see you. I watched them move, and saw them glitter as they disappeared into the darkness. When they had quite vanished I knew that I was cold all over. I shivered with a most awful sense of dread. My first desire was to run straight to Aunt Sophia, tell her the whole truth, and beg of her to share my room for the night. But on reflection I resolved not to do this. I did not want Aunt Sophia to know. She would certainly not have believed my tale, and she would put down the vision which I had seen to the same cause to which Rudolf would doubtless attribute it.

"There was no repose for me that night. The thought of those eyes kept me company—the eyes themselves and Rudolf's significant words: 'If you encourage those morbid fancies you will share the fate of poor Aunt Ethel. The pupils of your eyes point to a disordered brain.'

"In the afternoon of the next day I went for a solitary walk by myself. We have pine woods at the back of our house. From there I could see at intervals the tower which is the oldest part of the mansion. It is situated at the end of a long, rambling building, and was in existence at least four centuries ago. It is a curious old Norman tower, with arches over the windows and a castellated roof. The tower contains only two rooms, the lower one being the library of our house and the upper my father's study. Since his death no one has been near that part of the building. I felt a sense of reproach as I remembered his room now. Was his study neglected and covered with dust? Were the flowers in the vases dried up and dead? I would go to the study to-morrow and see that it was made fresh and clean. I would open the windows and let in the sweet air. Nay, more, when the long-looked-for and eagerly expected letters arrived from South Africa I would read them in my father's study.

"That evening I paced up and down for a long time in the pine woods, then I returned to the house. I took up a novel and tried to read, but the book did not suit my mood. I remembered another which had begun to interest me, and which I had left in one of the drawing-rooms. I went downstairs to fetch it. There was no one in the room. I found the book in a distant corner and returned slowly to my bedroom. To do this I had to go down a long corridor into which many rooms opened. For some extraordinary reason the electric light in this corridor was not turned on. I noticed how dark it was, and just as I reached my own door I looked back, impelled, I suppose, by instinct. In the darkness at the farther end of the corridor I again saw the gleaming eyes. They stared fixedly at me without blinking, and with a horrible leering expression in their gaze. Again I screamed, rushed into my room, and locked the door. I could scarcely endure my misery.

" 'Am I going mad or am I the victim of an apparition?' I said to myself. 'Is my brain giving way? What am I to do? How am I to endure this? How am I to live?'

"The next week or ten days passed without any further disturbance, and I was beginning to recover my mental balance. Rudolf was away from home during the greater part of that time, engaged on some very special business in the North of England. I was undoubtedly happier and less nervous when he was absent, but when he returned his affectionate and concerned manner about me made me self-reproachful, and I almost wondered at myself for the intolerable feeling of repugnance which I always felt towards him.

"Two or three nights after his return I saw the eyes again. On this occasion they stared at me from the centre of the rose-lawn. The night was black as pitch, and there were the eyes raised between five and six feet above the ground, and staring full at me with unblinking directness. After this visitation I determined to see you at once. Now, can you help me? Have I been visited by an apparition or am I mad? Tell me what you really think."

For reply the Professor said, quietly:—

"I will examine your own eyes before I pronounce an opinion."

I rose at once. He placed me in a chair in front of a large window and, taking up some powerful lenses, carefully looked into both my eyes. When the examination was over he said:—

"You are very nervous. Some of the higher nerve centres are in a state of irritation. Your father's death, joined to the shock of this apparition, trick, or what you like to call it, has been too much for you. You ought really to leave home."

"But am I going mad?"

"There is no trace of a disordered brain. Nevertheless you are nervous, and nerves are kittle-cattle, and ought to be attended to."

"But, Dr. Ellicott, why should I be nervous? Why should I see those ghastly eyes? What is the mystery?"

"I should like much to unravel it," he said, with a shrug of his shoulders.

"How I wish you would!"

He looked thoughtful for a minute or two; then he said:—

"Would it be possible for you to invite me to stay at Courtlands?"

"Would you come?"

"Could you give me a room where I could continue my business without interruption?"

"I could hand you over the library in the old tower. There you need never hear a footfall, for the tower is at the end of an unused wing at a remote part of the building."

"In that case I will bring my things and spend a few days at Courtlands. I do not believe in your apparition as an apparition, nor do I think that you are becoming insane. Your case interests me. May I arrive in time for dinner this evening?"

"I don't know how to thank you," was my answer.

"Expect me at Courtlands about seven o'clock. And now leave me, like a good girl, for I have many things to attend to."

I returned home with a great sense of relief, just in time for lunch. The only people at table were Aunt Sophia and my Cousin Lionel.

"Why, Nora," cried my aunt, "how much better you look! Have you had good news?"

"Yes and no," I replied. "By the way, Aunt Sophia, can we entertain a visitor for the next few days?"

"A visitor now?" she said, raising her brows in astonishment.

Lionel laid down his knife and fork and looked hard at me.

"To receive a visitor in the house now would be unusual, would it not, Nora?" he said, gently. "My uncle has not been dead a month yet."

I took no notice of him, but turned again to Aunt Sophia.

"Dr. Ellicott, the well-known Professor, is staying at Ashingford," I said. "I met him some time ago at the Newcomes'. He is a remarkably clever man, and I may as well confess that I consulted him medically this morning. No more Dr. Jessops for me. I preferred to consult one who was well up-to-date on medical matters. The Professor interests me and I interest him. He wishes to come here for a few days in order to watch my symptoms. He will arrive in time for dinner. Please, Aunt Sophia, will you order the green room to be got ready for him, and also the library in the old tower?"

I spoke in a decided manner, and neither my aunt nor Lionel ventured to remonstrate, for, after all, I was really mistress.

Suddenly I turned to my cousin.

"Is Rudolf away again?" I asked.

"No," he replied; "Rudolf is unwell. His eyes are hurting him. He is obliged to stay in a darkened room."

"I did not know that Rudolf suffered from his eyes."

"He never did until lately. We neither of us can imagine what is the matter with them," was Lionel's response.

I said a word or two of commonplace condolence, and then left the room.

That evening the Professor arrived, and when I entered the drawing-room before dinner I noticed that my aunt and both my cousins were waiting to receive him. During dinner he made himself generally agreeable, and Rudolf in especial seemed to be attracted by his manner and powers of conversation. I noticed, however, rather to my amazement, that my elder cousin wore a shade over his eyes, and in the course of dinner I inquired what really ailed them.

"I don't know," he said. "I am in considerable pain. My eyes are very much inflamed."

"Will you permit me to do something to relieve your symptoms?" said Professor Ellicott, suddenly, turning as he spoke, raising his pince-nez, and fixing his gaze on Rudolf's face.

"I wish you would," was the reply.

"I will look at your eyes after dinner. And now, Miss Dallas," he continued, turning with courtesy to my aunt, "let me explain that knotty point to you."

He was discussing a little matter with regard to the growth of ferns, and Aunt Sophia, a keen botanist, was listening to him with rapt attention.

By-and-by I made the signal to leave the room, and the gentlemen were left to themselves. In the course of that same evening the Professor came to sit near me.

"I have examined your cousin's eyes. There is considerable inflammation both in the eyelids and the eyes themselves. Their condition points to a strange diagnosis, but as it seems impossible that it can be the right one. I am not prepared to say anything further on the subject—at least now. Tell me, are you going to have a good sleep to-night?"

"I hope so."

"I think you will, for I have prepared a small, but effectual, draught, which I want you to take just as you are lying down. Get your maid to sleep in your room, and believe me that, eyes or no eyes, you will be in a state of oblivion five minutes after you take my draught."

I smiled, with a sense of relief.

"I believe," I said, "that in any case I should sleep well with you in the house."

The next few days passed without anything fresh occurring. We saw but little of the Professor. He was absorbed with his own work in the old library in the tower.

At last the day arrived when we expected letters and news from the beloved dead. Even Aunt Sophia was agitated, and Lionel and Rudolf were like restless ghosts, hovering here, there, and everywhere. Rudolf's eyes looked worse than ever, and he also complained of a strange sore at his side. At dinner that evening the Professor said, abruptly:—

"By the way, Dallas, do you happen to know anything about that new substance—radium?"

"I have heard of it," was the reply.

Lionel's face became suddenly rigid and very pale. Rudolf, on the contrary, looked with the utmost composure at Professor Ellicott.

"You, of course, have studied its properties," he said. "Tell me about them. I dabble in many things, and, above all enjoyments, to peer into the mysteries of science delights me most. But give me an account of the properties of radium."

"They are too varied to mention here. I will but allude to one or two. In close contact with the skin, radium has the effect of absolutely destroying the epidermis and the true skin beneath, thus in time producing an open sore. Moreover," said the Professor, "were you really dabbling with this strange substance the state of your eyes would be accounted for."

"I have never even seen the thing," was the abrupt answer.

The conversation turned to other matters. After dinner we all went to the drawing-room. Professor Ellicott came and seated himself near me.

"You will receive a letter from your father by the next post?" he asked.

"Yes."

"Where will you read it?"

"In his study. I have always read his letters there. I made him a promise that I would do so. He said he would like to think of me sitting under my mother's portrait, reading his letters and thinking of him."

A few minutes afterwards the postman's ring was heard, and a servant entered with several letters on a salver. The one I had expected was handed to me, and there was also a foreign letter for Aunt Sophia. Rudolf, who had come into the room just before the servant brought the letters, came up to me.

"You will go away by yourself and read your letter," he said, kindly. "You will read it in your father's study, won't you?"

I nodded. He smiled.

"I felt sure you would go there, Nora. He will be with you in spirit."

As Rudolf uttered the last words he glanced towards Lionel, and the two left the room a minute or two before I did.

To reach the tower I had to go down a long corridor which was seldom used. At the farther end of the corridor was a baize door which opened on to some narrow stone stairs. They were worn with age. Mounting them, I soon reached my father's study on the top floor of the tower. It was octagonal in shape, with many windows. These windows were closely barred and the panes of glass were small. When I entered the room I gave a start of surprise. I expected to see it in darkness, but instead of that a small table had been drawn up within a foot or two of the high, old-fashioned grate, and on it were placed a pair of brass candlesticks with candles in them already lighted. But why were the blinds not drawn down at the windows? I felt a momentary inclination to repair this omission myself, but my father's letter occupied all my thoughts and I soon forgot everything but the fact that I was about to read the beloved words—in short, to receive a message from the dead.

The contents of my father's letter absorbed my complete attention, and I soon perceived that only the very early portion was written by himself; most of it had evidently been dictated to a certain Edward Vincent, whose name, as one of the young lieutenants in my father's regiment, was already familiar to me. The letter told me that my father was mortally wounded, and that he was now partly writing, partly dictating his last goodbye to me in the tent where they had removed him after the skirmish with the enemy. In the letter he told me that he had received my last communication, and, in consequence, had made inquiries, which took some little time to come to fruition. On that very morning, however, he had received a long letter from London, which contained a complete confirmation of what I had told him, and also many other revelations had been forthcoming, which filled him with the utmost displeasure and horror. He therefore resolved immediately to change his will, leaving none of his property to my cousins, but all to me. The last words of his letter desired me to turn to the opposite page, on which a formally-worded will was written. This will left everything to me. I turned to it and read it. It was very short, and was signed by my father, and had also the signatures of two witnesses.

Tears flowed from my eyes. In one sense I was relieved, and yet my heart was torn. I covered my face. Just then a slight noise, which might have been attributed to the tapping of a bough against the window-pane, caused me to turn my head.

I did so tremblingly. I felt convinced that I was not alone. Something, or someone, was looking at me. Fascinated, I gazed straight before me. Again came that ghastly tap, which, I felt sure, proceeded from no human hand. I looked towards the upper panes of one of the windows, and there were the eyes. Never had they seemed more malicious or horrible. I lost my nerve, gave one shrill and terrified scream, and rushed towards the door, altogether forgetting my letter, which lay upon the table.

I had just reached the door when a fresh thing happened. The room became full of a sudden and terrible wind. It caught at the table-cover, flapping it violently. The letter, written on thin foreign paper and consequently light as air, floated off the table with one or two other loose letters, was carried straight to the fireplace, and then up the chimney. The next instant I felt my dress dragged as by an unseen power. Something seemed to draw me back into the room, and the candles on the table flickered and went out. I was in the dark and alone, yet not alone. What awful thing had happened? My brain swam for a minute. I felt sick and cold; then I lost consciousness.

When I returned to my senses I was lying on the sofa and Professor Ellicott was bending over me.

"Now, control yourself, Miss Dallas," he said. "We have not a moment to lose. Tell me exactly what occurred."

I pressed my hand to my face. There was a light again in the room.

"Be quick," said the Professor. "What did you see? Why did you cry out? I was coming into the house in a hurry—in fact, I was on my way to this room—when I heard your shriek. I had been smoking and walking up and down in the grounds. Something induced me to look towards the tower. All of a sudden I saw—but tell me first what did you see?"

"The eyes," I answered. "They looked at me through one of the windows—that one exactly facing the table."

"Through what part of the window did they look?"

"Through one of the topmost panes."

"Good! I thought so. Now go on. Tell me the rest."

"I lost my nerve. I rushed towards the door, and just as I got there I turned, for the room was full of wind."

"Wind!" said the Professor. "Why, the night is as calm as death."

"Nevertheless, the room was full of a sort of gale, and the letter—my father's letter—was lifted and carried towards the chimney, up which it disappeared, and I myself was dragged back into the room. Then the candles were put out. Oh, I do believe at last in the ghost. Professor Ellicott, I wish I were dead."

"Don't be so silly, child. I assure you there is no ghost. Now, listen. I also saw something."

"The eyes?"

He nodded.

"They flashed at me for an instant. I fancy, Miss Dallas, this is a very tangible ghost. I saw a figure crouching on the roof, bending down over the turret towards that very window. I was just under the tower, hastening in, when you screamed, and I looked up and saw it disappear behind the parapet. The eyes were visible for about half a second. We shall catch your ghost, don't be afraid, and solve your mystery. I shall remain here for the present, but we must have the roof examined, and at once. Do you know of any other way to get to it except by a ladder from the ground? There surely must be a trap-door somewhere."

"There is," I answered. "There's a trapdoor at the end of this very wing."

"Good!" said the Professor. "Go downstairs at once and get several men, your cousins amongst them, to examine the roof from end to end, and in especial to look on the roof of this tower. I will stay here. Don't be long."

I ran away. The Professor's words had excited me, and my courage had returned. I gave the alarm. I could not find my cousins, but soon the rest of the house was in a state of ferment. Some of the men-servants and two of the gardeners immediately ascended to the roof. They carefully examined not only the roof of the house, but that of the tower. But look as they would they could not see a single trace of any individual hiding there. It is true that a rope, fastened to one of the chimneys, was hanging close to one of the parapets of the tower. This alone pointed conclusively to the fact that someone had been there. Nothing else, however, was to be discovered.

Accompanied by Aunt Sophia I returned to the Professor.

"Four of our men have been on the roof," I said, "and they brought away this rope. You can see it. There was no one there."

"Ah!" He shrugged his shoulders. "I thought there must have been a rope. He could not have bent over so far without being secured against the possibility of falling."

"The rope was fastened round one of the chimneys," I continued.

"Professor, what does this mean?" said poor Aunt Sophia.

"Where are your nephews, madam?" was his answer. "Why are they not helping in this search?"

"We cannot find my cousins anywhere," I answered. "The last I saw of them was when I was going upstairs to read my father's letter. They then left the drawing-room and went out of the house arm-in-arm."

"I will go and have a further search made for them," said my aunt. "They certainly ought to be acquainted with this most remarkable occurrence."

She gave me a suspicious and, I fancied, unbelieving glance. Did she really think that I was imagining the whole thing? The Professor's attitude, however, comforted me.

"Don't be alarmed, child," he said. "The clue which we seek is close at hand. I am convinced of it. Now we must do something. I shall remain in this room for the night, and one or two of the servants must watch on the roof of the tower. But you must go to bed and rest, otherwise you will be down with nervous fever. Now, tell me, please, Miss Dallas, who are the most trustworthy and absolutely reliable servants in your house?"

"Harris, the old gardener, for one," I answered. "He has been with us since before I was born."

"Who else?"

"Franks, the butler."

"Then Harris and Franks shall watch on the roof of the tower to-night. Now go to bed."

Against my will I was forced to go to my room. Another sleeping-draught, administered by the Professor, ensured my repose, and in the morning I was sufficiently calm even to defy Aunt Sophia's looks of suspicion, for suspect me now of incipient insanity she evidently did.

The mysterious disappearance of both my cousins caused a great deal of talk and speculation on the following morning, and I went to the tower to visit the Professor in a state of great excitement on the subject. His manners were absolutely non-committal. He refused to say anything about my cousins, and he also refused to leave the study.

"When I go someone else must take my place," he said. "This room must not be left unguarded for a single moment, nor must the roof above."

Towards the latter part of the day he suggested that I should take his place in the study while he himself examined the roof. In about half an hour he returned to me. I saw that he held a tiny glass tube in his hand.

"Can you make anything of this?" he said, laying it on the table before me.

"Nothing," I answered. "What is it?"

"A very valuable piece of evidence, I take it."

"What do you mean?"

"I will try to tell you. I found this tube in the gutter just above that window. It is, as you see, sealed up at each end. It looks innocent enough; nevertheless, it contains a very minute portion of that new substance—radium. You heard what I said to your Cousin Rudolf with regard to the effect of radium on the human skin, but I did not tell him that it does something else. When held for a short time in front of the eyes, the eyes take to themselves a certain amount of its properties, and they glow in the dark with a great luminosity which gives them a most terrifying appearance. It strikes me, Miss Dallas, that in this little bottle I hold the solution of your ghost. The eyes of a man who held radium a short distance from his pupils would also become very much inflamed. Consider the condition of your Cousin Rudolf's eyes. I found this tube in the gutter. We are getting near the clue; eh, don't you think so?"

I felt myself turning pale. I know that I trembled.

"Could any man living be so wicked?" was my next remark.

"Men will do strange things for money," was his answer. "But how your cousin would know that your father intended to change his will is a mystery which I cannot fathom."

"What do you mean to do next?" I asked.

"Watch for the scoundrels. They are hiding somewhere, and all in good time they will reappear. By the way, you say that your father's letter, containing the will, was blown up the chimney. James," he continued, turning to the servant who had just entered the room, "you and Andrews must come up here within an hour and take my place while I visit the roof. I may have to remain there for some hours this evening. Meanwhile, Miss Dallas," he continued, giving me a quick smile, "you shall go and take a constitutional."

I did not want to go out, but the Professor's word just then was my law. The evening was a lovely one, and I walked for some little time. As I returned I looked towards the tower. Suddenly I perceived the tall figure of the Professor. He was standing absolutely motionless near one of the chimneys. He evidently saw me, but did not make the slightest movement. A wild desire to be with him and to share his watch came over me. Quick as thought I entered the house, reached the trap-door, which was open, and soon was standing on the low roof of Courtlands. I walked warily and presently reached the edge of the parapet. There were two steps here leading from the roof of the house to the roof of the tower. I mounted them and stood by the Professor's side."

"Child," he said, in a whisper, "what are you doing?"

"I must share your watch," I said.

"I would rather be alone."

I shook my head.

"Something forces me to remain with you. Don't deny me my wish."

He held up his hand with a warning gesture to me.

"Then you must crouch by this parapet," he said, "and remain motionless. I shall hide behind the chimney. My suspicions are confirmed. There are men not far from here. I heard a movement not long ago. Absolute quiet will force the scoundrels from their lair."

I now perceived that he carried a revolver. Moving away from him a few paces I crouched down behind the parapet. He did likewise a little way off. We were the only watchers on the silent tower, but I knew that there were servants also on guard in the room below.

By-and-by the sun sank towards the west and twilight reigned over the scene. Twilight deepened into night.

The Professor and I had remained motionless, as though we were dead, for from two to three hours.

All of a sudden I saw Professor Ellicott raise himself and glance towards me. I could but dimly see his face, but I knew that something was about to happen. The next minute, peering hard towards the stack of chimneys, I noticed, to my unbounded horror, the head of my Cousin Rudolf show itself. He did not see us, and cautiously began to descend from the chimney on to the roof. Just as he was about to place his feet on the roof, Professor Ellicott, strong as steel, sprang upon him and dragged him by the shoulders and arms down upon his knees.

"I have been waiting for you," he said. As he spoke he held his revolver to my cousin's ear. "If you stir you are a dead man. Confess your crime at once. Your game is up! Now, then, what does this mean?"

Rudolf groaned.

"The agony in my eyes is past bearing," he said.

"Call to your brother to come out of his hiding-place. I will take you both to the Colonel's study. There you shall explain your villainies."

"Let me rise, and I promise you I will not try to escape," answered Rudolf. "I am in such pain that I am past caring for anything but the chance of relief. I will shout to Lionel. We have been starving, and have been in the dark. Oh, the agony in my eyes!"

The Professor allowed Rudolf to rise. He went to the chimney and called down. In a moment Lionel made his appearance. Professor Ellicott then escorted the two men across the roof, down through the trap-door, and back again to my father's study.

"I cannot face the light," said Rudolf at once, covering his eyes with his hands. "I have endured more than I bargained for. If I am happy enough to escape without the punishment of the law, I will confess everything."

"That remains with Miss Dallas, for she is the person you have injured," said the Professor.

"Tell the truth, Rudolf. I won't be too hard on you," I answered, my voice trembling. I saw him shiver slightly. His tall, athletic figure was bowed. He still kept his face covered with his hand. As to Lionel, he was crouching in the attitude of an unmistakable cur in a distant corner.

"This is the story," said Rudolf. "There is no use any longer hiding things. I was in serious money trouble—Stock Exchange debts, the usual thing. The money left to me in my uncle's will would, however, have put me again on my feet. Were it for any reason withdrawn, nothing remained for me but open disgrace and ruin.

"For years it has been my one effort to keep my transgressions from my uncle's ears, and only for the extraordinary instinct which you, Nora, possessed, and which caused you to watch me as a cat watches a mouse, I should have succeeded in securing the fortune which he meant to leave me. Lionel was much in the same boat. We decided, therefore, to act together. For a long time we have been in league with a certain Lieutenant Vincent, a young officer in the same regiment as my uncle. My uncle was much attached to Vincent. In the hour of his death Vincent happened to be near, and it was to him my uncle dictated his letter, the letter which you received last night. On the afternoon of the day when the news of my uncle's death was received here I had a long cablegram from Vincent, in which he gave me briefly the contents of the new will, which was already on its way to England, and also said that both the witnesses, privates in my uncle's regiment, had been shot dead shortly after he breathed his last. Thus there were no witnesses to prove this will. He said we must make the best of his information, and we had a month to mature our plans in. We put our heads together and resolved on a course of action. We knew the history of Aunt Ethel. Nora has always had very highly strung nerves, and we perceived to our satisfaction that they were terribly upset by her father's death. I had been reading a good deal about the newly discovered substance—radium, and thought it possible that it might serve my purpose. I purchased a minute portion and began at once to work on my cousin's fears. Radium, as you know, when held near the eyes, can give them a luminous and very ghastly appearance. I got Nora to believe that she was the victim of a terrifying disorder, and you are aware how successfully my purpose worked. I further arranged, with Lionel's help, to deprive Nora of the fresh will as soon as she had read it; our belief being that her story would not be credited, and that when she spoke of a new will having been sent to her the whole thing, in combination with her story of the ghostly eyes, would be put down to insanity.

"Now, this was our plan: We knew that her habit was to read all letters received from her father in his study. We investigated this room thoroughly and made an important discovery. A few feet up the wide chimney was a secret chamber. The entrance to this chamber was approached by climbing down the inside of the chimney from the roof. This mode of entrance was facilitated by projecting bricks left for the purpose. We resolved to utilise the chamber for our requirements.

"As soon, therefore, as the post arrived from South Africa, Lionel and I left the drawing-room. We immediately went by the trap-door on to the roof. Lionel disappeared down the chimney into the secret chamber, where we had previously taken an immensely powerful exhaust-pump. In the bottom of the chimney there was placed a short time ago a large register, thus closing up the space, except for a small hole in the centre, in order to let the smoke pass up. Leading from the exhaust-pump we had arranged a large tube, the mouth of which fitted exactly into the hole in the register. We had also put in order a small electric bell which communicated from the roof to the chamber. After Lionel had disappeared down the chimney I prepared my eyes, and at the right moment bent over the parapet.

"All the time Nora was reading her letter I was looking at her, and when I perceived that she had quite taken in its contents I attracted her attention by gently tapping on the window with a spray of ivy. She turned instinctively. Again I tapped, and she looked up and saw me. As my brother and I guessed she would, she uttered a scream and immediately tried to leave the room, forgetting the letter, which still lay on the table. I immediately rang the bell. Nora was too terrified to hear it. At the signal Lionel began to work the exhaust-pump by means of a hand wheel. It sucked the air out of the study, and drew the letter and other small papers up the chimney right into the tube. Thus we secured the letter and the new will.

"I then joined Lionel in the secret room, not forgetting to take with me the wires from the electric bell. We both immediately set to work to draw back the tube into the secret chamber, and by the time Nora had recovered consciousness all trace of our plot had virtually disappeared."

"What about the will? Have you destroyed it?" said the Professor.

"Strange to say, we have not," replied Lionel. "The fact is, we were in the dark and starving. We had hoped, but for your interference, to get away in a few minutes. We have been incarcerated for twenty-four hours. Rudolf was in agony with his eyes. We wanted to read the will before tearing it up."

"Then you can give it to me?"

"Yes. We have it here intact, and, if our cousin will permit us, we will leave the country to-morrow and never trouble her again."

They did so. I did not wish to pursue them, as I doubtless could, with the punishment of the law. My terrors were over. Never more would the ghastly eyes alarm me.

How I Write My Books

An Interview with Mrs. L. T. Meade

Mrs. L. T. Meade has probably written a greater number of stories than any other living author. A healthy tone pervades all her works, and her pictures of English home life in particular are among the best of their kind. Calling on the novelist (writes our Special Commissioner) at her City office, I found her at her desk hard at work. Her personality is like her writings—bright, fresh, vivacious; and to say that she is of a well-favoured countenance is to understate the fact. She retains much of her girlish appearance, though a rather worn look about the eyes suggests midnight oil and an ever-active brain. Knowing how Mrs. Meade values her time, I plunged at once into the subject of my visit by remarking that nowadays people take a very friendly interest in those who delight and instruct them by their writings, they like to know how their favourite books are written; and asked whether she was willing to satisfy this natural curiosity.

"I shall be happy to tell you anything you want to know," she replied in a soft, musical voice. "As to how my books are written, well, I simply get a thought and work it out. I have no particular method of writing. My stories grow a good deal as I write them. I don't think the plot out very carefully in advance. My children's stories, for instance, before they are written, are, as a rule, first told to my own children to amuse them—at least, I have tried that plan since the children have become old enough to be interested in them, and I have found it very successful; as a rule, what one child likes, another child will like. I write my stories a good deal because the publisher wants the book; I simply write it to order, and, of course, if he asks for a girl's story he gets it, and if he asks for a novel or children's story he gets that. I may say that I am a very quick writer; I produce four or five books in a season. I have written in less than three months a rather important three-volume novel."

"Do you ever take your characters from real life?"

"Yes, but not intentionally. I don't deliberately say I will put such a character here or there; I take traits rather than a whole character. I find that deliberately setting my mind to delineate a certain character produces considerable stiffness, and the character is not so fresh. Authors are a good deal governed by their characters in writing fiction. If your book is to be successful, your characters guide you rather than you guide your characters; they are so very living and real that you have not complete control over them."

"Your experience, then, is similar to that of Charles Dickens and some living writers, who have stated that their characters become their masters, and, as it were, take their destiny into their own hands?"

"Exactly. I find it a good plan, when a novel is in process, after a certain stage, to cut out every character that is not intensely alive. I am now speaking, of course, of my larger stories; in a short story there is not room for development of character."

"May I ask how many stories you have written?"

"I am afraid to tell you—between fifty and sixty volumes, besides a great many short stories. I have been writing now constantly for fifteen years. An enormous quantity to have produced?—so it is; I don't know any other author who has done so much work as I have done in that time. I will give you an example. I have recently brought out four volumes (none cheaper than 3s. 6d., which gives you some idea of the size) and a three-volume novel, not to mention a complete Christmas number of the *Sunday Magazine*, of nearly sixty thousand words. They have certainly all been written under two years. I write on an average every day in the year a little over two thousand words; on some occasions I wrote a great deal more."

"Do you write everything with your own hand?"

"I write nothing with my own hand—I almost forget how to write. I employ a short-hand writer, and I revise the type-written transcript."

"Do you write at regular hours or at uncertain intervals; in other words, do you wait for an inspiration, or do you sit down and write whether you feel inclined for it or not?"

"I never wait for an inspiration." Mrs. Meade added, with a laugh, "I might never write at all if I did. I write every day at a certain hour, and it would be impossible for me to write in the way you suggest. I have a great many books promised against a certain time. I always write against time."

"And you find that your work does not suffer from that somewhat mechanical method?"

"I don't think it does. I believe that to write against time puts your work into a frame, and is improved by it. To have to write a certain length, and for a certain publisher, who requires a certain kind of work, is splendid practice; it makes your brain very supple, so that you can turn to anything. It is a matter of habit with me now, and I rather like it."

"Are you never at a loss for ideas when working under such pressure? Don't you ever feel impoverished?"

"Sometimes, perhaps; but not as a rule. I often sit down, my secretary has a blank sheet of paper, I say, 'Chapter I' and that is all I know when I begin. I suppose my ideas do flow very rapidly, for some writers who are very much beyond me in power can't write quickly. They have to think out their subjects a great deal. I could not write if I gave much labour to my work."

"But surely you must sometimes stop and think when you are dictating?"

"No; as a rule, I dictate straight ahead continuously, and never pause for an instant. I see the whole scene, and I talk on as I see it."

I could not help feeling that, if Mrs. Meade dictates as rapidly as she was speaking to me, her stenographer must be exceptionally expert. Her readiness and fluency were such, that of all the people I have interviewed, not one covered so much ground in so short a time. To this hard-working novelist our conversation was but a momentary interruption.

"Then you create as you speak?"

"Yes. Of course all writers must feel they do better work one day than another, but there is no day I don't write except Sunday. *Atalanta* takes up a great deal of time; more than half my days are occupied with it. I have a very large life outside my books."

A portrait of a sturdy, happy-looking youngster in cricketing costume, which his mother showed me, was an illustration in point. Mrs. Meade told me that he was the original of *Daddy's Boy*—one of the most fascinating of her numerous children's tales.

"What do you think of our English fiction of to-day?" I next inquired.

"I think fiction is at a very low ebb just now. We have no giants; but the average writer has come to a much higher pitch of excellence than was the case ten or twelve years ago. I admire Barrie immensely. I think I like him almost better than Rudyard Kipling, but I have a great admiration for both in their way. Mr. Kipling has more sting than Mr. Barrie, but Mr. Barrie's character-drawing is inimitable. Mr. Barrie, Mr. Kipling, and Mr. Stevenson ranks first of all."

"Still, none of them, you think, are 'giants'?"

"I would not put them on a level with George Eliot, or Thackeray, or Dickens. We have no Dickens now, no Thackeray, no George Eliot; we have not even a Bulwer-Lytton."

"Would you put George Eliot at the head of all women novelists?"

"Yes. I don't think anybody else has touched her. I think Charlotte Brontë has exceeded her in some things—she has more passion; but, on the whole, I think George Eliot is greater."

"What is your opinion of the theological novel?"

"Frankly, I don't care for it. Edna Lyall has made a great success, and done some very fine and noble work, but I think theology in a novel is a mistake. It might be introduced, but ought not to be overdone."

"It is bad artistically, don't you think?"

"Extremely bad; absolutely wrong. I think Mrs. Humphrey Ward is not at all artistic. She is a remarkably clever woman, but she is not a fictionist. A fictionist is in her own way a painter; she writes pictures instead of painting them. I think the art of fiction is not half studied by writers; there is so much in it."

"Do you do most of your work at home, or here in the City?"

"I write in the morning at my own house at Dulwich. I do most of my original work at home, and my editorial work here, though I have done a great deal of original work here also. I don't go by any fixed rule. The only fixed rule in my life is that I never can get a holiday."

"I hope that is not to be taken literally?"

"Well, we are going away to-morrow for three or four days. Such an event is so rare that I can hardly believe it is coming to pass. I never get more than about a fortnight's holiday in the year. That is mostly because of my magazine work, which, of course, never ends."

Sources

The texts used in this collection are taken from the original magazine sources in which they first appeared. While some light editing has been employed to correct typographical errors, instances of racism and cultural insensitivity, though unfortunate and jarring to modern sensibilities, have been left intact.

"Very Far West" (with Clifford Halifax) first appeared in the *Strand Magazine* (September 1893), serialised under *Stories from the Diary of a Doctor* (First Series); it was collected in *Stories from the Diary of a Doctor* (London: Newnes, 1894).

"The Panelled Bedroom" (with Clifford Halifax) first appeared in the *Strand Magazine* (December 1896), serialised under *The Adventures of a Man of Science*; it was collected in *A Race with the Sun* (London: Ward, Lock, 1901).

"The Mystery of the Felwyn Tunnel" (with Robert Eustace) first appeared in *Cassell's Family Magazine* (August 1897), serialised under *A Master of Mysteries: The Adventures of John Bell—Ghost-Exposer*; it was collected in *A Master of Mysteries* (London: Ward, Lock, 1898).

"The Dead Hand" (with Robert Eustace) first appeared in *Pearson's Magazine* [UK] (February 1902), serialised under *The Experiences of the Oracle of Maddox Street*; it was collected in *The Oracle of Maddox Street* (London: Ward, Lock, 1904).

"The Doom" (with Robert Eustace) first appeared in the *Strand Magazine* (October 1898), serialised under *The Brotherhood of the Seven Kings*; it was collected in *The Brotherhood of the Seven Kings* (London: Ward, Lock, 1899).

"The Woman with the Hood" first appeared in the *Weekly Scotsman* (December 1897); it was collected in *A Lovely Fiend and Other Stories* (London: Digby, Long, & Co., 1908).

"Followed" (with Robert Eustace) first appeared in the *Strand Magazine* (December 1900); it was collected in *Silenced* (London: Ward, Lock, 1904).

"The Man Who Disappeared" (with Robert Eustace) first appeared in the *Strand Magazine* (December 1901); it was collected in *Silenced* (London: Ward, Lock, 1904).

"Eyes of Terror" first appeared in the *Strand Magazine* (January 1904); it was collected in *The Oracle of Maddox Street* (London: Ward, Lock, 1904).

"How I Write My Books: An Interview with Mrs. L. T. Meade" first appeared in *The Young Woman* 1 (January 1893).

Acknowledgements

I would like to thank Wayne Meckle and Brian J. Showers for their support and technical assistance. I would also like to thank the following people for their help in the preparation of this book: Brian Coldrick, Timothy J. Jarvis, Meggan Kehrli, Jim Rockhill, and Steve J. Shaw.

About the Author

L. T. Meade (1844-1914) was born in Bandon, Co. Cork and started writing at an early age before establishing herself as one of the most prolific and bestselling authors of the day. In addition to her popular girls' fiction, she also penned mystery stories, sensational fiction, romances, historical fiction, and adventure novels. Her notable works include *A Master of Mysteries* (1898), *The Brotherhood of the Seven Kings* (1899), and *The Sorceress of the Strand* (1903). She died in Oxford on 26 October 1914.

About the Editor

Janis Dawson received her doctorate in English literature from the University of Victoria (Canada). She has published articles on L. T. Meade, nineteenth-century women writers, Victorian girls' books and magazines, and children's literature. Her recent work includes a study of Irish girls in Meade's school fiction. She is the editor of a critical edition of Meade's popular crime series *The Sorceress of the Strand* published by Broadview Press (2016).

SWAN RIVER PRESS

Founded in 2003, Swan River Press is an independent publishing company, based in Dublin, Ireland, dedicated to gothic, supernatural, and fantastic literature. We specialise in limited edition hardbacks, publishing fiction from around the world with an emphasis on Ireland's contributions to the genre.

www.swanriverpress.ie

"*Handsome, beautifully made volumes . . .
altogether irresistible.*"

– Michael Dirda, *Washington Post*

"*It [is] often down to small, independent, specialist presses to keep the candle of horror fiction flickering . . .* "

– Darryl Jones, *Irish Times*

"*Swan River Press has emerged as one of the most inspiring new presses over the past decade. Not only are the books beautifully presented and professionally produced, but they aspire consistently to high literary quality and originality, ranging from current writers of supernatural/weird fiction to rare or forgotten works by departed authors.*"

– Peter Bell, *Ghosts & Scholars*

BENDING TO EARTH

Strange Stories by Irish Women

edited by Maria Giakaniki
and Brian J. Showers

Irish women have long produced literature of the gothic, uncanny, and supernatural. *Bending to Earth* draws together twelve such tales. While none of the authors herein were considered primarily writers of fantastical fiction during their lifetimes, they each wandered at some point in their careers into more speculative realms—some only briefly, others for lengthier stays.

Names such as Charlotte Riddell and Rosa Mulholland will already be familiar to aficionados of the eerie, while Katharine Tynan and Clotilde Graves are sure to gain new admirers. From a ghost story in the Swiss Alps to a premonition of death in the West of Ireland to strange rites in a South Pacific jungle, *Bending to Earth* showcases a diverse range of imaginative writing which spans the better part of a century.

"Bending to Earth *is full of tales of women walled-up in rooms, of vengeful or unforgetting dead wives, of mistreated lovers, of cruel and murderous husbands.*"

– Darryl Jones, *Irish Times*

"*A surprising, extraordinary anthology featuring twelve uncanny and supernatural stories from the nineteenth century . . . highly recommended, extremely enjoyable.*"

– *British Fantasy Society*

NOT TO BE TAKEN AT BED-TIME

and Other Strange Stories

Rosa Mulholland

In the late-nineteenth century Rosa Mulholland (1841-1921) achieved great popularity and acclaim for her many novels, written for both an adult audience and younger readers. Several of these novels chronicled the lives of the poor, often incorporating rural Irish settings and folklore. Earlier in her career, Mulholland became one of the select band of authors employed by Charles Dickens to write stories for his popular magazine *All the Year Round*, together with Wilkie Collins, Elizabeth Gaskell, Joseph Sheridan Le Fanu, and Amelia B. Edwards.

Mulholland's best supernatural and weird short stories have been gathered together in the present collection, edited and introduced by Richard Dalby, to celebrate this gifted late Victorian "Mistress of the Macabre".

"It's a mark of a good writer that they can be immersed in the literary culture of their time and yet manage to transcend it, and Mulholland does that with the tales collected here."

– David Longhorn, *Supernatural Tales*

THE DEATH SPANCEL
and Others

Katharine Tynan

Katharine Tynan is not a name immediately associated with the supernatural. However, like many other writers of the early twentieth century, she made numerous forays into literature of the ghostly and macabre, and throughout her career produced verse and prose that conveys a remarkable variety of eerie themes, moods, and narrative forms. From her early, elegiac stories, inspired by legends from the West of Ireland, to pulpier efforts featuring grave-robbers and ravenous rats, Tynan displays an eye for weird detail, compelling atmosphere, and a talent for rendering a broad palette of uncanny effects. *The Death Spancel and Others* is the first collection to showcase Tynan's tales of supernatural events, prophecies, curses, apparitions, and a pervasive sense of the ghastly.

"Of remarkably high literary quality . . . a great collection recommended to any good fiction lover."

– Mario Guslandi

"Tynan's fiction is of a high standard, crafted in relatively simple yet still lyrical prose . . . a very assured craftswoman of the supernatural tale."

– Supernatural Tales

"Lovers of late Victorian and Edwardian ghost fiction will assuredly adore the restrained literary quality . . ."

– The Pan Review

CPSIA information can be obtained
at www.ICGtesting.com
Printed in the USA
BVHW070401290921
617680BV00007B/326